A SAILOR'S DELIGHT

I0687266

Beverly Ovalle

Contemporary Romance

Contemporary Romance

A Sailor's Delight

Copyright © 2016 Beverly Ovalle

ebook ISBN: 978-0-9967973-4-4

ISBN: 978-0-9967973-5-1

First E-book & print Publication: July 2016

Cover design by Dawné Dominique

Cover photo by Capture Life Photography

Edited by M.S. Daniels

All cover art and logo copyright © 2016 by Beverly Ovalle

PUBLISHER

MIDWEST DRAGON PRESS

CONTENTS

DEDICATION

To my family who puts up with my crazy schedule of a full time job plus my insane need to write! Ed, Nick, Suzy and my wonderful granddaughter Brileigh who will one day question why Grandma has to run away by herself for a while.

To Bailey at Capture Life Photography who took this wonderful picture that I used for my cover. Again to my daughter Suzy who is the model for my cover! Thank you for letting me use such a wonderful moment.

Thank you to my beta readers Cendi, Josephine, Robin, Tamara and my editor, Molly. Despite your harsh critiques! LOL. This book wouldn't be what it is without you!

To all the men and women in uniform. You are an inspiration to me. Thank you for your service.

A SAILOR'S DELIGHT

Beverly Ovalle

Contemporary Romance

ONE NIGHT HE DOESN'T REMEMBER

ONE NIGHT SHE'LL NEVER FORGET

Lee Santiago went from one mistake to the next. When a friend dies, exposing his mortality all too well Lee's family steps in to force him to make something of himself. He can't be a party boy all his life and if he wants to sign his life away, it will be on the dotted line. He doesn't even have time to say goodbye. Anyway it was only a drunken one night stand.

Isabelle was always the good girl. Until that night. When the man she'd always worshiped finally noticed her. She couldn't say no. She's heartsick to find out he doesn't remember it. Isabelle's life crashes around her when the results are in. The truth comes out and she has nowhere to turn. She looks for Lee, but he's gone.

Will he be man enough to step up and face the consequences when he learns the truth?

CHAPTER ONE

Lee groaned, the light seeping through his blankets. The nasty cotton flavor in his mouth assured him he had once again gone on a bender; another one he couldn't remember. Turning his head had him groaning. The heavy throb in his temples set off flashing lights behind his eye lids. He couldn't breathe. Flat on his belly, pillow over his head he tried to rise. Pushing up, he encountered smooth warm flesh.

"Shit."

Dropping back to his stomach Lee tried to remember last night. Flashes of laughter and too much booze clouded his memory. He knew he was home. Finding a drunken slut beside him wasn't how he wanted anyone in his family to find him.

Pushing her, not even bothering to look at her, he shoved her out of bed. After all, what did it matter if he saw her? He'd probably never met her before.

"Go away." He pulled the cover over his head. "Get dressed and use the back door so no one sees you."

A sharp intake of breath told him she hadn't been expecting that.

"But…"

"Just go. My abuelita and mama will be pissed to find you here. I don't need no more trouble."

"But…"

Her voice wavered. She sounded close to tears.

"Go. I'll call you later." A lie, Lee had no idea who she was. He didn't want to know. Scenes flashed in front of his eyes. He groaned. God knows what was real and what wasn't anymore. Party after party rolled together.

"Okay."

He heard the rustling of clothes as she quickly dressed.

"The back door?"

Her hesitant question brought a face to mind. One that never used the backdoor. Wishful thinking on his part.

Without looking he pushed a hand from beneath the covers and pointed in the general vicinity of the door leading out of his room.

"There. It leads straight out into the back yard. Take a right around the house or you'll be going past the kitchen where my familia is probably at. I'm sure you don't want to be seen. And I don't need the hassle."

"Okay. I'll talk to you later, Lee."

Shit, she knew his name. It didn't matter, when he didn't call her she'd get the hint. She sounded young, hopefully she wasn't underage! He prayed no one in his familia saw her leaving.

He heard the creak of his door opening.

Shit.

"Mi hijo, it's time to get up." The sound of Mama Rosa's voice reached him. Half the time he and his siblings called their grandma Mama. Despite their own mother being there, their abeula practically raised them.

A soft squeak from the girl, and the back door opened and shut in a flurry of noise. He forgot it screeched in protest as it opened. At least that's what it sounded like to his sensitive ears. Hopefully his abuela hadn't heard it.

"Je je je!"

Fuck! Hurried steps back to the kitchen and his abuela's mild wording told him his visitor leaving hadn't gone unnoticed. He groaned and buried his head deeper into the bed, pulling the pillow tighter over his head.

The *woosh* of the front door and yelling told him that he was in for a world of shit. Quiet, then the patter of his abuela's footsteps heading his way. He groaned, his eyes pounding from his own noise.

"Malo! Bad Lee!"

Abuela's broom came down on top of him, again and again. The babble of Spanish dropping from her lips too fast to follow.

"Parar! Abuelita, por favor, stop!"

Lee rolled out of the bed to her screeching. It got louder when he rolled naked out from under the covers.

"Wicked boy!" Her broom coming down on top of him had him grabbing his shorts from the floor and running from the room.

"Jesus! Someone stop her!"

Lee leaned against the wall, hopping into his shorts. Despite the wicked sting of Abuelita's straw broom, he had his prima's, his cousins, to think of. They were always around since they lived next door. You never knew who was over. He couldn't go running out there naked even if he wanted to escape the pain.

He pulled them up with a snap and escaped. Running into the hall he heard his hermano, his brother, laughing.

"Stop her, jackass."

Alejandro just laughed harder.

"You deserve that and more." His madre sounded pissed. She stood to the side, watching grandma hit him with a broom.

He hunched under another blow. "Stop Mamacita. Por favor."

"No. I'll beat the demons out of you." Another swat and Lee ran. He had his shorts on. Leaning over and grabbing his gym shoes from the front door on his way outside. His head throbbed and the sunlight made him curse.

"Think fast."

Lee turned his head.

"Fuck." Lee swore. His eyes ached, the blood pounding in his temples. The sunlight had his head exploding. He reached out and caught a pair of Oakley's Alejandro tossed before they hit the ground. Jandro was an ass, but at least he understood Lee's pain.

"If I were you, I'd find a place to lay low for a couple of days. And stay out of trouble."

"Son of a bitch." Lee slid the sunglasses on, muting the bright sunlight against his aching eyes.

The door shut, cutting off the stream of invectives from his uncle, his mama, and abuelita's chanting to remove the demons from his soul. His brother's laugh intertwined with their sister's. A shit storm of trouble, God knows how he would get out of it this time.

Lee stood in the driveway, sweat forming at his nape, shoes in hand and only a pair of boxers on.

Fuck.

The door opened and jeans, a shirt and his wallet flew outside.

"Get going before mama lets grandma back after you with the broom. Oh, you'll need these too." Alejandro tossed his car keys at him. "Don't fuck up my car, hermano. I can get a ride if I need it." They landed on the cement with a jarring jangle.

"Where's my phone?"

"Fuck if I know, dude. Check your pants."

Lee walked over and grabbed the clothes, sliding the jeans on and slipping his wallet into his back pocket, tossing his shirt over his shoulder. Reaching into the front pocket of his jeans, he found his phone. He leaned over grabbed Alejandro's keys, one hand holding his throbbing head.

"Thanks, bro."

A taste of bile when he straightened had him wanting to heave into the bushes. That would really set his abuelita off again if she saw him.

Alejandro leaned against the door, closing it softly behind him. Probably so he didn't alert the family inside that he was talking to him, the black sheep of the familia.

"Where you gonna go?"

"Dunno. Maybe Lenny's. I need a shower."

"No shit. You stink."

"Fuck you."

"No thanks. Looks like you already did that this morning."

His pulse pounded harder, his stomach churned. He had a bad feeling, a real bad feeling. What the fuck had he done?

"What do you mean?" Maybe he could bluff his way out of this, at least with his hermano.

"You think grandma, didn't see her leaving your room? How wasted did you have to be to bring her back here?" Alejandro shook his head. "Estupido. And on the heels of Nico's visit? He's abuelita's hero, the perfect grandson. Then you do this. The day after he leaves."

Lee shook his head. Lights shot behind his eyelids. He swallowed down his rising bile.

"Fuck. I don't know what to do anymore."

"Don't worry, I don't think you'll have a choice."

"What? Whatcha talking about?"

Alejandro nodded his head toward the raised voices that could barely be heard inside the house.

"When you come home, your life will change. I guarantee it. I think this was your last chance."

"Fuck you. No one can tell me what to do. I'm not Nico."

"You don't think anyone tells him what to do, do you? He chose his path. Just like you've chosen yours." Alejandro looked down. "Like I've chosen mine."

"Maybe I like the path I'm on." The stink of his own body, and the heat of the sun had him sweating and his stomach churning. He could taste the lie on his tongue.

"Don't be a fool. I can tell you don't."

"You know nothing." Lee couldn't admit Alejandro was right. But it was his life and he'd live it how he wanted. Stuck in place with no future and a past that could no longer be ignored. What the hell was he supposed to do?

"Don't waste your life, pendajo. You're the only hermano I have." Alejandro sighed. "Figure it out. Before we lose you."

Fuck. Lee didn't know if he meant to jail or to the grim fucking reaper. He didn't want either, but he was on a path he didn't know how to stop. Sometimes shit just happened.

"I'll figure it out, don't worry."

Lee turned and hitching up his pants, headed to where Alejandro had parked his car.

"No drugs in my ride, pendajo! Get some cajones and tell them no."

Lee glanced back in shock. Fuck. He didn't know how Alejandro knew what he had gotten involved in, but what the hell could he do? Once you started, there wasn't much option to quit.

"What the hell are you talking about?" It seemed he spent his life lying and hiding from his familia.

"I know what I know. You're not in too deep. Fix it, bro."

Alejandro turned and went in the house, shutting the door quietly behind him.

Fuck.

It seemed like nothing was going right in his life anymore. He'd done one job. One. How the hell Alejandro knew about it, he didn't have a clue. It's not like he ran the drugs himself. He'd just driven a man. Told where to go, he'd followed directions. It wasn't like he was a dealer. He assuaged his conscious by telling himself he was just a delivery driver. Hell, just helping out his best friend.

He'd lost his job, too much partying, coming in late to work and hung over. His productivity spiraled and the third week in a row he didn't meet his quota, they let him go. With no cash, no job, no way to pay his bills he'd taken the easy way out.

He drank to drown his problems. Maybe his abuelita was right. Maybe he needed an exorcism. Maybe he did have demons inside.

* * * *

The hard bed, stifling air, and noise like a freight train pulled Isabelle from sleep. Stale beer, cigarette smoke and sex assaulted her nose. She sucked in a breath; her eyes widening. What had she done?

Along her side hot warm flesh pressed solidly against her. Squeezing her eyes shut, she prayed she hadn't done anything stupid. From the nasty air under the unfamiliar scratchy covers and the heat all along her naked body she knew it was in vain. God could only help so far. She'd no evidence that a miracle would remove her from the situation she found herself in.

Isabelle stuck her head out from under the covers. She recognized this room. The smell of coffee and bacon told her she wasn't the only one awake. She glanced over and her heart stuttered. The large mound, the hot flesh could belong to only one man. Lee. Lee Santiago.

Naked under the covers, Isabelle flushed, glancing around for her clothes. Flung haphazardly on the thankfully empty bed across the room, they twined together with Lee's.

Her body ached in unfamiliar places. A flush covered her from head to toe. Thank goodness Jandro hadn't come in. Lee shared a room with his brother. Isabelle didn't know how she would have stood the embarrassment if he had been there.

She glanced over. Despite only the top of his unruly black curls showing from beneath the blankets Isabelle recognized Lee. She'd always hoped to catch his eye. Her shyness stopped her from trying. She worshipped the ground he walked on regardless of her BFF telling her that her hermano was bad news. Jacinta loved her brother but hated his wastrel lifestyle.

Now Lee had noticed her, Isabelle hoped that things would be different. He had been so gentle with her once he found out that she had never been touched. Isabelle didn't regret one minute. Snuggled up against him, pressed against his strong body, tingles raced from her toes to her cheeks, filling her body with warmth. A low throb settled in her abdomen and her loins clenched and heated in remembrance of the night before.

Isabelle smiled and snuggled closer to Lee, thinking of the night before. Her sister drove her to a party for her birthday. Isabelle turned eighteen and decided to cut loose and have a little fun. Caroline urged shots on her to celebrate. The two of them sat and giggled at the wildness around them as drink after drink was downed. The dim lighting hid more than it exposed, but what Isabelle could see left her shocked and squirming.

Her sister's boyfriend tried to persuade Caroline to leave with him, but she insisted on staying with Isabelle. Then Lee showed up. Isabelle ignored Caroline's frown. Lee swore he'd take care of her and make sure she stayed safe. Jack finally coaxed Caroline away. Lee settled next to her, his arm around her body, pulling her in close to his side.

"I've never seen you at a party before. I thought you were a good little girl." His teasing voice sent thrills throughout her body.

"Today's my birthday." Isabelle snuggled closer to him. His body seemed to surround hers.

"So, does that make you legal today?"

Isabelle nodded vigorously then groaned. Her head swam from the movement. Maybe, just maybe she'd had a bit much to drink. Lee would take care of her though. He'd promised.

"But not legal for drinking yet."

Isabelle pouted then sniffed.

"So what? Most of the people here aren't twenty-one."

"Doesn't make it right."

Isabelle craned her head around to look at him. Surprised at the hard note in his voice.

"But you've been drinking since you were in high school."

"Again, doesn't make it right. So, you decided to cut loose now that you're an adult?"

The small smirk at the side of his mouth fascinated her. Somehow the tip of her finger made its way there. His lips were strong but soft, warm against the softness of her finger. The scruff around his mouth prickled her finger as he rubbed his face against it.

"Don't play with fire, little girl." He nipped the tip of her finger as he winked at her, sending a zing through her body.

Isabelle giggled. Normally she thought herself out of Lee's league, but tonight that didn't bother her in the least. She'd had too many jello shots to care. Snuggled in his arms, his hands on her affected her more than any bit of alcohol could. Combining them gave her a warm glow.

Isabelle wiggled, the trail of his fingertips tickling her neck and circling her ear. She could feel her nipples tightening, glad for her push up bra. It made her boobs look fabulous, but was thick enough to hide her body's reaction.

Lee chuckled in her ear, sending warmth pooling low in her belly. Isabelle caught her breath as he trailed his finger down her breast unerringly circling her nipple.

"Cat got your tongue, little girl?"

His warm breath in her ear, followed by a flick of his tongue had her gasping. She shifted, wiggling, trying to relieve the ache building in her. Lee pulled her closer, positioning her across one leg. One hand held her tightly by the hip. The other skimmed the top of her camisole dipping in to tease her nipple.

Isabelle gasped at the sensation. "Lee." She didn't know if she was encouraging or warning him away.

He chuckled, stroking her nipple until it stood out, obvious to anyone that bothered to look. He lowered his head, bending Isabelle over his arm as he nibbled her through her shirt. With a tug he pulled it aside exposing her breast before quickly sucking it into his mouth.

"Ah." Isabelle arched offering herself to the warm suction of his mouth. She caught her breath, liquid heat pooling between her legs with each pull. Her toes curled. The noise of the party disappearing, all her senses focused on the sensations swirling in her body.

"Beautiful." His voice muffled as he nursed.

Isabelle groaned and shifted. Her body yearned for more. She wrapped her legs around Lee's other leg, pulling it toward her.

He hummed against her breast. She shivered, her hips rising, yearning for something more. Lee's hand slid down her thigh leaving goosebumps in his wake. He slid it up her skirt, his fingers rough against her softness.

"Wet for me." He pulled up her camisole covering one breast and quickly exposed her other before taking it into his mouth. Lee stroked her through her thong, sliding easily under to tease her. "Hot. God." Lee slid his finger inside, stroking her. His thumb teased her clit.

Isabelle sobbed, the sensations almost too much to handle. She could feel her own wetness. Her clit throbbing with each stroke. Her body tightened in anticipation. Of what, she wasn't sure. Lee pressed against her and Isabelle gasped. She shattered into pieces, warmth running from her body.

"Good little cat."

One more stroke had her shivering as his finger slid out of her.

"Lee." Isabelle shuddered and reached to pull up her shirt.

Lee beat her to it, settling it over her aching nipple. "Shhh. It's okay." He slid his finger into his mouth. "Mmm. You taste delicious."

Isabelle felt her cheeks heat. "Lee."

"Come on, let's get out of here." He set her upright in front of him, pulling her skirt down and her camisole up higher. He stopped at the keg in the corner. "One more for the road."

He grabbed two solo cups and filled them, handing one to her. He tilted his head back and guzzled the beer down. He quickly poured himself another.

"Happy Birthday." He toasted her and drank.

Isabelle sipped hers. It didn't seem so bad anymore. She drank more, attempting to cool down. The party was packed, but she thought fuzzily that it mainly had been from Lee.

"One more, it is your birthday after all."

Isabelle blinked and realized her cup was empty. She giggled and handed it back to Lee. He poured them both another.

Quenching her thirst, downing the bitter taste of brew, her last coherent thought. She had flashes of heated touches, calloused hands and a hot mouth worshipping her body. She smiled, her body sated until he had pushed her out of bed. The shock had her gaping.

Isabelle swallowed, tears filling her eyes. Surely Lee wasn't kicking her out? Most of the night was missing, but what she did remember heated her insides. She'd dreamed of being awoken with firm kisses and heated touches, not being shoved out of bed to land naked on the floor.

"Lee?" She didn't understand. Isabelle drew in a calming breath, trying to calm her racing heart.

"Go, before anyone sees you."

His words stole her breath. Maybe he was trying to protect her. But the callous note in his voice as he spoke unnerved her. Her stomach twisted. Surely Lee knew it was her. His pointing toward the backdoor, telling her the way to sneak out of the house, spoke otherwise. She knew this house as well as he did. He knew that.

"Lee."

"Go, I'll call you later." Buried under the covers, his words were mumbled. He didn't even look at her.

Swallowing a sob, Isabelle heard steps coming toward the door. She hurriedly finished dressing. Lee would call. He said so. Ignoring the niggle of doubt churning in her belly, Isabelle escaped out the back door and around the house. She kept her head down, trying to hide. She'd be so embarrassed if Lee's family saw her leaving.

Wiping her cheeks Isabelle glanced at the closed door and she sniffed. He would call. Her aching heart wasn't so sure. Isabelle pushed the doubts away. She had to leave without being seen.

She peeked around the corner of the house and slid into the front yard. She had the gate open when she heard the front door squeak and Lee's abuela came out. Eyes wide, she glanced up into her disapproving face. The shock, then disappointment on her features had Isabelle turning and running away.

Her stomach churned. How would she ever face Lee's family? How would she ever be able to look Jacinta in the eye again? What if she disapproved of her being with Lee too? She was her best friend. Isabelle couldn't bear to lose her friendship with his family. They kept her sane in the too strict, overzealous life she had to live at home.

Thank goodness her father would be at the church

working on his sermon. She could get in and take a shower without him seeing her. She wondered how Caroline always managed to not get caught. She pulled up the bottom of her camisole and wiped her eyes. No use worrying about Lee calling her yet.

She opened the door and slipped into the living room. Isabelle blinked, her eyes adjusting to the darkness. The curtains were pulled to keep the sun out and the cool in.

"Where have you been?"

Isabelle jumped. Her father sat on the couch. She hadn't seen him. If she had known he'd be there, she'd have grabbed the shirt Caroline had hidden in a planter near the door. He'd be sure to mention her clothes. They weren't modest enough for a preacher's daughter.

"At Jacinta's. I spent the night."

"Why didn't you call? You know you're supposed to call. I don't like you running around, especially wearing clothes like that. Anything could happen. Where is your shirt? You look like you're wearing your underwear."

She was right. It was always one of the first thing he mentioned. "I told you last night. Caroline was dropping me at Jacinta's after the movies. My shirt is there, I spilled on it and her abuela is washing it."

He shook his head. "I worry. I have reason." He sighed

and shook his head. "I had to go over to a parishioner's home today. Their son died last night. A drug overdose, they think. They came home and evidently there was a party while they were gone. Their house was trashed and they found their son dead on the couch."

Isabelle gasped. "Oh no! Was it anyone I know?"

"He was older than you by a couple of years, so maybe not. They swore he didn't use drugs but the police are investigating. You just never know." Her father sniffed the air. "You smell like cigarettes."

"One of Jacinta's tios, her uncle Mateo, smokes." She knew her father knew little of the Spanish words she was used to from hanging with the Santiago's.

"Well, you better go get a shower. I have to help Len's parents make arrangements." With a sigh, her father stood up. He patted her on the head. "I just want to keep the evil out of your life. If you leave, text me where you're at."

Isabelle stared as he shuffled away. Her father had never been so human before. Usually full of fire and brimstone, but maybe the death of someone so young had shaken him. Then she realized the name he'd spoken.

"Dad, did you say Len? Len Ramirez?"

He turned and looked at her.

"So you did know him?"

Isabelle nodded her head. "He was Jacinta's brother's best friend. I saw him over there all the time."

"Too bad he wasn't there last night. He might still be alive."

Her stomach knotted. Isabelle took a deep breath, trying to relax the tightness in her lungs. God, what would Lee do when he heard the news? He was going to freak.

"I'm gonna take a shower and head back to Jacinta's, okay? When their family gets the news..." She shook her head. "I don't know how they'll take it."

He looked at her and nodded.

"Provide comfort as best you can." He placed his hand on the door knob. "This is the worst part of my job." The obvious ache in his voice had Isabelle's heart thawing toward him.

Bowing his head, Isabelle heard him whisper a prayer, a brief flash of sunlight then the darkness enveloped her again, and he was gone. She supposed her father wasn't a bad man, just too strict for her liking.

"Crap."

She tore up the stairs and into the shower flinging off her clothes as she headed in. Lee will be devastated. She knew that he and Lenny had been friends since kindergarten. The warmth beaded on her skin and rolled down her back. Her hair became heavy and wet from the spray. She groaned, taking a moment to enjoy the liquid heat as it slipped down her body. Grabbing the scrubby, she soaped up, being very careful of the tender spots on her body.

Shampooing quickly, she rinsed off the bubbles and stepped out, grabbing a towel. She went to her room, wiggling her toes in the soft carpet as she stood in front of her closet. She didn't want to upset her dad more than he appeared to be, so she grabbed a modest sun dress. It would be cool enough in the heat.

Drying off, Isabelle quickly dressed, the spun cotton soft against her skin as it fluttered down, settling on her curves. She clattered down the stairs, grabbed her purse and slung it across her body as she slid her feet into her flip flops. She opened the door and fumbled in her purse for her sunglasses, sighing in relief as she slid them on.

Isabelle locked the door and headed back to the Santiago's, the embarrassment of the morning gone as she hurried back to comfort Lee and his family. If his abuela said anything, Isabelle would just pretend she was coming to see Jacinta and left when she heard all the arguing. Nothing outrageous about that. Isabelle just wasn't sure that she'd believe her.

CHAPTER TWO

Lee cursed, blowing at his fingers as they stung. Chrome door handles were so damn lame. Alejandro really needed to spring for better ones. Cheap is one thing, burning yourself was another.

A loud creak accompanied the opening of the door, grating on his ears. He tossed his shoes in, then his shirt and slid in the driver's seat.

"Fuck."

He jumped, leaning forward away from the pain. The leather seats were hotter than hell. The stifling air had him gasping. He jammed the key in, blasting the air as the engine rumbled over. He smiled, the rumble vibrating through him from the power of the engine.

He'd love to race this baby, but Alejandro would break his neck. He eased back, the seats branding his shoulders, and stretched. Lee relaxed, the tightness easing from his muscles with the heat of the seat and the whole body massage the Charger gave.

Shifting gears, he backed up and headed toward Lenny's. He'd help him clean up if he needed it, and then they could go play in the hills with Alejandro's car. Maybe a trip through Dead Man's Curve for some thrills. The growl of the engine soothed him as he prowled the streets, heading toward his buddy's.

Lee took the long way there. Savoring the smooth ride and the finely tuned engine of Alejandro's car. Turning the corner onto Lenny's street, past the raggedy assed palm trees haphazardly planted on the abandoned corner lot, Lee slowed. Police cars lined the road. He pulled over a couple of houses before Lenny's. The jacked up rides, iron bars on the doors and windows proof the police were familiar sights in this neighborhood. Police tape blocked the front door and Lenny's parents were in the yard crying as the police spoke to them.

Lee had a sinking feeling in his gut. He rolled down the passenger window and called out to one of the men there. The neighbors were all out gawking and gossiping in groups.

"Hey, muchacho, what's going on?"

One of the men slinked over and leaned in the window. A couple of others followed.

"Shit, I think the vato was murdered. We heard

screaming and crying, the police came, an ambulance, and then the coroner."

Lee's stomach sank. Lenny was the only one that still lived at home. He wasn't out there. Maybe the police were talking to him inside. Another man stuck his two cents in.

"I heard it was a drug deal gone bad." The wanna be thug, bandana wrapped around his head, his dirty wife beater showing better days, eagerly added.

"There was a party there last night. I heard it. The cops are looking for anyone that was there." Another, prison tattoos flashing while he cracked his knuckles spoke.

"I heard it was a break in." The first man spoke again.

"No, pendajo!" The thug pushed his friend, shaking his head. "I was there for a bit. It was a party. Booze and drugs and easy cholas."

Lee shook his head at the comments. Everyone had their own opinion. If the cops were looking for the party goers, maybe they needed to identify the body. God knows that anyone had been welcome, especially if you paid to get in or brought booze, drugs, or easy women. Hell, he had been at the door taking money when it first started. He didn't care what they brought as long as they paid to get in.

He knew that some of the guys would let the pretty girls in, hoping to hit on them. Some of them would let them in if they got a hit of H or a bit of blow. Hell, some were happy with just a toke. Lee wanted the cash. He had bills to pay at home. The drugs didn't interest him and girls were easy enough to come by.

Lee hadn't seen this guy though. Maybe he'd prettied up for the party, looking to score some pussy. Right now, he looked like a street thug. If he hung around long enough, the cops probably would recognize and arrest him.

"Thanks, dude." Nodding, Lee eased the car into reverse, backed up, and drove away from Lenny's. He'd call and check out the situation before barging in. His stomach in knots, Lee only hoped that Lenny answered.

He felt the pocket of his jeans. His cash from the party was still there. Alejandro had obviously just grabbed the pants he'd tossed onto the floor. Thank God or he'd have no place to go and no money. Lee drove aimlessly, his gut knotted. Finally he drove toward home. He pulled into a parking stall at the park, across the street from his grandma's. Pulling out his phone he called Lenny.

The phone rang and went to voicemail. Lee slowly left a message. He swallowed, clearing away the lump forming. Definitely something wrong, Lenny always answered when he called.

"Lenny, my man. Alejandro loaned me his car and I wanted to hit Dead Man's Curve. You up for some fun today? Call me back, dude."

Closing his phone he stared at it. He willed his phone to ring. Len never left him hanging. They'd been tight for as long as he could remember. A sick feeling twisted in his stomach. He had to know the truth. He dialed the number that they'd only used in emergencies.

It rang and rang. Not good. Lee was getting ready to hang up when it was answered.

"Hola."

He'd never heard her like that, voice deep and raw.

"Mrs. R. It's Lee. Can I talk to Len?"

She burst out crying, deep sobs that tore from her gut.

"Mrs. Rodriguez. What's the matter?"

"Who is this? What did you say?" The phone had changed hands. Mr. Rodriguez answered, his voice hoarse.

"Mr. R. It's Lee Santiago. I just asked to talk to Lenny. He didn't answer his phone. I drove by the house earlier." Lee could hear the tremble in his own voice. "The police were there. Is Lenny okay?"

Lenny was his best bro. He had to be okay. Lee would be

lost without him.

"Oh God, Lee." Lee could hear the heaviness in his voice. "Lenny's dead. We came home early and found him on the couch. We thought he was asleep."

Lee squeezed his phone. It couldn't be true.

"No. He was fine last night. Laughing and joking."

"The police think it was a drug overdose."

Lee was silent, heart aching and gut churning.

"Lee, did you hear me?"

"Yes."

"Lenny didn't do drugs. He didn't do drugs, right Lee?"

Lee couldn't answer. Lenny had started running with a harder crowd lately. His throat felt raw. How could he respond? He didn't really know for sure.

"Answer me, Lee."

"Mr. R." Lee swallowed. "I don't know. Some of the people he knew..." He drew in a deep breath. "Some of the people he knew weren't so good."

The line was silent. He could hear Mr. R's breathing and Mrs. Rodriguez crying in the background. He leaned his head on the steering wheel. A tremor shook his body. He just knew what was coming.

"Will you tell the police what you know, Lee? Please. Lenny was your best friend."

His gut clenched. He knew it. What could he say? No? Yes? Lenny was his best friend. Sometimes his only friend. If he told what he suspected, he might as well pick out his gravesite. Hell, his mom already had it. He'd be planted next to Papa, pushing up the roses.

"I don't know." He drew in a ragged breath and swallowed. "Maybe."

"What went on last night, Lee? Was there a party here? The place is trashed."

Lee could hear him crying. A hopeless sound that twisted his heart. Mr. R had stepped in when Lee's dad had died years ago, taking him under his wing. How could he say no?

"Yeah, there was a party. I was on my way over to help Lenny clean up when I saw the cops."

"Why didn't you come over?"

Lee swallowed and leaned his head back against the seat.

"I didn't want to hear what you just told me."

"The police will want to question you. They need to find out what went on last night."

Lee swallowed and nodded. He squeezed his eyes shut.

The damp tracks on his cheeks were drying in the heat leaving his skin tight.

"I know. I... I'll talk to them." He drew a deep breath. "I'll be over in a bit, okay?"

"We'll be here, Lee."

He closed his phone, his hand crushing it. A moan worked its way out of his throat as his nose clogged up. Lee hit the steering wheel, again and again.

Dammit! What would he do now?

He gripped the wheel and turned off the car. Looking up, he saw Isabelle open the gate and knock at the front door before entering. His gut knotted. He grabbed his shirt and wiped his face, tossing it back on the seat. Lee needed his family.

He looked up and saw a police car pull in front of his house. His belly churned. He'd promised Mr. R. he'd talk to them, but was surprised they'd arrived so quickly. He got out of the car and stood up, taking a deep breath. He could do this.

The door opened, Tio Mateo frowned and ushered the cops in. Straightening his shoulders, Lee hit the lock on the car remote. At the beep he swallowed back the tears that threatened and stepped toward la casa and his familia.

His phone rang and he glanced down. It was Alejandro. He could answer it or just go in and talk to him. He walked around the car, toward the house. He looked up and Alejandro looked straight at him, his phone to his ear.

Frowning Lee looked at him. Alejandro was shaking his head. Lee's phone rang again.

"What dude? You can see I'm here."

"Get lost, bro." Alejandro whispered into the phone. Lee saw him slip into the window seat, the curtains blocking the view of him from anyone inside the house. "The police are looking for you."

"I promised Mr. Rodriquez I'd talk to them."

"No, dude. They're here to arrest you."

"Que? No way."

"Si, hermano. Go. Take my car and lay low. I'll call you when it's safe to come home. You got money?"

"Si. A bit."

"Don't go to any of the family. Ernesto is one of the cops here. He knows them all."

"Hell, where am I supposed to go?"

"Get a hotel. Go on, before they see you."

"Okay. Let me know when it's clear."

Lee opened the car and sat down. He breathed in deep, the hot air burning his lungs. He didn't know why the cops were there to arrest him.

He'd take Alejandro's advice and get a cheap room. There were a few dives in the industrial park. No one would look for him there and he could pay cash.

He started up the engine and left, his hands gripping the steering wheel until they were white. It had been a hell of a day and it wasn't even noon yet.

* * * *

Isabelle stuck her head in the door.

"Hola! Is Jacinta here?"

Jacinta's tio, Mateo, waved her in.

"In the back yard, Izzy."

Isabelle entered and headed to the rear door in the kitchen. Lee's abuela frowned as she passed. Isabelle's cheeks heated. Ducking her head, she slipped out the door. She had seen her leaving this morning. Isabelle hoped she hadn't known it was her.

"Hey, Isabelle. Did you have a good birthday?"

Jacinta watered the small orchard in the back yard. The shade from the banana tree kept the yard fairly cool.

"Yes, Caroline and I went out."

"Where'd you go?"

Isabelle swallowed, the news she'd received overshadowing the joy from last night.

"We went to a party." She forced a smile, feeling her lip tremble.

"Did you enjoy yourself?"

"Yes."

"Oh ho. Tell me all about it." She waggled her eyebrows at Isabelle, turned off the hose and flopped down in a lawn chair. "C'mon, spill girlfriend."

Isabelle bit her lip and sat on the other chair. It had been the scene of many of their confidences over the years. This news wasn't hers to tell. Her tummy churned at keeping it in.

"You don't look so good." Jacinta peered at her. "You said you enjoyed yourself, watsa matter?"

Before she could start a loud bang came from the front of the house.

Jacinta sat forward, an ear cocked toward the house. Isabelle could hear Mateo cursing and Jacinta's abuela crying.

"Let's check out what's going on."

The girls crept to the kitchen door and looked in. Everyone appeared to be in the living room.

"C'mon, or we'll never know what's going on."

Jacinta slipped in the door and Isabelle followed her.

"Maybe I should go home. It could be a family matter."

She really hoped they weren't here about Lenny. She hadn't said anything, not figuring it was her place. Besides that, Lee should hear it first before his family did. He had been Lee's best friend.

"Don't worry. It's probably nothing. C'mon and be quiet so they don't kick us out."

Isabelle could hear the officers questioning Jacinta's family. They were looking for Lee. He was under suspicion for Lenny's death. Isabelle looked at Jacinta. She swayed, her face white. Isabelle grabbed her to keep her steady.

"Lee would never hurt Lenny." Jacinta's whisper only reached her ears.

Isabelle nodded in agreement. Her stomach felt hollow as

they listened to the officers. If they saw him they needed to call the police. Her arms crept around Jacinta's waist. The girls held each other up.

"Are you telling me Lenny is dead?" Alejandro stood in the living room.

Isabelle hadn't seen him there earlier. He must have been in the window alcove. She wondered why he'd been hiding.

"Yes. He was found by his parents when they arrived home this morning."

"We have a witness that said Lee Santiago gave something to Lenny. We'd like to find out what."

"The witness said that it happened when the party started winding down. Whether he knew it would kill him or not doesn't change the fact that it did."

Isabelle stepped forward, dragging Jacinta with her. She knew Lee hadn't been there then. They had left shortly after midnight. She vaguely recalled Lenny complaining because Lee was leaving so early.

"What time does this supposed witness say it was?" Alejandro asked before Isabelle could.

"Around four a.m."

"Lee was home." Alejandro gestured to the back of the

house. "We share a bedroom."

The officer looked at his notebook. "You were seen downtown at that time. We have witnesses that were with you." He looked at Alejandro. "We have a witness that places him at the crime scene."

Isabelle shook off Jacinta's arms and stepped forward.

"I was with Lee all last night." She stiffened her spine, swallowing before she continued. "Mrs. Santiago even saw me leave this morning." Isabelle looked down, and pulled out her phone. She flipped to her picture gallery to see if she had any selfies with Lee. She did. Isabelle grimaced. It was obvious they were both drunk. "Here, you can see the time it was taken." She handed her phone to the officer.

"We'll have to verify your story."

Isabelle nodded, her stomach in cramps. Her father wouldn't be happy if he found out. Alejandro and Jacinta were staring at her in shock.

Her voice came out in a whisper. "Lee helped me celebrate my birthday." Isabelle cleared her throat. "My sister and her boyfriend can probably verify what time it was when I met up with Lee."

The officers nodded. The one looked relieved. Isabelle wondered why.

Jacinta's arms wrapped around her again. Their warmth comforting her. Isabelle hadn't realized she had gone cold.

"Thank you, amiga." Jacinta's whisper in her ear had Isabelle hugging her back.

"Ernie, can I ask who the eye witness was?"

"Jandro, you know we can't tell you that."

The officer was a friend. No wonder he looked relieved when Isabelle stepped forward. Lee's tio still looked pissed. After her announcement he looked livid. Isabelle didn't know what to think. Did he want Lee to go to jail? She was too timid to ask.

The one officer, Ernie, turned to her.

"We need these pictures. Your phone will have to go into evidence."

"But I need my phone. I'm not allowed out without it."

Mateo stepped forward placing a hand on her arm.

"We'll make sure you have a phone." He turned to the officers. "You just need the pictures, right? She can change her number to another phone, can't she?"

"Si. That shouldn't be a problem."

"We'll change it right away. I have a spare phone we can

set up for you."

"Thank you. Will I get my own phone back at some point?"

"Yes. When the investigation is over."

"Ernie, if the witness is by any chance Luis Alverez, I'd double check it. He's been trying to get Lee to run drugs for him and Lee's refused. This might be his way of getting revenge." Alejandro looked grim. "Lenny would never have him over at his house, so I have to wonder if he was the witness, how he got there and when."

Ernie and the other cop looked at each other. He flipped his notebook closed and placed it back in his shirt pocket.

"We'll be in touch. If his alibi checks out, Lee should be cleared." The officer shook hands with Mateo and Alejandro and left through the front door.

"Thank you for stepping forward with Lee's alibi. That couldn't have been easy." Alejandro came over and gave her a hug and whispered in her ear. "I didn't want to say anything. I walked in when you were asleep. I figured you wouldn't want to say anything."

Isabelle hugged him back. "I couldn't let Lee be arrested. Not when I knew better."

Jacinta tugged on her arm, pulling her away. "Spill, girlfriend."

"Later." Mateo laid a hand on her arm. "We need to get you a phone set up. If you don't mind, I have an iPhone 4 sitting upstairs, since I upgraded you can have it. What company do you use?"

Isabelle's eyes widened at Mateo's words, her jaw slipping open.

"An iPhone? Are you sure? They're so expensive." Isabelle frowned. "I'll give it back when I get my phone back."

Mateo laughed and ruffled her hair. "No problem, mi hija. You can keep it if you'd like. It's a couple of years old. Now, what company do you use?"

"Thank you! I have straight talk. Since I have to pay for my own phone, it's the cheapest I could find."

"Perfect. So do I. All we have to do is go on the computer and change your number over. It already has a sim card for that plan."

Isabelle was thrilled. Instead of being condemned by Lee's family, they all seemed to take it in stride. Maybe because she prevented him from being arrested. She wasn't sure, but she sure didn't want them to look down on her. They'd always treated her like family and it had her worried.

Isabelle glanced at Jacinta's abuela. She didn't look

happy. From the movements of her fingers on the rosary, she was praying. Isabelle kind of figured she prayed for her soul.

"Come on, let's have a seat." Jacinta dragged Isabelle to the table. "Tio, will you bring your laptop down so we can change her phone?"

Isabelle laughed, then sobered and let herself be dragged over. "I can follow you, you know."

Jacinta giggled. "I know. I just figured I'd get you comfortable and find out all the dirt." She plopped down in a chair, toeing another out for Isabelle to sit in. "You're so lucky. An iPhone. I've been trying to get Tio Matteo to let me have it but he keeps refusing. He has a couple of extras. He keeps upgrading and lets them go to waste."

"Do you think it's all right to take it? Maybe I should pay him for it."

"Nonsense. I wouldn't think of it. Even when you get your phone back you can keep it."

Isabelle jumped. She hadn't seen Mateo come back down. He set up his laptop and started to sit in Jacinta's lap.

"Tio!" She laughed and pushed at him.

Mateo chuckled and grabbed a stool from the counter

behind them to sit down on. "I didn't see you there, flackita."

"Isabelle, you'll have to log in so we can get this set up." He turned the computer toward her. "Just log in."

Isabelle gave him a shy smile. "Okay." Pulling the laptop closer, she brought up the site and logged in. She soon had her account pulled up. "I don't know what to do from here."

"No problem. I can do the rest." He turned the computer around and quickly entered the information.

Isabelle quietly listened to the sound of the clicking of the keyboards. She wondered where Lee had gone. He said he'd call, but with her phone not working and now in police hands, she didn't want him calling her. She didn't want them finding him until he had been cleared.

A plate slid in front of her. A savory scent wafted up from it as she breathed the savory aromas in. "Thank you, Mama Rosa."

The soft click of metal against porcelain and more plates appeared on the table. Isabelle's stomach growled and Jacinta laughed.

"Hungry?"

"Si. Yes. I haven't had anything to eat since last night." Isabelle swore the Spanish was catching.

"Eat up. Abuelita makes the best grilled cheese." Jacinta spoke around a mouthful.

Isabelle could believe it. The smell of the butter on the toast and the wonderful aroma of melted cheese filled the air. Isabelle couldn't resist and happily dug in.

Mateo sat back. "All done." He slid a slim silver phone over to her. "Here you go." He grabbed his sandwich and took a healthy bite.

The contented sound of crunching surrounded Isabelle. Alejandro was talking to someone quietly on the phone in the living room. Seeing her watch him, he turned away. Taking a last bite, Isabelle popped the last corner into her mouth and sighed contentedly.

"Mama Rosa, that was delicious."

"Gracias. Everyone needed to eat." She talked with her arms, her expansive gestures including everyone in her statement. "Jandro, where is that brother of yours?"

"Don't know, Mamacita." He came over and gave her a kiss on her cheek. "Got a sandwich for me?"

"Of course. Eat. Then we have to decide what to do about Lee."

"Don't you think we should wait until Mom gets home?"

"If your mother could control him, do you think he'd be

in the trouble he's in? Even though he didn't do what the police think, it's only a matter of time until he's in serious trouble. It's time to settle this once and for all."

Alejandro shook his head. "We'll see." He looked at his watch. "I need to get going. Ric's picking me up for work. I'll be back later." He grabbed his sandwich and headed out the front door, phone once again glued to his ear.

Isabelle wondered what they would do. Mama Rosa and Mateo shot ideas back and forth. Isabelle sat, her heart sinking. Everything they mentioned meant sending Lee away. If they did, Isabelle wasn't sure if she'd ever see him again. Maybe he'd come home periodically. If he went to school, he'd come home for the holidays and breaks. She had finally caught his interest and wanted to keep it.

The suggestions were getting wilder thanks to Jacinta. Her giggles made it obvious she wasn't serious with her suggestions.

"Mi hija, hush." Mama Rosa scolded her. "You are just getting silly."

Isabelle smiled. Sending Lee away to apprentice on a pirate ship was ridiculous.

"Fine. I think that would be right up Lee's alley though." Jacinta sniffed, but ruined her pretend outrage with a giggle. "C'mon Isabelle, let's go back to the garden."

Laughing, they pushed their chairs back and both girls grabbed their plates, setting them in the sink as they left the kitchen. A phone rang and Mateo called out.

"Isabelle, it's your phone that's ringing."

"Oh, I didn't realize it was activated already."

"Si, it only took a couple of minutes. You better answer it."

"Hello."

Isabelle glanced around the kitchen and sighed. Jacinta waved her to the back yard. Mama Rosa and Mateo were watching her.

"Yes, okay. I'm at Jacinta's. I told you." Isabelle made a face at the phone. "Can't I just stay a little longer?" She sighed. "Fine. I'll come home." She nodded and hung up. "I have to go."

"Are you sure? Just stay a little longer."

Twisting her lips in a scowl, Isabelle shook her head. "No, I have to go home. He is not happy." Giving Jacinta a hug she waved good-bye. "Bye, Mama Rosa, Mateo. Thank you so much for the phone."

"Bye, Isabelle."

"Behave mi hija, listen to your father." Mama Rosa made the sign of the cross as she left.

Isabelle figured she probably began praying for her soul the moment she left. Jacinta came with her, walking her to the gate.

"Give me a call later on. Maybe your dad will let you come back." She gave Isabelle a hug, squeezing her tightly. "You have some explaining to do."

"Maybe. I'll call you later and let you know." Isabelle ignored her last comment. She didn't have to explain anything, best friend or not. She sighed. She probably would though, who else could she talk to? Her sister wouldn't really care. She was too wrapped up in her own life.

"Bye."

"Call me later!"

One more hug and she left, feet dragging. Her father had sounded pissed. The last thing she wanted was to find out why.

CHAPTER THREE

Lee yawned and groaned, grabbing his head. His mouth tasted nasty, glued together. The result of the cheapest tequila he could buy. The polyester bedspread lay in a crumpled heap at the foot of the bed. The drab green carpeting had seen better days. With the color it was hard to know if it was even clean. Probably the reason for the color.

The window had a fine crack in it, while the ancient air conditioner wheezed what sounded like its last breath. The sweltering air inside the room this early attested to the fact it was only making noise. His temples pounded in the stifling air. His belly gurgling. He probably shouldn't have stopped at a liquor store before checking in yesterday. No, make that two days ago.

He'd called Jandro the day before, drunk as a skunk and slurring his words. Lee vaguely remember Jandro telling him to sober up before he came the fuck back.

Lee hadn't been sure he even wanted to go back. He'd grabbed another bottle, figuring, what the hell? His phone had rung and he'd fumbled trying to answer it. He'd talked to someone but between guzzling whatever was in his hand, Lee had grunted and hung up.

His phone started beeping with messages and he threw it across the room, the noise echoing through his head. Screw them. His best friend was dead, the cops thought he'd killed him, and his damn family wouldn't leave him alone to breathe, let alone grieve.

Now he was paying the price.

"Fucking hangover." He swore and rolled to his stomach. His breath hitched. Lee stilled, letting the bile settle back down before sprawling across the bed.

He'd driven until the tank was nearly empty. Then found a dive to crash in. Lucky for him it was across the street from a liquor store. He'd eaten nothing but pickled eggs, Slim Jims, and chips in the last two days. Along with more "to kill ya" than he should have. His stomach roiled just thinking about it.

At least he didn't wake with some unknown slut in bed with him. Lee didn't date. He fucked. If he had an itch to scratch, he found the easiest hole to plug and went for it. He never brought them home and they never spent the night. That night was an aberration.

He only wanted one woman and she was out of his reach. Hell, she was too fucking young for him, and not just in age. Experiences alone separated them.

His phone rang. Lee eyed it, laying on the floor. It was probably Jandro. He dragged himself up, groaning at the pounding in his head as he bent to pick it up. "'lo." He barely got that out. Lee swallowed, clearing his throat, shuffling back to the bed. He needed to lay back down.

"You need to get your dumb ass home." Alejandro didn't even bother with a greeting. "You can thank Izzy for saving your ass. Fuck head."

His hermano hung up.

"What the fuck?" Lee stared at his phone then tossed it on the nightstand next to him. How the hell did Isabelle save him?

Flashes of giggles, sighs, and soft skin flashed through his mind. Lee rolled over careful not to move his head too much. He slid his hand down, circling his cock. Pastel pink nipples, the faintest hint of honeysuckle on his tongue as he sucked.

He pulled, his erection throbbing. Imagining supple curves, heavy breathing, and clothes flying. Lee slid his hand faster. Pre-cum dripped, lubricating his hand. The swing of long, dark hair brushing his collar bone followed by soft lips leaving butterfly kisses down his body to settle over his cock sent a shock through his body, his hand jerking.

Lee groaned, his cum pulsing across his belly. Not the first time he'd jacked off imagining Isabelle's lips wrapped around his cock. He froze. No. It couldn't be.

First he'd take a shower. Then he'd find out what his hermano meant. Dropping his boxers on top of the pile of his clothes, he headed into the bathroom. Stretching, he aimed at the toilet, letting loose with a belch and a groan. The heated release relieving the uncomfortable fullness of his bladder.

Finished, he flushed the toilet and turned on the shower. For all the rattiness of the room, the shower was strong and steady, steam rising from the stream as it hit the tub. Stepping in, Lee groaned. The water massaged deep into his muscles, loosening the tightness in his shoulders. The heat permeated the air, soaking into his skin.

Lee relaxed. The shower spray mingled with his tears. What the hell was he going to do without Lenny?

He'd drank to stop the memories. It hadn't helped. The laughter, the fights, and the mischief they'd been in. An ache Lee couldn't push away when he thought of him. His eyes were sore and his sinuses swollen from the tears he couldn't stop again last night. Silent, they were pulled from the deepest part of him. He'd alternated between sorrow and anger. Drinking until he passed out. One thought kept going through his mind. His best friend was gone.

"Damn it, Lenny. Now what?" Talking to himself was not going to help. Lee slammed his fist into the tile, pain shooting through his arm. He hung his head, taking a deep gulp of air. "Fuck."

Lenny didn't do drugs, not really. Sure, he'd sampled some, who hadn't? But he wasn't habitual as far as Lee knew, and he was pretty sure he'd know. Lenny did deal, though. He'd never pushed Lee into it. Lenny just accepted that Lee wasn't interested. Lee knew he'd been doing it for the past year. Maybe he'd fucked up. Pissed off the wrong man. More than likely, he'd received a new batch and tested it. Some mother fucker had probably laced it with something they shouldn't have. Killing his friend. He hadn't known how to answer Mr. R. Lenny had done some drugs, nothing serious. He'd swear to it.

Lee's anger beat back his sorrow. If he ever found out who had given it to him, Lee would kill them. Then he sighed and breathed deeply. The heated moisture of the shower calmed him. He would probably never know what happened.

Unfortunately, in his world, an overdose was all too common. No one would believe him that Lenny didn't use. Then again, his parents wouldn't want to know he sold them either. They were part of that strict Baptist church that Isabelle's dad preached at. Fire and brimstone was the word there. Many of the Catholics he knew started going there. The hard core, unforgiving ones. The new, softer, more forgiving Catholic Church wasn't what they wanted.

They wanted the black and white, good and bad spelled out. Unforgiving and strict, the word of God was law that they wanted obeyed. Lee shook his head. His thoughts were jumbled. His life spiraling out of control. He needed a change. He just wasn't sure of how to do it.

Leaning against the back wall of the shower, Lee let the water beat down on his shoulders and back. Letting the steam rise and envelope him with each deep breath. His muscles loosened the longer he stood there. He turned and raised his face to the water. It washed away the evidence of his emotions. Helped him calm and push them back down where they belonged. Back where they didn't rise up and hurt.

He took a deep breath and slowly let it out. He turned off the shower and stepped out, grabbed what passed for a bath towel and dried his hair. He stepped into the bedroom and tossed the towel on the unmade bed. The heat in the room had him dry in moments. Stretching, he contemplated his clothes.

Toeing the pile, the aroma of beer floated up. Lee scowled. He wished Alejandro had grabbed a clean set to toss to him yesterday when he brought them to him. Dirty clothes were better than no clothes, though.

Wrinkling his nose at the smell, Lee sniffed. His boxers were rank. He grabbed them and tossed them toward the small trash can in the room. They dangled half in and half out. Close enough.

He swiped up his jeans and put them on. Tucking himself in, he zipped up. The well-worn denim was soft against his dick. Flashbacks of a soft small hand sliding in his jeans and caressing him flashed across his mind. He shuddered, hardening a bit. He gave a quick squeeze and released himself. Masturbating in bed should have been enough, had to be enough.

He had more important things to think of. Like what his family was thinking. Finding out what Alejandro meant. He knew he was in trouble. He'd broken every rule his family had set. Now that the police had come looking for him, he knew he'd have to change.

Drugs, alcohol, and too many women to put names and faces together. The night of the party was a prime example. Add getting caught by his abuela, Lee knew he had to face the music. An uneasy feeling crept over him. The glimpses he was seeing seemed too real to just be his imagination. Lee shook his head. It couldn't be.

Picking up his shirt, Lee shook it out and sniffed it. The faint odor of sex wafted to his nose. Honeysuckle had him breathing deep. The scent of beer overwhelmed it easily. Honeysuckle. His gut clenched. What had he done? He only knew one girl who smelled like that.

Shaking his head, Lee snapped his shirt one more time before slipping it over his head. Glancing around the room to make sure he didn't leave any of his scant belongings behind, Lee scooped up his wallet, phone, and keys from the nightstand. Filling his pockets, he let himself out. It was time to go home.

Crowded with vehicles as usual the drive passed in jerks and starts. Lee passed a couple of squad cars but they didn't notice him. They wouldn't be looking for him in Alejandro's vehicle. He thought about calling Lenny and laughing about it. Reality hit. His breath stuttered, his eyes dampening. He couldn't believe Lenny was dead.

"Fuck!" His hand pounded the wheel.

What the hell? He felt lost. It'd been Lee and Lenny since they were in grade school. They clicked. Ever since they'd met they ran together. Maybe they didn't always see eye to eye, but who did? Hell, they were always like, bros before hoes. No one had ever come between them. There'd been a little bit of tension with the drug thing, but hell, that was life here. Drugs touched every family.

It wasn't enough to break up their friendship, and as long as Lenny kept it away from Lee's family, he didn't care. Lee looked on it as Lenny's job. It just gave Lenny the time and money to party more, happy to take Lee along for the ride. Lee kept up with him, but it had cost him his job. With Lenny gone, Lee knew he had to get another one. First, he had to find out why the cops thought he'd killed his best friend.

Lee pulled up by the curb in front of the house. Jacinta's friend Isabelle was just leaving. Lee could see her walking home, her ponytail swishing in counter point to the sway of her hips. He sat, watching her until she turned the corner. He wondered if she had spent the night with his hermana once again. He swore she lived there, her delicious body keeping his dick hard whenever he caught sight of her.

Cursing under his breath at his own stupidity, Lee got out and locked the car. He gazed down the sidewalk. Never would he deserve her, his behavior had made sure of it. Rubbing his neck, Lee headed inside. He hoped his abuela would have calmed down. He hadn't talked to any of his familia since he'd left, other than Jandro. He told him to leave until things got straightened out then called and said it was safe to come home. From the cops maybe, but he had a feeling not so safe with his familia. He'd never seen his grandma so upset.

The cops weren't sitting there, that was one good thing. He didn't see any squads in the area either. Regardless, Lee knew that his family was going to demand changes. He was so used to just telling the world to fuck off that he didn't know if he could stop. Approaching the door he could hear arguing. Fuck.

His shoulders tensed as he opened the door. Teeth clenched, Lee stepped inside. A glance showed his mama, Tio Mateo, and his abuela arguing. He rolled his eyes. Mama Rosa wouldn't get anywhere waving her rosary in front of his uncle's face.

Alejandro waved him over and shoved a coffee cup in his hands.

"Thanks." Lee took a long sip, setting the cup down on the table.

"My car in one piece?"

"Fuck you, dude." Lee pulled out a chair and flopped down, sprawling in it while he glared at Alejandro who just laughed.

"Is that any way of behaving toward your hermano? After I saved your ass and everything?"

"'Preciate it." He grunted the words, the argument going on in front of him. Grabbing his coffee, he took a gulp of the lukewarm brew. He glanced over at Jacinta. "I just saw Isabelle leave. I'm surprised she didn't stick around. You two being thick as thieves, after all."

Jacinta's mouth dropped open. She gave him a glance he couldn't interpret. "Her dad called her home. You know what he's like. We didn't even get a chance to finish putting away the Christmas tree."

Lee nodded. Her dad's word was law. Lee didn't know how she managed to live under his thumb. "Lucky she's a goody two shoes. She doesn't have a problem listening." The rest of what Jacinta said sunk in. He'd missed Christmas. "Crap." He closed his eyes. If his grandma found out how he spent his Christmas he might as well just leave. He couldn't believe his familia hadn't called him to come home. Then he remembered Jandro's call, the one after, and throwing his phone. Lee looked at his messages and swore. They had.

Jacinta frowned and gazed curiously at him. Alejandro looked puzzled as well.

Lee glanced toward the argument in the living room and turned back to his siblings. He'd missed most of it anyway, they were speaking so rapidly. He knew it involved him from the glances his way, but that was about it. He wasn't surprised.

"Dude, what do you remember about the night Lenny died?" Alejandro leaned toward him, speaking low.

Lee shrugged and yawned. "Not much. I was wasted. I know I woke up to a slut in my bed but that was about it." He scratched his groin. "I need to change clothes. These stink."

He saw Jacinta frown and gave him a disapproving stare. Alejandro slowly shook his head.

"Why? Other than the cops thinking I killed my best friend that is."

"Don't worry about it. I can smell you from here, go change." Jacinta waved a hand in front of her face. "Phew. Go."

He stood and saw his uncle and mama glaring at him. He waved and grinned at them, drawing curses from them both. He headed back to his room.

"This is going to kill her."

His stomach sank at Jacinta's whispered words. What did he do?

"She'll get over it. He's no good for her." Alejandro stood. "I'm going to the park."

Hunching his shoulders now that he wasn't in the line of sight of his family, Lee felt like an ass. He continued to act like one too. He wasn't sure that he would like the outcome of the argument, but he supposed he'd have to live with it. He shrugged out of his shirt, and dropped his pants as he entered his room.

He could always leave. The idea seemed a bit easier than it had yesterday.

Lee grabbed a towel from his bedpost and wrapped it around his hips. He may have had a shower but the stink from his clothes needed to be washed off before he got dressed. Grabbing deodorant and clean clothes, Lee headed across the hall to get cleaned up. Time enough to face his family then.

Turning on the shower, Lee stuck his hand under it until the temperature heated up. He wished the shower had more vigor, instead of a water saver, low flow and no power. Good enough to get clean but it wasn't enjoyable.

Lee slipped in and showered up, rinsing quickly. Sooner or later someone would come looking for him. He wanted to be dressed and clean before they did. Stepping out, he dried off and got dressed. Shorts and a tank top were good enough, too damned hot for anything else.

Lee headed back to the kitchen. Mama Rosa had made eggs and chorizo. Lee grabbed a tortilla and scooped some up. He took a bite and groaned. The spicy sausage cleared his nasal passages in a heartbeat, while the eggs and cheese set his taste buds dancing. His abuela was a damn fine cook. His mama on the other hand, well, Lee happily lived with his grandma to prevent starvation.

"Sit down."

Crap, Lee hadn't seen his uncle there. He sounded pissed. Steeling his nerves, he sat. Lee knew better than to make a smart ass comment with the look on his face. Hell, he'd be better off not talking and just sitting there until he asked for a response.

"I'm tired of your mother and grandmother being upset. The police showing up looking for you for the death of your best friend was the last straw."

Lee stared in fascination at the veins throbbing at Mateo's temple. He quickly finished his breakfast, licking his fingers and humming low in satisfaction.

"The depths of depravity you've hit are unconscionable. Drag yourself down, but to take an innocent with you?" He shook his head. "I don't know what you're thinking anymore. But it is going to stop."

Lee stayed quiet, his shoulders hunched up to his ears as he listened. He didn't know for sure what the hell he was talking about but figured he better not say so.

"The police looking to arrest you was bad enough. Lucky for you your alibi was solid. Finding out you dragged Isabelle into your sordid life style." Mateo shook his head. "I'm so angry I haven't put my foot down before now. It makes me sick."

The look Tio Mateo gave him made him feel ten inches tall. What the hell had he done that night? He knew he hadn't hurt Lenny, but Isabelle? The eggs were sitting precariously in his stomach.

"What did I do?"

Mateo ignored his question.

"Your mother and I have discussed what to do with you. We made arrangements this morning. You're coming with us to finalize them. You're leaving as soon as possible."

Lee frowned and stood up. He realized that nothing he said was going to change the outcome. His chest tightened. He was going to lose everything. He could and would try to fight it.

"I don't know what you've planned, but that doesn't mean I have to go along with it."

"Sit your ass down now!" Mateo turned to his sister gesturing wildly. "This is what happens when you have no control of your children."

"Mateo…" Lee's mom patted her hermano's arm timidly.

"It's not going to work. He's going. I'm tired of his behavior. Never knowing if he'll be alive the next morning or not. Whether his ass will end up in jail or not. It stops here and now." He practically growled. "He may be your baby, but he's a grown man. It's time he pays for his actions."

Lee knew better than to answer back, but it seemed he had lost all of his common sense. "I don't have to do what you say. You can't force me. You can't kick me out." Lee turned to his mom. "Mama, you don't want me to leave, do you?"

She shook her head no. Before she could speak, his abuela stood up, shaking her finger in his face.

"But I can Leonardo! This is my house. You've disgraced it for the last time." Mama Rosa ran her beads nervously through her fingers. "I can't bear to see you throw your life away. It's killing me." She clasped her hands over her heart, her rosary beads rattling wildly.

Lee stood there, mouth open and eyes wide. He'd never seen his grandma so upset. His shoulders sagged and the burn of tears filled his vision. He moved forward, pulling her into his embrace. God, she felt so small. He never realized how frail she was. Her personality made her seem huge.

Lee hugged her, her arms tightened around his waist. Her head only reached his lower chest. He'd laughed at how she looked in Nico's arms, but she was just as small in his.

"I'm sorry, Mamacita." Lee couldn't help but address her like he had when he was little. He felt shamed to his toes to have upset her. She never raised her voice. She never had a harsh word, but he'd had her yelling for the past two days. "I'm sorry. I'll do what you want me to."

"Gracias, Leonardo." She pulled his head down and kissed him on the cheeks, then blessed him. "Por la gracia de dios."

Lee had a very bad feeling. Where were they sending him that she was sending him off with a blessing for God to be with him? He looked over at his hermana. She was eating and watching everything, absorbing every word. Probably to spill it all into Isabelle's ears. The two of them were as tight as he and Lenny were. Maybe it would be better if he left.

No job and his best friend dead, Lee had no idea of what to do with himself. He'd only ruin the life of the one girl he wanted if something didn't change. If he hadn't already. His abuela was right. He'd probably end up dead.

His little cousins ran in through the kitchen door at that moment.

"Mama Rosa, did you make breakfast? Mama is being sick again and we're hungry."

"Sit, sit mi hijos. Of course Mama made breakfast."

Lee stood and watched his familia step back in place. Like nothing had happened. The little ones crowded into a chair, sharing and giggling, while their grandma served them breakfast.

"Lee, Jacinta, finish eating. We need to go." Mateo stood up, placing his plate on the counter.

"I need to wash my hands. I'll be ready in a minute." Lee headed to the sink to wash.

A heavy hand fell on his shoulder. "It won't be so bad. Maybe in a couple of years you'll thank us."

Lee shook off his hand. "Maybe, Tio, but it won't be today. I'm only doing this for mi abuela." He swallowed. Where the hell were they taking him? He wanted to ask, but the look on Tio Mateo's face had him giving up that idea. How bad could it be, anyway?

Mateo shook his head, exiting through the kitchen door.

Jacinta sidled up to him. "Are you going to call Izzy?"

Lee frowned. "Why the hell would I do that?"

"Because you said you would."

"When…" Lee turned and looked at her. "That really was Izzy? Oh God." Lee ran his hands through his hair, wincing at the pain with each tug. "Fuck."

"Bastard!" Jacinta viciously pinched his side.

"Fuck. Why'd you do that?"

"You shouldn't have messed with her." Jacinta whispered. "Call her."

"I don't want to mess up her life. You know I'm a fuck up. Whatever is going on won't make it better."

"I don't care. Call her."

"I don't even remember what happened."

"Call her. She's not one of your putas."

"Fine, I'll call her later. After whatever is going on." He looked at Jacinta. "You know I'm going away. I don't know where. How fair is that to her?"

"Doesn't matter." Jacinta walked away. "Call her."

His cousin jumped from his chair. Lee's mom snagged him and carried him outside. Lee could see her point at the park. Alejandro was over there with his buddy Ricardo. From the sweat dripping down their faces, they'd been playing soccer.

He ran across the street and Alejandro picked him up and settled him on his shoulders for a piggy back ride, tossing his shirt over his primo's head. Lee could hear the giggles from here.

"Time to go."

Lee dried his hands and went over to Mama Rosa, giving her a hug. "Abuelita, I'm sorry. For everything. My behavior and missing Christmas."

"Mi hijo. Te amo."

Her arms pulled him to her. Lee felt peace settle over him. No matter what else happened he knew his family loved him. He kissed the top of her head, a reluctant smile breaking out as she scolded him and swatted him with her ever present towel.

"I'm going. I'm going." Lee followed Tio Mateo outside and slid in the car. Nervousness eating at his belly, he couldn't even appreciate the soft seats beneath him.

He looked at his phone. Fuck it. He punched in a number he never thought he'd use.

"Hello."

"Izzy? It's Lee."

"Lee." She was silent for a moment. "How are you doing?"

"Fine."

"Really?"

He swallowed. "No. Lenny's dead. My family is pissed. I don't remember anything about the night of the party and I don't know what to do."

"Nothing?" A hitch in her voice made him wince. "Maybe that's better."

Crap. Lee pinched his nose. "Yeah, maybe it is." What had he done? Lee would bet it was Isabelle he'd pushed out of bed. He thought about the elusive sent of honeysuckle that wafted from his sheets. His chest ached. "Are you okay?"

"Fine."

He wasn't fine and he'd bet neither was Isabelle. "Izzy, was it you?" He didn't know what else to say.

"Bye, Lee."

She was gone. Lee rested his head against the window. He'd royally screwed up. He didn't know what to do anymore.

Lee watched Jandro swing their little cousin down. "Go find your mamacita, primito." Jandro straightened up and looked at their mom. "Lo que está pasando, Madre?"

"What's happening is that we are going somewhere. Get in the car." She gestured into the car, holding open the door.

Alejandro shrugged, slid into his shirt and slipped in the car, pushing Lee further in as he did so. "What's going on? Where are we going?"

"Just get in." Tio Mateo's voice was harsh. He was already in, waiting for the rest of them to get settled.

"What's going on?"

"Not sure, bro. I'll fill you in later, 'kay?" Lee whispered back. Their madre sat shotgun and behind her, Jacinta waited to get in the car. Jacinta shut the front door, closing it for their mama. She then crawled in next to

Jandro and leaned over.

"Lee, you're in so much trouble." Her voice was low, obviously trying to not be heard in the front.

"All of you, shut up." Tio Mateo started the car. It was a tight fit in the small car their mama owned. The little Vibe was good on gas, but three in the back seat sucked.

Jandro pushed Lee over. "Move over, dude. You're hoggin'." Lee glared at him, an excess of emotions and an upcoming dread of what was to come churning in his belly, but he shifted closer to the door. He promised abuela he'd do it.

Alejandro and he alone filled the back seat. Jacinta was squished, off to the side. Of course she probably didn't have to come along, but was too nosy to stay home.

They pulled out, heading west on Beverly Boulevard. Lee watched the scenery go by, dirty run down houses, graffiti on every surface imaginable. Not even the sign for Saint Agnes was spared, the gang symbols sprayed across the frame, though the glass had obviously been cleaned. *God*, Lee thought, *I'm going to miss this place. I hope whatever they have planned keeps me near home.*

Lee ignored the pointing and kept staring out the window. His reflection showed a bone deep weariness in his eyes. He knew that whatever was coming wasn't what he'd planned for his life.

Mateo parked the car and got out. He shut his door and pulled open the rear passenger door, gesturing Lee out.

"We're here."

Lee frowned. A card shop, a few eateries, a couple of

clothing boutiques, and the recruiters' office were here. Nothing he could see that would have the family so grim, or necessitate them all coming.

They exited the vehicle, Lee silent as he followed his uncle across the parking lot. Jacinta and Mama got out, following behind like ducks in a row. Jandro was last. Tio Mateo held the door to the recruiters' office open, pushing Lee inside and waiting for Alejandro to get there. Lee stopped inside the door and looked around. Despite his cousin's and uncle's service this was never something he'd wanted.

Lee sighed and stood straight. If this was what grandma wanted, he'd do it for her. He knew that he'd have to behave. It didn't mean he'd like it.

Jandro pushed open the door, entering last. The innocuous tinkle of the bell sounded like a death knell to Lee's ears. The final tinkle of the bell that closed the door on the life he'd been leading.

He saw Alejandro take a deep breath and look around.

"Jandro." The Marine recruiter stepped over to shake his hand.

Lee and his familia turned, staring at him.

"You've brought your family. Wonderful." The recruiter turned to the family. "Bet you're proud of this young man. Do you have any final questions for me?" He turned to Jandro. "Are you excited?" He clasped his shoulder. "I'm proud to have you joining me."

"Thank you." Jandro smiled.

Lee stared, struck dumb. *What the hell? Why did Jandro*

never tell me?

"I can't wait. It's what I've always wanted to do." Alejandro turned to face everyone. "I'm not sure why we're here, but you need to know. I've enlisted and I leave for boot camp at the beginning of the year."

Mama burst into tears. Tio Mateo and his sister looked stunned. Lee cracked the first smile on his face that he'd had in days, then he started laughing. He leaned against a desk grinning while the rest of Jandro's family were whispering together. He just knew his mama was going to start her hysterics. She didn't disappoint.

"Mi hijo." His mother was wiping her eyes and sniffling. "Why are you doing this?" She clamped her lips together as Mateo spoke to her, too low for Lee to hear.

Jacinta hugged him. "I'm going to miss you. Why didn't you tell me?"

Jandro hugged her back and ruffled her hair. "To tell you was to tell the world, little media queen."

She laughed. "I've already tweeted it."

"See what I mean?" Jandro rolled his eyes grinning down at her. "You have no secrets, and neither does anyone else in the family with you around."

Lee snorted. God's honest truth. Certain that the cops would have found him if she'd have known his location.

"Alejandro." Mateo stepped over to his side. "I'm proud of you, mi hijo." He pulled Alejandro into a hug.

The rest of their conversation was carried out too low for Lee to hear. He wondered when they'd get around to remembering him. Not that he was in any hurry, obviously. He had a damned good idea why they were there. Lee glanced around and headed over to the water fountain.

He was still thirsty from his hangover. He looked over. The water fountain was one of those fancy ones with a spigot.

He looked for a cup and glanced over at the sailor behind the desk. "Is there a cup I can use?"

"Sure." The man leaned over and pulled a cup out from the bottom drawer of his desk. "Here you go."

Lee poured a cup and drank. He watched the man watch him.

"What?"

"Lee Santiago?"

"Who's asking?" He narrowed his eyes at the man. He really wasn't in the mood to play games. "Look, I'll make it easy. My family wants to get rid of me. I'd like to stay but I promised my abuela that I'd go. How can I stay near home?"

The man looked him up and down. He leaned back in his chair.

"It sounds like you're trouble. Boot camp will curb that, even if you think it won't." He leaned forward. "If you want a duty station near here, the closest we have is Oakland or San Diego."

"That will work for me."

"Let's get your Asvab done ASAP. We can take the

prelim now and there is one scheduled in LA for tomorrow." He gave Lee a hard look. "Don't miss it. I'll pick you up in plenty of time to make it, so all you have to do is be there when I arrive."

Lee nodded. "Fine. Let's do this."

He stood and shook his hand. "I'm Chief Johnson. I'll be your liaison until your induction. Follow me. Let's get you the initial test."

Lee followed him into the room that Alejandro had exited. Small and basic, exactly what Lee expected from a government building. None of the glamour of the outer office. Lee guessed this room wasn't shown unless you were serious.

The chief shut the door.

"Now, please have a seat." He gestured at the plastic molded chairs facing a computer. "Lee, do you want to enlist?" He sat down, pulling out a seat to face Lee. "I need to ask. Your uncle and mother called and talked to me early this morning. They don't seem to understand that no one can force you to enlist."

"I promised my abuela I would." He swallowed heavily, closing his eyes. "She's worried about me. I didn't realize how much."

"They mentioned the police. They didn't seem to understand, but if you have an arrest record, or are wanted for a felony, the military won't take you. At least, the Navy and Marines won't. There are too many people wanting to join despite the war. So, what is going on?"

Lee sat up straighter, running his hands through his hair,

tugging slightly on the overlong tips. He gave a strangled laugh.

"God. My best friend died of an overdose. The police were blaming me. I don't know why. But evidently I had an alibi. Even if I couldn't remember it." His voice raw, his heart twisting in pain thinking of it. "I'd never do anything to hurt him. He didn't even do drugs, nothing serious at any rate. I don't understand it, nor why they'd blame me. I don't do drugs."

"Do you have an arrest record?" The chief shifted, leaning back.

"Surprisingly, no."

The chief laughed. "So you haven't been caught."

Lee felt a flush rise, his cheeks heating. "No, I haven't been caught."

Johnson pointed to the markings on his lower arm. "Neither have I. These are hash marks for every four years I've served. Each time I've also gotten a good conduct medal." He laughed. "We call them haven't got caught medals."

Lee snorted and couldn't stop the grin. "Maybe the Navy would work for me."

"Maybe." Johnson waved at the computer. "First, the pretest for the Asvab. We can then look at ratings, see what you'd be interested in. Sign the papers and be ready for me tomorrow for the real test. I'll need to get your High School transcripts and any college transcripts if you've gone."

Lee nodded.

"Then at induction we do a drug test. Don't fail it."

His stomach sank, this was real. His family wanted him gone. They were guaranteeing it with this move. His nostrils flared as he sucked back what he really wanted to say. It wasn't Chief Johnson's fault. He rubbed his hands over his face. He had to suck it up. Regardless of his mom and uncle, he'd promised his abuela. He couldn't break his promise to Mama Rosa. She'd been there for him no matter what he'd done. He could do this for her.

"I won't." Lee faced the computer. "Let's do this."

"Good man." Johnson clapped him on the shoulder and stood. He slid a sheet of paper in front of Lee. "Follow these directions to log on and take the test. I'll check on you periodically. It should take about an hour."

Lee watched him leave, shutting the door behind him. He looked at the paper and shook his head. Simple and easy to follow directions. Lee fired up the computer and got started.

Lee sat back, stretching his hands and cracking his knuckles. So far the questions and problems had been interesting. The chief had looked in a few minutes ago, nodded and backed out. With a quick twist to his back, and arms overhead to stretch, Lee shook them out and went back to the questions. He loved puzzles, surprised to find enjoyment in the odd questions and brain teasers, though some of the questions were so easy he had to wonder why they were in there.

Lee glanced at his watch to see how much time had passed. He'd heard Johnson checking on him a couple of times but hadn't looked up. Lee stood up and stuck his head out the door.

"I've finished."

"Good." Johnson stood up and headed toward him.

Lee backed up, opening the door all the way.

"Let's see your score."

The chief slid in Lee's vacated chair and saved his work, typing in information into a program. He sat back and looked at Lee in surprise.

"Were you in the honor society in High School?"

Lee laughed. "No way. All that work and having to deal with those stuck up assholes and bitches? No way in hell. I've only known two people that I'd ever even consider hanging with that were in it. My sister and her best friend. How they stand it, I don't know."

God, Izzy. What the hell was he going to do about her?

"Hmm. Well, you did really well on the test. We'll see how you do on the real one tomorrow. Follow me; I need to get the information on your High School and college."

"Sounds good."

Lee sat in front of the chief's desk. Maybe this wouldn't be so bad.

* * * *

Isabelle wondered what was going on at the Santiago's. She'd been grounded when she got home. Her father had found out somehow that she and Caroline had gone to the party at Lenny's house. She hadn't heard from Jacinta or Lee for the past couple of days. Admittedly, it was Christmas, but usually they at least called each other. Worried, she'd slipped out and taken Jacinta her gift and found out Lee still wasn't home. Her heart sunk. He hadn't bothered to call her either, like he'd said.

They'd taken part of the tree down when her father must have found out she wasn't home. He called, demanding she return immediately. She left with still no glimpse of Lee.

Her dad was waiting for her when she got home. "Where were you?"

"Jacinta's. I dropped off her Christmas gift."

"You were grounded."

"Dad, it's Christmas break. My best friend's family is mourning and I wanted to help. I wasn't doing anything here. I was helping them clean up from Christmas."

"No more parties, Isabelle. I don't want to see you in an early grave." He turned away, rubbing his temples. "I just want you girls safe."

"I'm sorry." Isabelle sniffed. "I promise. No more parties."

Her dad looked tired.

"Then, I suppose you can help out your friend. Just make sure I know where you are."

Isabelle nodded, she could do that. She didn't often see the softer side of her father. "I will. I'll text you if I leave."

"Thank you." He sighed. "I have to finish up the funeral arrangements for your friend. I'll be home later. Just save a plate of supper for me."

He left, the door shutting softly behind him.

Isabelle started supper in the slow cooker and then headed upstairs to read.

Her phone rang. Glancing at the caller ID, her heart sped up. Lee. He'd finally called. She swiped it and spoke.

"Hello." God, how stupid could she get?

"Izzy? It's Lee."

"Lee." Her nipples perked at the sound of his voice. Thank God he couldn't see her. "How are you doing?"

"Fine." His voice was rough. No way was he fine. He probably didn't want to talk about it. Guys were funny that way.

"Really?"

"No. Lenny's dead. My family is pissed. I don't remember anything about the night of the party and I don't know what to do." Lee sounded hoarse, like he'd been crying and screaming at the same time. Maybe he had.

"Nothing?" Isabelle thought she would cry. "Maybe that's better." Her heart ached. She knuckled her eyes. He really didn't know it was her that morning. She'd been afraid of that.

"Yeah, maybe it is." He was silent for a bit. "Are you okay?"

"Fine." She wasn't. Her heart was breaking.

"Izzy, was it you?"

She sniffled. Why should she confirm it? Her face heated, trying to stop her tears from falling. "Bye, Lee."

Isabelle made sure she hung up. She set her phone carefully down on her nightstand grabbed her pillow, hugging it to her body, burying her head and letting loose a scream. Her chest ached. Her breath hitched. Tears leaked out no matter how hard she tried to stop them.

Shortly after that, she got a text from Jacinta that Alejandro had signed up to join the Marines and was leaving at the beginning of the year.

It wasn't even personal. Jacinta was the queen of multiple messaging. She had it down to an art.

Isabelle didn't call her. Breathing hurt. She couldn't just lay here in bed. Her thoughts were tearing her apart. Despite her father liking the tree up through New Year's Eve, Isabelle took it down. She cleaned the kitchen, the living room and the bathrooms. Finally, it was time for bed. She couldn't help but cry herself to sleep.

Morning came early. Isabelle tromped down the stairs, phone in hand.

"Morning."

Isabelle grunted.

"I want you to stay around the house today. No sneaking out."

"But, Dad, I was going to go to Jacinta's. Her brother is leaving for the Marines and I wanted to say good-bye."

"Right." He didn't sound like he believed her.

"Look. I'll prove it." Isabelle opened her messages and scrolled to the one. "Here, see." She pushed it across the table.

"I'll look." He picked it up and read the message. "Hmm."

Isabelle wiggled. He didn't give it back. He was doing something to it. She looked over, trying to see. He set it back down and slid it over to her.

"Where did you get that phone? It's not yours."

"My old phone had pictures of me, Jacinta, and Lee on it. The time stamps backed up Lee's alibi that he wasn't anywhere near Lenny when he died. His uncle Mateo had let me use an old phone in gratitude until I got mine back."

"That's not an old phone. It's an iPhone."

"Dad, it is to him. He's upgraded twice since he had this one."

Her dad shook his head and grumbled.

"He let me have it because the pictures gave Lee his alibi. Mateo was grateful."

Not that Isabelle cared if she ever got the phone back. If she did, she'd delete every one of them.

"Fine. Keep the phone then. I'd rather you had one anyway."

"Can I go over to Jacinta's later?"

He glanced at the phone and frowned. "No. I'm sure they'll be at the Rodriguez funeral. You can say good-bye then." He stood up, taking his bowl to the sink. "Stay home or you can come to the church and help there this morning."

Isabelle shook her head. "I have a book report due for English. I need to finish it before break is over."

"Do that, but don't even think about leaving. The funeral is today at two."

She watched him leave. Her lip trembled. Damnit. She didn't want to cry anymore. Her eyes stung, her nose was stuffed, and all she wanted was to cry on her best friend's shoulder.

It hurt. She wanted to say good-bye to Alejandro and spend time with her best friend. She refused to think about Lee. Alejandro had always been like her big brother. He treated her the same way he treated Jacinta. Their house wouldn't be the same without him there.

With him gone and Lenny dead, it would never be the same. She was afraid that Lee would get worse. There was absolutely nothing she could do about it.

Isabelle went back to her room. She knuckled a tear away. At least her father accepted her explanation as to why she had a new phone. Especially as he already knew about the party. Luckily he knew nothing about Lee.

She sniffled and looked out her window. She could just

see the tip of the Santiago's roof. Isabelle wondered why she hadn't heard from Jacinta since yesterday.

Isabelle turned away from the window. Her jaw tight, she swallowed, trying to keep the tears back. How could Lee have not known it was her?

She checked her phone again. Dammit. Nothing. She swore every Santiago had fallen off the face of the earth. Isabelle had never seen Jacinta not on social media this long. It could only mean that something serious had happened. Isabelle couldn't help imagining the worst.

She was an idiot. Dialing, she called Jacinta. It rang and finally went to voice mail. Now she was worried. Maybe she just couldn't answer. Time to text her.

Is everything okay?

Yes. You won't believe what happened!!!

What?

GTG. TTYL

At least she knew everything was okay. It was less than satisfactory. She couldn't even cry on Jacinta's shoulder. Now she just wondered what the news was. It had to be good for three exclamation points.

Isabelle scrolled through her phone wondering what her dad had been looking at. Nothing interesting was on it.

She opened her cloud account. The pictures of her and Lee were uploaded. Oh God. Isabelle felt the tears slide down the side of her face. She flicked through them.

How could he not remember?

Her stomach ached, her head ached, her eyes and nose

burned from crying. Isabelle threw herself across the bed, burying her head in her pillows. She lay there, trying to keep the memories of that night at bay. She nodded off, letting oblivion take her thoughts away.

A heavy tread echoed up the stairs, waking her. It had to be her father. He didn't believe in the luxury of carpet. His words. Isabelle snorted. Right, carpet… a luxury, one she happily did without. She couldn't imagine having to vacuum carpet. The wood and tile were bad enough to sweep every day.

A knock sounded on her door.

"Come in."

Her father stepped in and looked out the window, giving her a sidelong look. "Take a shower and get ready." He turned to leave. "You know you can talk to me about whatever is bothering you."

Right, like he wouldn't blow a gasket. "I'm fine."

"Get ready. I'll wait for you downstairs." He stood at the door, his back to her. "His family and friends need comfort in their time of grief."

"Okay. I'll hop in the shower." She stood up. "Can I go to Jacinta's after? I'm worried about how they are doing. Lenny spent all his time over there. Plus, Alejandro leaves soon and I want to say good-bye."

"I don't think that's a good idea."

"Please, Dad. Alejandro's always been like a big brother to me. I just want to say good-bye."

He looked at her. Isabelle knew her red rimmed eyes and

swollen nose made her look like hell.

"We'll see. If he's at the funeral you can talk to him there. Tell him good-bye. If he's not there you can go over."

Isabelle sighed in defeat. "Okay. But you won't forget, will you? You'll let me go if I don't see him?"

"Yes. Now you probably should get ready." He shook his head. "You don't look so good."

Her father left, closing the door behind him. Isabelle stuck out her tongue at the closed door. She wanted to scream at him, but she knew that would only make it worse. She'd learned to pick her battles with her dad.

If she could avoid seeing Alejandro at the funeral maybe she could go over there, talk to Lee and say good-bye to Alejandro. She missed the whole family but she couldn't help wanting to see Lee. She knew he had to be upset about Lenny. She just wished she could be there to comfort him. She was an idiot.

Opening her closet door, Isabelle quickly pulled out clothes for the funeral. She'd have to look appropriate, or her father would send her to change. Laying them out on her bed, Isabelle headed to the shower. She had to hurry or her dad would leave her behind.

Turning on the shower, Isabelle undressed, dropping her dirty clothes on the floor. Stepping in, the hot drops splashed on her skin, stinging her eyes as she turned away. Backing into the spray Isabelle arched, her muscles loosening in the heat. She stood and let the water run down her body. The rhythm of the drops against her back relaxed her.

Before it got too late, Isabelle soaped up quickly, rinsing off in the stream of warm water.

"Are you ready?"

Isabelle heard her father yell up the stairs. She turned off the shower and grabbed a towel, wrapping it around her. Isabelle opened the door and stuck her head out.

"I just have to get dressed."

"Don't take too long. I have to make sure everything is ready for the funeral."

"I won't."

She grabbed another towel and rubbed it through her hair. She headed to her room, leaning over and wrapping her hair in the towel before throwing it back. The turban would keep her hair out of the way while she dressed and put on a little makeup.

Quickly dressing, Isabelle grabbed her makeup. She'd feel naked without her mascara and a bit of lip gloss. Any more than that would set off her father about the evils of prostitution. As if she'd ever!

Looking around her room, Isabelle grabbed her purse and headed downstairs.

"I'm ready, Dad."

"Good. Can you grab the tray of cookies? I've got the coffee grounds already at the church."

"Sure." Sliding her purse strap over her head, Isabelle grabbed the tray of cookies that were on the counter. "Are there more than this?" She knew how much the boys, or rather young men, could devour.

"There are more at the church. The ladies have been bringing food and storing it in the church kitchen since yesterday."

Isabelle nodded. At every funeral some of the food was better off never seeing the light of day, not that she could say so. Isabelle or Caroline just kept their mouths shut and put it out. Maybe someone would like it. Doubtful, but you never know. Thinking of Caroline had her calling out to her dad.

"Dad, where's Caroline?"

"She's already at the church. She volunteered to be there when the ladies dropped off their offerings."

"Oh. Hmm. Okay."

"You sound surprised."

"She just doesn't usually volunteer is all."

"Maybe she's turning over a new leaf."

Isabelle snorted. Sure she had. Caroline had probably snuck her boyfriend into the church. Isabelle was surprised Caroline had stuck around as long as she had on her birthday. It wasn't that Caroline didn't care, she was just hugely self-centered. Whatever she did would profit her in some way.

"Maybe Dad." What else could she say?

Her dad was out the door and opening up the rear doors to the van. He'd had it as long as Isabelle could remember. An old VW paneled van that he'd had since he was a young man. He liked to tell the story of how he'd fixed it up. Lee and Lenny used to call it the shaggin' wagon.

A twist hit her heart, a bit of pain as she realized she'd never see Lenny again. Isabelle stopped and took a deep breath. She'd never thought of him as a close friend or anything. But she'd known him for years. He hung out with Lee like she hung out with Jacinta. Buddies and best friends since they were little.

There'd be no more teasing and chasing. No more changing channels when they got home regardless of what Jacinta and she were watching. No more stealing snacks or noogies when the girls weren't looking. Isabelle swallowed, tightening her lips.

"Are you all right?"

Her dad's voice had her sniffing and straightening her spine.

"Yes. I just realized I'll never hear Lenny teasing me about your van again." She let out a breath of air. "It suddenly became real he's gone."

Her dad wrapped an arm around her shoulders and gave her an awkward hug.

"Unfortunately, that's life. It goes on no matter what happens. Young lives or old lives, time passes and takes a toll on all of us. You just have to have faith and continue to live."

"I guess. I've never really had someone I knew die. At least not that I remember."

"It eventually happens to all of us. We get older and our friends die. It's part of life."

"I know." Isabelle walked the rest of the way to the van. "It just seems weird is all. Not in a good way." She put the cookies into the back of the van and clambered inside. "I'll get used to it."

Her dad nodded and closed the doors. He circled around and climbed in the driver's seat. Inserting the key, he turned it on. He carefully checked both ways before he backed out of the driveway.

"By the way, what did Lenny call my van?"

"Er, you really don't want to know."

"It can't be that bad."

Isabelle sighed. She'd hoped her father hadn't caught that. He could be tenacious, so she knew she'd have to tell him sooner or later.

"He called it the shaggin' wagon."

To her surprise her dad let out a bark of laughter.

"That's what I used to call it when I was younger." He smiled. "Until your mother found out. I was dating her when one of my buddies called it that. She wouldn't talk to me for days afterward."

Isabelle involuntarily wheezed, her jaw dropping. Her dad always seemed too strict to ever have been any fun. She wondered what changed him. She rolled her eyes. Oh yeah, her mom's death probably. She barely remembered her. She probably wouldn't if she hadn't watched the videos of her. Her mom holding her or Caroline in most of them. She died when Isabelle had barely been one. Her dad had always been a sourpuss. The only softness in his voice was when he talked about her.

Isabelle couldn't be really sad for someone she never felt she knew. Most of the time she didn't really feel the loss. She'd never really known any difference. Her dad was always there. Too strict, but all her friends said that about their parents. Isabelle just knew her mom died in a car crash.

Her teachers commented on how sad it was that she lost her mom. True, but Isabelle never knew what it was like to have a mom in her life. As strict as her father behaved, she knew he loved her, but he did not tolerate mistakes or what he called bad behavior.

If he knew what she'd done on her birthday, he would definitely call it bad behavior. She didn't know what he would do. Grounding for life, maybe. She'd gotten past the age of being spanked. To punish her, he knew to take something she cherished away.

Isabelle grabbed the seat as they turned a corner.

"Put your seatbelt on."

Isabelle pulled it over her shoulder and clicked it into place. "Sorry, I forgot." No way would she tell him he'd surprised her. He had actually seemed human. Then he'd put on his serious face again, like he'd never cracked a smile.

Her heart pounded. Isabelle hoped she'd get a chance to see Lee while they were there. Maybe he'd remembered that it was her that night. Isabelle shook her head. She knew he'd too much to deal with to worry about what was probably a common occurrence to him. Her heart twisted. Despite the pain that thought caused, Isabelle would be there if he needed a friend. If something happened to Jacinta she didn't know how she'd deal with it. Isabelle would do what she could, offer her sympathy and a shoulder to cry on.

The van shut off. Isabelle released her belt and went around to the back of her van. Her dad went to greet the men from the funeral home. They were pulling up with the hearse.

Her breath caught and her eyes stung. God, Lenny lay in there, silent and cold. Her nose stung trying to hold the tears back. Isabelle hated wakes. This was her first time attending one for a friend. She leaned against the door of the van and took a deep breath, and another. She couldn't imagine the pain his parents were going through. Or Lee.

Regardless of her hurt, Lee would be hurting more. She had to ignore her pain. He would need her friendship to get through the day. One more deep breath and Isabelle straightened her back. She'd be strong, for herself, and for Lee. Even for her dad, he needed her to help make the church ready for Lenny's family.

Isabelle grabbed the tray and closed the van doors. She headed to the doors they'd just brought Lenny through. She turned before reaching the doors of the nave. The room they'd use for refreshments was just off the narthex. Normally for those parents who needed to feed or change a child during services, for wakes and funerals they used it for refreshment, a break from the emotional turmoil of grieving. Behind the doors on the far wall was the church kitchen. On the other side of the narthex were the bathrooms.

She proceeded to help with the set up. Volunteers were

already setting up the light snacks. For the funeral tomorrow a meal would be served after the burial. For now, light snacks to help keep people occupied, and any children from getting cranky.

Isabelle grabbed boxes of tissues and set them out in the narthex and on the pews in the church, near where the family would be sitting and standing. The florists were arriving, placing their offerings where her father directed. If she could just forget this was for someone she knew, she could get through it.

Finally everything settled down. Isabelle went back into the waiting room. She could hear her father speaking, a woman crying and another man's voice. It could only be Lenny's family. She didn't know what to say. Isabelle figured she'd stay here until she did. Or until her father called her out. Maybe she'd stay here until Jacinta found her.

She'd text Jacinta her location. They could hide in here.

The voices moved nearer, entering the room.

"Isabelle."

She looked up.

"This is my daughter."

Too late to escape. Mr. Rodriguez looked broken and Lenny's mom was even worse.

"Mr. and Mrs. Rodriquez…" Isabelle didn't know what to say.

Mr. Rodriguez held open his arms.

"I'm so sorry about Lenny. So sorry. I'll miss him so

much." She could hear herself babble.

"Me too, Izzy." His arms hugged her to him. "Me too." He passed her off to Mrs. Rodriguez.

She just squeezed her tight, silently crying into Isabelle's shoulder.

"I didn't realize you knew my daughter."

Mr. Rodriguez nodded at her dad.

"Of course we do. From church and from her hanging out with Jacinta. Lee would have to drag them along to our house from time to time. The boys delighted in teasing them." He smiled and then the sadness returned to his eyes. "Our house will be too empty now." He closed his eyes, a tortured look on his face. "Too full of ghosts and memories."

Isabelle held onto Mrs. Rodriguez. She didn't have much of a choice as she clung to her.

"I can't believe it. I can't believe my Lenny is gone."

Her whisper broke Isabelle's heart. Isabelle hugged her tighter. She didn't realize they were the same height. Mrs. Rodriguez seemed frail in her arms.

"I'm sorry. I wish it weren't so."

"Lorna, come on. We need to say our good-byes before everyone arrives." Mr. Rodriguez pulled her away from Isabelle. "The family should be arriving soon."

Her dad escorted them toward the front of the church where Lenny lay.

The doors to the church opened. Lenny's siblings arrived. It was obvious they were related to Lenny. Isabelle could see what Len would have looked like if he'd lived another twenty years.

Lenny was his parent's oops baby. At least ten years separated him from his youngest sister, even more years separated him from his brother. Lenny's older brother and his wife looked stunned, walking silently up the steps. Len's sisters looked harried, too busy trying to corral their children while their husbands just watched.

Isabelle grabbed a tissue and wiped her eyes. She wouldn't be able to pretend she didn't know the family. It just wasn't going to work. She watched from the doors as Mr. and Mrs. Rodriguez said good-bye to their son. Their sobs reached her across the room. Their embrace, obviously to hold each other up as they faced their heartbreak.

"Your parent's are through there." Isabelle gestured into the church proper. "With Lenny."

They nodded, not speaking. Isabelle couldn't imagine what they were going through.

The taste of her tears reached the edges of her mouth. Isabelle felt them tracing down her cheeks, soaking into the neckline of her dress. The doors to the church creaked open heralding the first attendees to pay their respects. Snagging a tissue, Isabelle scrubbed her face and slipped into the side room without looking to see who had arrived.

CHAPTER FOUR

Lee stared at the doors to the church. Inside his best buddy lay dead. The place looked deserted. Only a couple of cars were in the parking lot. His familia slamming doors and getting noisily out of their cars. Everyone came. They'd known Lenny most of his life. Mama Rosa had her rosary beads and her handkerchief. Everyone shifting, uncomfortable in their nicest clothes.

Lee could hear his Tio Juan hushing his children. Lee knew they had no clue as to why they were there. He smashed down his anger when his cousin asked to see the dead body. He didn't know better; Lee knew that. He didn't know that Lee's life was spiraling beyond his control because of this catastrophic event. Lee swallowed back a sob. He didn't know that Lee had lost his best friend.

Lee grabbed the handle of the church door and pulled it open. The creak of the door surprised a chuckle out of him. It sounded like a door in a bad horror movie. His mouth turned down. It was a bad horror movie for him. It still didn't feel real. Lee had a feeling it would seem real all too fast.

Not waiting for the rest of his slow moving family, Lee stepped inside. The sun through the stained glass windows had him walking through a rainbow as he moved forward. The cheerfulness of the entry eased him in some indefinable way. He headed for the short rise of stairs. Looking up, he saw a shadow slip into a room to the side.

Ignoring everything but the open doors that would lead him into a world filled with pain, Lee ascended. One step after another bringing him closer to saying good-bye to his best friend. He gripped the railing, his knuckles white as he forced himself closer.

His throat swelled as he held back the pain. His vision blurred as he looked through the doors of the nave and saw the casket sitting there. He made a choking sound, moving forward to grip the doors. He couldn't step forward further into the room. Wetness spilled down his cheeks. Lee moaned, a low sound of pain escaping him.

Lee took a deep breath, easing the pain in his chest. He closed his eyes, a sob escaping. Arms circled him, offering comfort. He turned and wrapped his arms around the warm body. The scent of honeysuckle filled his lungs. He silently cried, his face buried against her hair. Loss assailed him. The loss of his best friend, of a life he could never have, of a girl he could only dream about. The girl he knew he had to give up to keep her out of his fucked up life.

"I'm so sorry, Lee."

The whisper broke another sob from him. He couldn't push his anguish away. The sight of the casket tore him apart.

"Do you want to sit down, or did you want to go

forward?"

It was the question he'd been asking himself for days. He wanted to go forward with his life. Lee knew that wasn't the question she was asking though. Opening his eyes, everything was blurry. He spied the tissue box, and releasing one arm, snagged a handful.

"Forward, Isabelle." He straightened up, keeping an arm around her waist. "But stay with me, chiquita, okay?"

"Okay, Lee." She snuggled into his side.

Lee warmed at how good it felt to have her by his side. Isabelle, the one girl he always knew he needed to stay away from. Besides being his kid sister's best friend, her father always showed his disdain for him and his family. He never seemed to approve of them. Lee wasn't sure why, but he didn't let it bother him. Right now, he didn't care. Lee needed her to get through the nightmare in front of him.

"I need to pay my respects." Lee leaned over and drew a deep breath, breathing in the sweet scent of Isabelle's hair. "Stay with me."

Her arm tightened around his waist. She felt so delicate against him.

"I will. As long as you need me."

Lee paused a moment longer, drew a deep breath and headed toward the front of the church. He ignored the evil eye of Isabelle's father. His eyes were drawn to the casket. He moved slowly down the aisle, his steps faltering the closer he came. His breath stuttered and he came to a halt.

The arm around him urged him forward. He took step after step. His eyes and nose stung as he stared into the face of his best friend. Dressed in a damn cholo suit that he'd only be caught dead in. Fuck.

He caught movement in his peripheral vision but he couldn't stop looking at Lenny. He took a deep breath, shuddering as he drew it in. He looked up and saw Lenny's parents behind a haze of tears he refused to let fall.

Mr. R. came over and hugged Lee. The tears he'd tried unsuccessfully to hold at bay, running down his face in silent grief. Lee hugged him back with one arm, the other holding Isabelle tight to his side. Her arms encircled him, her unspoken comfort easing his soul.

"Lee."

Mr. R. said nothing else. His arms tightened, his grip almost painful. Lee figured he didn't know what else to say.

"I'm going to miss him."

Mr. R. nodded. Mrs. R. stood turned toward the casket, her gaze cloudy as she stared at Lenny where he lay inside. Lee thought she looked lost and confused. He felt the same way. A piece of himself lay in the casket, a spark of life that had been extinguished.

Mr. R. cleared his throat and stepped back. His hand squeezing Lee's shoulder convulsively.

"Thank you for coming." Mr. R's voice harsh, and rough from the tears he'd already shed.

"I'm so sorry." Lee had to say it. What else could you

say at a funeral? Especially when your best friend lay in front of you.

Lee moved and Mr. R's hand fell away. He turned to face Mrs. Rodriguez. Isabelle's arms slid away, leaving one hand on his back. Amazed at how much comfort her touch held.

"Mrs. R., I'm sorry." Lee pulled her hand toward him. She continued to ignore him, her attention on Lenny.

"It fits him well. I knew it would. I got it for church services. I told him he needed something formal to wear. He wouldn't wear it, until now." She turned to Lee. "He looks nice, doesn't he?"

Spooked, Lee regarded Mrs. R. She didn't appear to be all there. She spoke as if Lenny were still alive. He glanced at Isabelle. She looked at her with pity on her face.

"He sure does, Mrs. Rodriguez."

She nodded at Isabelle's agreement. She turned back and continued to stare at Lenny.

Mr. R. came over and put an arm around her, the pain evident in his face.

Lee swallowed, pulling Isabelle fully into his arms, resting his chin on top of her head while he looked at Lenny.

Right now, only the feel of Isabelle against him kept him sane. Her warmth chasing away the cold. A hand landed on his shoulder and he started. Lee glanced over to see Alejandro looking at Lenny, tears in his eyes.

"God, it doesn't seem real, does it?" Alejandro was as choked up he was.

"No." Lee's voice sounded hoarse even to his own ears. "No, and I hope that I wake up and it's all just a nightmare."

Alejandro's hand tightened on his shoulder. He said nothing.

"Lee, you need to move on." Jacinta nudged him. "There are people waiting."

Lee looked behind him and could see the line forming. Mr. and Mrs. R. were looking uncertain, glancing from Lenny to the people moving into the church. He felt Isabelle pulling away, holding on to just his arm.

"Lee, why don't you sit down?" Isabelle tugged him away from the casket to the front pew. "Let me help Lenny's mama and papa get situated. I'll be right back."

Lee held on to her hand, only to feel her tug it away. His body turned cold with the loss of her contact. Her touch was the one thing that was getting him through today.

"Sit. We'll be right here with you." Alejandro and Jacinta sat on either side of him. Jacinta grabbed his hand, seeking and giving comfort.

Lee watched Isabelle go over to the Rodriguezes. She guided them to the side of Lenny's casket and brought forward Lee's abuela and family. She introduced each one, letting them hug Lenny's parents and urging them on until the line was moving. Once she wasn't needed, she turned back to Lee. Stepping closer she held out her hand.

Lee reached out and pulled her back to him. Nudging Alejandro over, he fitted her next to him. He needed her near and he didn't really care what anyone else thought.

"I see where I rate, bro." Alejandro gave a low laugh.

"Shut up."

His teasing didn't even bother Lee. Isabelle was the only one that quieted the screaming voice in his head. Glad, finally, that he'd agreed to enlist. He needed to be away from here. Watching Lenny, his family, and all of their friends pay their respects brought home that it could have been him lying there, his familia the ones grieving.

His chest ached, pain and grief swirling. Lenny's loss one he wouldn't easily get over, if ever. He glanced down as Isabelle. Leaving meant losing the chance of ever getting to know her better. Lee decided it would be better to let her go. She had the whole world in front of her. He wouldn't drag her down.

Looking at the line of people, hearing the tears and grief surrounding them, Lee swallowed. If he stayed, this was his future. It was only a matter of time.

* * * *

Isabelle felt her stomach lurch. Nothing seemed to settle it lately. After the funeral her father had brought her straight home. Sitting next to Lee, Alejandro, and Jacinta she couldn't say she hadn't said good-bye. She had.

Then, her father took her phone. He wouldn't even say

why. She had a feeling it was because Lee wouldn't let her go until he'd left. Her dad didn't want her involved with him.

Caroline had let her send a text to Jacinta, but refused to let her use her phone again. She'd had no contact until break was over and school started back up. Her dad reluctantly gave her phone back to her then. It was dead. Once it was charged, Isabelle laughed. Jacinta had blown up her phone messaging her. She didn't have time to read them all.

She searched and took a deep breath. She wouldn't cry. She wouldn't. There wasn't one call or message from Lee.

Lunch rolled around and Isabelle sat next to Jacinta and sniffled.

"Amiga, what's the matter? You're gonna look like a raccoon."

Isabelle gulped, drying her eyes, trying to stop her tears. "It's Lee."

"What did he do now?"

"He didn't call." She tried to suppress the ache in her voice. From the look on Jacinta's face, she hadn't succeeded. "I thought for sure he would call again. He didn't let me go during Lenny's funeral."

"I know. I thought for sure he'd call, too." Jacinta hugged her hard. "I need to tell you…"

"What?" Isabelle wiped her eyes.

"Lee is gone."

Isabelle pushed her away. "What? When? Why didn't you tell me?"

"I texted you. He left the day after Jandro." Jacinta's eyes watered. "I lost both mi hermano's right after Lenny's funeral."

Isabelle threw her arms around her, pulling her in for a hug. She hated her friend hurting.

"I haven't had a chance to read them. Dad just gave me my phone back." Isabelle whispered. "Lee never called or texted."

"He went…"

"Don't talk about him. I don't want to know." Isabelle interrupted. Her eyes ached. Her silly dreams were down the tubes.

"Let's go outside. Everyone is starting to stare." Jacinta stood, pulling her up. She grabbed a napkin and noisily blew her nose.

"Okay. I could use some air." And to let the breeze blow away her pain.

Isabelle erased the messages without reading them. Her BFF was persistent, trying to bring up Lee's name but Isabelle shut her down each time. It hurt to hear his name. Jacinta finally stopped trying to mention Lee to Isabelle. Lunches were subdued as they talked. The funeral and both Lee and Alejandro leaving seemed to cast a pall over both of them.

Isabelle refused to ask about Lee. Grief stricken at the funeral, clinging to her for comfort Lee wouldn't let her go. Lenny's death had shaken Lee. Isabelle could see it.

Maybe he was taking a good long look at his life. She hoped so.

Much as Isabelle loved Lee, she also knew it would go nowhere unless he got his life together. Hearing the facts come out about Lenny, knowing Lee involved himself in the same things brought that home.

Isabelle didn't want a man that did nothing but party. She didn't want a man that went from one woman to another. She didn't want a man that did nothing but drink and do drugs. She didn't want a man who sold drugs.

That was why she didn't ask about Lee. If he got his life together and he wanted her, he knew where she lived. She knew he had her phone number. Lenny's death had made Isabelle take a good long look at her life. She couldn't sit, pining away for Lee. She had to think of her future.

She'd always planned to go to college. Jacinta and she talked about it constantly. Isabelle checked out the local community colleges, but hadn't decided on which she'd prefer, let alone a course to study.

She kept hoping that Lee would notice her, fall madly in love, and sweep her off her feet. The night they'd spent together only fueled her dreams more, giving substance to her imagination. Isabelle laughed bitterly. What a fool she was. Lee had left without even a good-bye.

Without Lee around, Isabelle finally talked to her counsellor and started to apply for scholarships and colleges. Late to be doing that, but Isabelle figured she might as well try. She rubbed her chest. She would go as far away as she could. Staying home to go to college would hurt too much.

The front door opened and closed. Caroline had gone out after school with friends, so this had to be her dad.

"Dad, is that you?"

"Yes." He looked in the kitchen. "Did you make supper?"

Isabelle rolled her eyes. She always made supper. If they relied on Caroline, they would all starve. She burned everything she touched.

"Yes." Thinking about it made her stomach roll. The taste of bile in her mouth made her shudder. "I don't know if I'll eat. I don't feel well."

"Hmm. Maybe you're just hungry."

Swallowing, Isabelle shook her head. "I don't think so. Maybe I'll just eat a slice of bread."

"See if that helps." Her dad grabbed a plate from the cabinet. He checked the pans on the oven sniffing appreciatively. "Smells good."

He served himself and sat at the table. The aroma of beef and noodles wafted by her nose.

Her stomach lurched and Isabelle jumped up, heading for the bathroom. Leaning over the toilet, she retched. The acid burning her throat and nostrils. Her stomach twisted painfully, bile burning as it rose again.

She could hear her father eating. The remembrance of the smell made her heave again. Isabelle rested her forehead against the cool seat. She must have picked up a bug at school. She'd been feeling ill for the last couple of weeks. She'd feel better, then sick again. Maybe she'd set up an appointment with the doctor. She'd had too many days ill recently and she wasn't getting better.

Isabelle sat hugging the toilet. The cool porcelain against her skin soothing. The throbbing in her head subsided and her stomach settled back down. She could hear her father moving around the kitchen. Hopefully putting dinner away. Isabelle didn't know if she could handle the smells again.

She was glad she'd cleaned the bathroom earlier. She'd been neglecting cleaning lately, but had felt a burst of energy earlier in the day. She'd cleaned her room, the up and downstairs bathrooms. Now she felt wrung out, a sour taste in her mouth and her stomach had her debating whether or not she'd stay sitting right here.

"Isabelle, I'll call tomorrow and make you a doctor's appointment." Her dad was outside the door. "You don't seem to be getting better."

"Okay." She took a deep breath and choked. Isabelle snaked an arm up and flushed the toilet. "I think I'm going to go to bed."

Isabelle pushed up, leaning heavily on the toilet to do so. It had to be the flu for sure. She rested against the vanity and pulled open a drawer. She needed to get the sour taste from her mouth. Hoping the flavor of the toothpaste wouldn't set her cramping stomach off again, Isabelle quickly brushed her teeth and slowly made her way upstairs.

She crawled into bed after changing. All Isabelle wanted to do was sleep. Her stomach had settled as she headed upstairs. Snuggling into bed she tried to sleep. Her mind couldn't help but repeat the last couple of months, regardless of her tired body.

The night she'd turned eighteen had been the best night of her life. Lee finally noticed her. Not that it did her any good.

Isabelle's chest ached each time she thought about him.

Despite the welcoming she always received at the Santiago's, she cringed each time she saw the pity in Mama Rosa's eyes. It made it hard to go there.

Her father unconsciously aided her in her cowardness. Rarely letting her go anywhere but church, home, or school. She wasn't sure why, but she had a feeling it had to do with Lenny's death. Not that she didn't manage to sneak out now and again. Sitting at home all night drove her a little bonkers.

Caroline had been extra careful not to get in trouble. She didn't want to be grounded. Her sister followed the rules to the letter, for now at least. Isabelle couldn't help being envious. She knew Caroline had a bit more leeway due to her age, but not much. Maybe because Isabelle was still in high school. She wouldn't be forever. Four more months to go until she graduated. The future held anything she could imagine.

Her stomach growled. After losing everything earlier, Isabelle wasn't willing to fill it back up. She still felt a bit queasy. Food, and thinking about Lee, two things she didn't need right now. He'd shown that he had no interest in her. He hadn't bothered to contact her at all since he'd left. Isabelle had to stop thinking of him. One night didn't matter. It obviously hadn't meant anything to him.

Isabelle cuddled her pillow, the softness cradling her head. She yawned and pulled up her covers. Her eyes closed, sealing in the darkness.

The sunlight shown through her eyelids. Isabelle yawned and stretched. She felt better this morning. She rolled over and checked her clock. Isabelle sat up quickly. Late for school! She must not have set her alarm last night. Getting up, she quickly hopped in the shower. In and out and dressed in a matter of minutes.

Isabelle grabbed her backpack and headed downstairs. She found her dad sitting at the kitchen table.

"Good morning. Are you feeling better?"

"Yes. I must not have set my alarm. I'm going to be late to school."

"You're excused from school for this morning. You have a doctor's appointment at nine o'clock."

"Oh. Okay." Isabelle sighed and sat down. "That's good to know, though I do feel better this morning."

"Go anyway. You haven't been feeling well lately." He took a sip of his coffee. "Do you need a ride in or are you okay?"

"I'm okay. I'll take the car if it's here."

"Mmm hmm. Your sister had a friend pick her up for classes. I let her know you'd probably need the car today."

"Thanks, Dad." Isabelle looked at the time. "I might as well head over. There will probably be paperwork to fill out."

Her father pulled out his wallet, and pulled out a card.

"You'll need this."

Isabelle grabbed it and looked. It was the health care card.

"Cool. Just give this to them?"

"Yes." He handed her a twenty dollar bill. "There is a twenty dollar copay. Just make sure you get a receipt."

"Oh. Okay." Usually her dad came with for emergencies, but this wasn't really. Isabelle wasn't sure how to take it. It felt good, not being treated like a child, but kind of scary too. "Thanks, Dad."

He looked at her and gave her a smile. It looked a little sad.

"It's time I realized you are growing up. You're eighteen and soon you'll be out of the house. I just wanted to make sure you had your head on straight." He sighed. "I know you and your sister think I'm too strict."

"No." What else was she supposed to say? He was strict, look at how long she'd been semi-grounded. But she couldn't agree could she?

He laughed. "No need to lie. I know you do. I just want to keep you alive and away from the party scene that ruins so many young lives."

"Oh."

"Go on, head to your appointment. Let me know what they say."

"Okay."

Isabelle grabbed her purse and the keys to the car. She glanced back at her dad. Reading the paper and shaking his head. He'd been different lately. Maybe because he realized that she and Caroline were grown up already. But he'd been a lot stricter also. Isabelle attributed that to Lenny's death. Too close to home, even for Isabelle.

She hadn't really rebelled because Lenny's death hurt her. She hadn't realized how much contact they'd had until he died. It felt like something was missing with him gone. Isabelle hadn't been eager to confront it. Hiding behind her father had been safe.

"Bye."

Her father nodded as she left. Isabelle unlocked the car door and slid in. She unlocked the club from the steering wheel. She shook her head. Dad insisted they use it all the time. The car was so old, Isabelle had a hard time believing someone would try to steal it. He insisted it hadn't been stolen because they kept it locked. Who could argue against that?

Starting up the car, she drove to the clinic. Parking, Isabelle looked at the club and put it back on. She shrugged, better safe than sorry. If she came out to the car missing and she hadn't put it on, she'd feel horrible. The fumes of traffic reached her nose as she pulled open the door. Isabelle grabbed her stomach and covered her mouth. It churned from the smell of the fumes. She made a beeline for the restroom hoping to make it before she lost what little she could possibly have in there.

A few minutes later, she wiped her face and headed to

the reception desk to check in.

"Are you all right?" The receptionist must have seen her sprint across the room.

"Yes. That's why I'm here. I've been sick on and off for a couple weeks."

"No problem." She handed Isabelle a clip board. "Fill this out, and I'll get you checked in."

Isabelle complied, and handed back the completed form.

"Thank you," the receptionist glanced at the page, "Isabelle. What time is your appointment?"

"Nine o'clock."

"Thank you. There is a twenty dollar copay. Do you have it or did you want it billed?"

"I have it." Isabelle pulled the money from her wallet. "I need a receipt."

"No problem. Let me get it printed." She entered information on the computer, leaned over and pulled off a sheet of paper and handed it to Isabelle. "Here you go. Have a seat and the nurse will call you when it's time to go back."

"Thank you." Isabelle nodded and took a seat, folding up the paper and stowing it in her purse. She looked at the clock. She still had a little time. Isabelle grabbed up a magazine and flipped through it. She frowned and looked at the cover. AARP, ugh, an old people's magazine. She set it down and looked up when they called her name.

"Hi, I'm Peggy. I'm Dr. Cahill's nurse. Follow me and let's get your weight."

"Hi." Isabelle stood and followed the nurse to the scale for her weight and height. She toed off her flip flops to step on the scale. Peggy adjusted a lever to get her height, scribbling the information in a notebook.

"Now to the exam room."

Isabelle followed her and Peggy took her pulse and blood pressure.

"Your blood pressure is good. So, why are you in today?"

"I've not been feeling good. I think I have the flu. My stomach had been upset for the last couple of weeks."

"Okay. Any other issues?"

"No. Well, I'm tired a lot."

"Okay." The nurse entered the information on the computer. "The doctor should be in shortly."

Isabelle flipped through her phone, checking her accounts. Jacinta had posted pics from Biology Class of the frogs they were set to dissect in different poses. Isabelle giggled, in the last one she could see Mr. Brown frowning and heading her way. Busted.

A knock and Isabelle looked up, sliding her phone back in her purse.

"Come in."

Peggy stuck her head in.

"Dr. Cahill wanted me to run a couple of tests before she came in."

Isabelle's eyes widened when Peggy pushed a cart in.

Needles. Ugh. She suppressed a shiver.

"Are you sure they're necessary?"

Peggy laughed.

"Don't like needles?"

"Not really."

"Well, I'll make it as painless as possible." Peggy tied a band around her arm. "Make a fist."

Isabelle did, the rubber band pinched her skin, digging in.

"This will pinch a bit." Peggy slide the needle into her arm.

Isabelle swallowed and looked away. The prick hurt, followed by an uncomfortable pinch inside her arm. She glanced over and saw the vial filling with deep red blood. She glanced away, stomach turning and gulping in air.

"There, all done."

Isabelle gasped as the needle slid out from underneath her skin.

A wad of cotton pressed against her elbow.

"Hold this." Peggy guided Isabelle's finger to the cotton. She pulled off a piece of tape and placed it over the cotton, nudging Isabelle's finger out of the way. "Here you go. You can take it off in about fifteen minutes."

"Thanks."

"It wasn't that bad, was it?"

"Yes."

Peggy laughed. "Well, that should be all the poking for

the day." Peggy placed a sticker on a cup and handed it to her. "Now time to pee in a cup. Take this down the hall and leave it in the door in the bathroom. I'll get this out of here and Dr. Cahill should be in shortly." She labelled the vials and left, the wheels squeaking on the cart as she pushed it out of the door.

Isabelle looked under the cotton and the color drained from her face. Ick, blood on the cotton. She pulled her finger away and glanced out the window. She only minded blood when it was hers.

Grabbing the cup, Isabelle slipped out and headed to the bathroom. Done, she placed it in the little door and headed back to the exam room. She sat and waited.

A knock on the door and Dr. Cahill entered.

"Good morning, Isabelle. I hear you think you have the flu. Let's get you checked out." She sat down in front of the computer and logged in. "I have a few questions. You haven't been in for a physical lately, so I want to get caught up."

"Okay."

Dr. Cahill asked Isabelle questions about her general health and any concerns. She entered the information on the computer. Quietly, she double checked her notes.

"Good, some of your tests results are back." She read over them. Nodded and turned back to Isabelle. "Tell me why you are in."

"I've been sick to my stomach for the last couple of weeks."

"Has anything else been bothering you?"

"I've been really tired lately. But it's been a stressful winter, plus graduation coming. I've been applying for scholarships besides my homework. Checking out colleges."

Isabelle tapped on her arm. The doctor gave her a look she didn't like. If she didn't know better, Isabelle would think it was pity.

"Busy with your boyfriend?"

Isabelle shook her head. "No, no boyfriend."

"Hmm." Dr. Cahill looked grim. "Isabelle, there is no easy way to say this. You're pregnant."

Isabelle's jaw dropped and her breath caught. Her heart raced and Isabelle pressed her hand against her heart.

"Oh God."

"I take it, this wasn't planned."

Isabelle shook her head frantically. Her father would kill her.

"What am I going to do?" Her mind raced. Pregnant. She didn't know what to do. Her eyes filled. Her whole future crumbled before her eyes. She needed to talk to Lee.

"I can go over options."

Isabelle stared at her. Options? What options did she have left? She was pregnant. One night that would affect the rest of her life. Isabelle's mind raced. What was she going to do? How would she tell her dad? Lee? Oh God. She swayed. Pregnant. Oh God.

"Isabelle." The snapping on fingers in front of her face had her focusing. "Do you know how far along you are?"

Isabelle blinked, trying to process the question.

"Isabelle, how often do you have unprotected sex?"

"Once, just once." It came out as a whisper. She looked down and realized her hands were clenched together. She was going to lose it.

"Okay. When was that?"

"December. Over Christmas break." Her father would ground her forever.

"What was the exact date?"

"It was the twenty-third."

"So you know who the father is?"

Isabelle looked up, surprised. "Of course. Why wouldn't I?"

Dr. Cahill placed a hand over Isabelle's.

"Plenty of young girls don't. Now, how about I discuss those options?"

"What options do I have?"

"You can terminate the pregnancy."

Isabelle sucked in a breath. One hand involuntarily covered her tummy, protecting it instinctively.

"I see you don't like that option. But many girls that are raped prefer that option. You can give the baby up for adoption. Or you can carry until full term and keep the baby."

"I wasn't raped." She flushed thinking about that night. She'd tried not to since Lee hadn't called her after Lenny's funeral. Isabelle thought about the options. How fast she instinctively protected the life inside her.

"That's good." Dr. Cahill sighed. "Since you knew the exact date, I wasn't sure. A lot of girls that know the exact date are raped. Then we have a whole other issue to deal with."

"I wasn't, but I don't think I could kill my baby."

"You're still within the first trimester. It would be safe. No one would have to know, you're of age."

Isabelle shook her head. "No. I couldn't kill my baby."

The doctor sighed. "You wouldn't be killing it. Medically, it's not a life yet."

"No. It is to me." Isabelle laughed softly, her hand stroking her abdomen. "I've always been pro-choice, but I've never been pregnant. I suppose that makes all the difference in the world. I couldn't even begin to think about terminating my baby."

"Well, that eliminates one option. I'll give you pamphlets on pre-natal care and get you a prescription for vitamins. We'll set up your first appointment in a month at the end of your first trimester. I'll also give you pamphlets about adoption." She typed as she talked, then turned to Isabelle. "Will the father of the baby be notified? He should also have input, especially if you are considering adoption."

"Okay." Isabelle's head whirled with the information. "Are you sure I'm pregnant?"

Dr. Cahill laughed. "I wondered if you were going to ask that. When you told Peggy your symptoms, she came and said that she recommended I have her do a pregnancy test. She can pick out a pregnant woman by practically looking at them."

Isabelle wrinkled her nose. "Is that why I had to pee in a cup?"

"Yes. The bloodwork gives me more information. If Peggy recommended a pregnancy test, I assumed you already were. This way I'll be able to see if you have any deficiencies in your blood and I can treat them right away so you have no problems going forward with your pregnancy."

Her breath shortened, becoming choppy. She was going to have Lee's baby. What would he say? What would her dad say? What was she going to do? Isabelle swayed in her chair, her hand reaching out to grab the desk.

"Whoa. Take deep breaths. Put your head between your legs." Isabelle leaned over, following her directions. She felt the doctor's hand rubbing her back. "It's going to be okay. Women have babies all the time."

"I don't know how to tell my father. He's going to kill me. And Lee? He hasn't bothered to call me again."

"Is that the baby's daddy?"

"Mm hm."

"Sit up, slowly. Are you feeling better?"

Isabelle swallowed and nodded. "Yes."

"Are you scared of your father hurting you?"

Isabelle turned and looked at the doctor, raising her brows. "My dad?"

"Yes. You said he's going to kill you."

"Oh. He'll be pissed. I'll be grounded the rest of my life." She exhaled a deep breath. "I don't know what he'll do, but he won't physically hurt me. He's a minister." Isabelle shook her head. "He is not going to be happy."

"But he won't physically harm you?"

"Of course not."

"Okay. If you feel physically threatened call or come here immediately. There are places you can go to be safe. If we are closed you can go to the hospital or the police station."

Isabelle smirked. Her father raising a hand to her? He didn't believe in violence. Not since she and Caroline had reached their teens.

"I don't think that's a problem."

Dr. Cahill nodded. "Good." She handed Isabelle a handful of pamphlets. "Here is one on nutrition for you during your pregnancy. Another for the baby's development. This one has a timeline of how your body will be changing. The last one is on adoption." She turned to the computer. "What pharmacy do you use?"

"CVS."

"I'll send a prescription there for pre-natal vitamins." Dr. Cahill finished tapping and shut down the computer. "Read them over." She nodded at the pamphlets in Isabelle's hands. "Call if you have any questions or concerns."

"Thank you." Isabelle frowned. "How long do you think I'll be puking?"

The doctor laughed. "That's right. That was why you originally came in. Well, you don't have the flu. Morning sickness usually lasts about two to three months if you're lucky."

"And if I'm not?"

"Let's not borrow trouble."

"I don't get sick in the morning. It's usually at night."

"It can happen anytime during the day, or all day."

"Oh man. So far it's just in the evening."

"Avoid greasy foods. Have some crackers or toast and ginger ale or tea. They should calm your stomach. Don't eat huge meals. If you do snack, make sure they're healthy."

"Okay." Isabelle looked at her stomach. "When do you think I'll start to show?"

"It is different for every woman." She looked at Isabelle's clothes. "I'd recommend not wearing skin tight pants, especially skinny jeans. Nothing that pinches your abdomen. You'll just be more comfortable that way."

Isabelle rolled her eyes. "That's not a problem. Dad wouldn't let me leave the house like that anyway."

"Any more questions for now?"

"No. I don't think so."

"Well, feel free to call if you do. Ask for Peggy, she can answer just about any question. She'll ask me if she doesn't know. Now, you do have options depending on your insurance. You can stay with me through your pregnancy, or see either an OBGyn or a midwife. Let's check." Dr. Cahill entered some information in the computer. "You can do any of those. Which would you prefer? Bear in mind if I think you are having any issues, I'll refer you to an OBGyn."

"I'll stay with you if that's okay."

"That's fine. Babies are the best part of my practice. Now, make sure you make another appointment with the receptionist before you leave." Dr. Cahill stood up.

"Okay. In a month, right?" Isabelle couldn't stop the quiver in her voice. Pregnant, what was she going to do?

"Yes. The paperwork should be at the appointment desk." She shook Isabelle's hand. "Call if you have any problem. That's what we're here for."

"Thank you."

Isabelle followed the doctor out and returned to the reception area. She was waved forward.

"Name?"

"Isabelle Rivers."

"Do you need a follow up appointment?"

"Yes. In a month."

"What time works best for you? Morning or afternoon?"

"I'd prefer morning."

"I have a morning appointment available with Dr. Cahill on the twenty-fifth. Will that work?"

"Sure."

"Do you need an appointment card?"

"Yes, please."

The receptionist handed her a card. "Here you go. If you need to cancel, please call twenty-four hours in advance."

"Thanks."

Isabelle turned and left. She'd head over to CVS to get her prescription. Isabelle shoved the pamphlets from the doctor in her purse. She'd look them over in her room. She needed to figure out how to tell her dad.

Isabelle picked up her prescription. She sat in the car in the parking lot and dialed a number she thought she never would. It rang and rang. When she'd just about given up hope a recording came on.

"You have reached a number that is no longer in service. If you have reached this recording in error, please hang up and dial again."

Numb, knowing the number was correct, Isabelle hung up her phone. Resting her head on the seat, knuckles white from gripping the steering wheel, Isabelle took a deep breath. Not knowing what else to do she headed home. Her stomach churning, a sour taste starting to filter up. She swallowed, hoping to keep it down until she got home. Luckily the curb in front of the house was empty. Isabelle slid in, parking and jumping out. Hitting the fob to lock it as she jogged to the front door.

She hurried to the door, pushing the key into the lock, her stomach rising in her throat. Isabelle tossed her purse on the kitchen table not caring when she heard it crash to the floor as she ran to the bathroom.

Isabelle made it just in time. Her stomach heaved and she

fell to her knees, throat burning as she expelled the little in her belly. She rested against the seat. This sucked.

She heard grumbling and the jingle of keys. Her dad must be home. Obviously he found her keys still in the door.

"Isabelle, why are your keys in the door?"

She didn't have the energy to reply. She could hear his footsteps as he followed the same path she had taken, albeit slower.

"What is the matter? Your purse is on the floor and your junk all over. Why do you put so much junk in there…"

Isabelle heard him trail off at the same moment she heard the rattle of her prescription. She tensed and bile rose again. She leaned over the toilet, her stomach painful as it tightened with each heave.

"Son of a bitch."

Isabelle knew she wouldn't have to tell her dad. Miserable, head hanging over the toilet, she didn't even care that he'd found out. Tears formed and spilled down her cheeks as she heaved again.

She heard her father's heavy tread as he came to the bathroom door.

"Isabelle."

She heaved again over the toilet, moaning. Nothing coming out, but her stomach twisted in knots each time it rose in reflex.

"Damn it." He sighed. "We will talk about this later when you're done." His hand hit the wall.

Isabelle flinched and moaned, cheek resting on the seat.

Nothing could be worse than this.

CHAPTER FIVE

Lee looked around him. Maybe he should have done this straight out of high school. Older than the average recruit, but now that he was graduating, he looked forward to starting a new career. Being away from home had its positives and negatives.

Isolated from the drugs and gangs that kept popping up in the area. Away from his familia for the first time. Harder than he thought until he remembered how they pushed him away. He hadn't bothered to call them other than the mandatory call to let them know he'd arrived. He had been required to send letters home, though. Jacinta had written him all the latest gossip. In her weekly letters she hadn't mentioned the one person he was interested in hearing about. Not that he would ask.

Lee had taken the chance and sent a letter to her. He wrote Isabelle to tell her he'd joined the Navy. He knew he'd been an ass not calling her back. Grief stricken and shocked at his family's ultimatum, he'd made the wrong decision, as usual.

He wasn't ever able to talk about his feelings, but he put them down in words. He told her about his family's disappointment in him. His anger and grief at Lenny's death. Lee told her about how he floated aimlessly through life. How his family had forced him to enlist. Lee told her about finally feeling like he had a place to belong, a future. In the Navy.

He never told her he missed her. Lee never told her how she eased his grief at Lenny's funeral. He never told her that he wouldn't have made it through it without her by his side. He should have.

Lee waited but Isabelle never wrote him back. Instead, his letter came back marked unknown. Large masculine letters. He knew Isabelle never received it. He was pretty sure her dad had though. Knowing he'd never send them, Lee wrote each week to Isabelle. Maybe one day he'd give them to her.

Alejandro wrote from boot camp and he wrote back to him. Lee chuckled reading them, damn glad he'd joined the Navy rather than the Marines. Sounded like pure hell to him. The only bad part about boot camp, freezing his ass off. Winter in Illinois sucked big time, especially for this born and bred California boy. Lee couldn't put on enough layers to keep warm. He'd survived though.

He looked at all the families around him heading into the drill hall, craning their necks looking for their sailor. He knew his familia wouldn't be able to come to his graduation. Alejandro was still in boot camp, so a no brainer there. Jacinta, a senior in high school, couldn't get away. His mom and abuela couldn't afford to fly to Illinois for just one day. If you could even force his abuela on a plane.

Lee had been offered the option of leave between boot

camp and A school but he'd turned it down. Nothing waited for him at home right now. Maybe someday. His choice of schooling had been based on location of the school. He didn't want to end up back in California just yet. Illinois was so damn cold he swore his balls were frozen. He thought long and hard about it. He needed warmth.

Lee liked the idea of being a Damage Control Specialist. The idea of being a fire fighter appealing, until he found out the school was in Great Lakes. He'd had enough of the cold. Lee hadn't known the half of it until he'd spent the winter here. Glad he'd chosen and been accepted to the Information Technician Specialist School, he'd be spending the next six months warming back up in Florida. It would take that long to thaw out.

From there, who knows? He wouldn't get orders until he was done with school. Maybe at that point he'd go home on leave. Lee grinned and patted his stomach. He'd actually dropped weight. His family wouldn't believe it. Without the cerveza and chips he'd slimmed down. Boot camp had gotten him in shape. Lee had double the energy, which seemed strange as his days were twice as long. Up before the sun and in bed after it set. Not a schedule he would ever have thought would agree with him.

Lee shrugged and glanced at the guests arriving. He saw arms waving and turned away. Lee heard his name being shouted. He stopped and turned back. Lee looked closer and grinned. His aunt and uncle from Wisconsin were there. He didn't even know they knew he was there. He waved back. His spirit lightened. Not all of his family were ashamed of him. He suppressed a smile. Lee guessed he would be seeking liberty after all.

He ducked back out of view and turned back to formation. The Company Commanders were turning a blind eye as everyone took a turn peeking in at the families arriving for the graduation ceremony. The practice pass in formation brought them close enough to glance inside. It least it kept them warm.

Lee looked forward to the graduation now. It wasn't just something to get through. He wouldn't be the only one in his company left behind with no family there.

"Santiago. You seem a lot happier. I swear you just smiled. What's up?"

Lee glanced at Severson. They'd been stuck together due to their last names, kind of like in Kindergarten. Severson had grown on him like mold.

"Some of mi familia made it."

"And here I thought you were found under a rock, eh?"

Severson snickered.

Lee just rolled his eyes and ignored him. Severson claimed to be a comedian. Lee figured the Navy took him without knowing. Lee got aggravated just looking at him. His peacoat flapped open and he didn't seem to feel the cold. Severson came from somewhere called the U.P. Swore this weather felt like spring to him. Lee had no idea where that was at and decided never to go there if this seemed warm to him.

"Back in formation, recruits!" The Company Commander was back to giving orders. One more practice round before they had to officially be ready for the ceremony. "I didn't hear you!"

"Yes Sir, Company Commander Sir!"

Lee and Severson separated, moving back in formation, into their unit, the lead company for graduation. If they screwed up all the companies behind them would be out of sync. An honor given to the company that had won the most awards.

Lee couldn't help but smile when he saw the flags they flew proclaiming their prowess. A sense of pride filled him, something he'd never really had before. They'd worked hard to win everything they could, ready to be proclaimed one of the Chief of Naval Operations Honor Divisions. Their company picture would be displayed on the wall in the Hall of Fame. He didn't have a whole lot to be proud of in his life, at least in his actions. Now he did. He wondered if it would make a difference in how they treated him back home. Not that he'd find out anytime soon.

He already had his tickets to Pensacola, Florida with his orders. He looked forward to the warmth. Lee held back his glee. No smiling on the parade grounds. Knowing some of his familia had made it to graduation, icing on the cake.

It had been hard, not receiving mail from anyone back home but Jacinta. Alejandro didn't count. He wasn't home. He'd gotten one letter from his cousin Nico. Short, just saying hi and giving him shit. Lee grinned. He'd sent an equally insulting letter back. He ignored the kernel of hope he'd had of Isabelle writing, but held back the hurt that she hadn't scribbled on at least one of Jacinta's letters.

Lee sighed. His fault. He hadn't called her but once. The desire to reconnect, to see if Isabelle liked the new, responsible Lee swam through his head. Maybe he'd call her. His hands sweated, his throat tight. Later, when he was alone. Just in case she hung up. He needed to get a phone though. His old one was back in Cali, service turned off.

Lee pulled his head out of the clouds. He had to pay attention during Graduation. The Pass in Review, the culmination of all eight weeks of their training, and no one wanted to screw it up.

"At close interval. Dress right dress!" The Company Commander had the thankless task of pulling them into a working unit. "Ready front. Right face. Forward March!" At the drop of an arm it began. They headed into the Midway Ceremonial Hall for graduation.

Lee and the rest of the recruits fell into place. They had become a well-oiled machine during their weeks together. "Eyes right." They effortlessly responded to each command, coming to a halt in their designated location.

Each company followed, the nine graduating companies following each after the other. They stood still, in formation, at attention.

"Section leaders fall out and collect outer garments."

Lee tried not to grimace. It was fucking cold in the drill hall. He shrugged out of his peacoat, handing it off.

"Dress right dress." They all shuffled around, realigning themselves once again. "Ready front. Right face. Parade Rest!"

Then the rest of the two hour ceremony began. The rifle squad had a performance. Great Lakes Navy Band played and the choir, off key but enthusiastic sang.

Lee's heart swelled. He'd made it. Standing at attention, he didn't dare move. Despite the itch on the end of his nose. Soon, they would be done. He'd even miss Severson. Glancing sideways at him, well, maybe not.

The Commanding Officer began to speak. He welcomed the guests and asked any Navy Veterans to stand up. Lee suppressed his smile when both his aunt and uncle stood. His eyes widened when he asked if any other Veterans or active duty were there and he saw his primo, Nico, there. His chest swelled. He had no idea that he would come. Nico stood proudly in his dress uniform. His prima, Savina, sat, the only one in that branch of la familia that hadn't enlisted. Lee swallowed and took a deep breath. They had all come just to see him graduate.

The ceremony seemed to last forever. The Navy definitely taught the meaning of patience. Lee stood at parade rest along with the rest of his company. No one moved at all. With their families out there, every recruit made sure their family would be proud of them. No one wanted to be called out in front of them. Knowing his familia supported him made the day that much better.

The speeches and ceremony drew to a close. The band and color guard exited. The buzz of excitement flittered through his belly. The bigwigs left. Their outer gear was handed back out, thank God. It was done.

"Now here this, now hear this, liberty call, liberty call. Fall out."

Finally they were dismissed. The families surged off of the bleachers to find their recruits. Lee kept an eye on his familia, sliding back into his peacoat. Nico in his blues made them easy to keep track of. He leaped down easily, heading Lee's way, a grin on his face. Lee couldn't help but match it.

"Lee! I couldn't believe it when Gramma Rosa told me you joined the Navy." Nico shook his head with an exaggerated sigh. "What was wrong with the Marines?"

"Why would he want to be a jarhead?" His Tio Esteban slapped Nico on the back. "Not everyone has that little sense."

"Dad!"

The two of them were laughing, joking back and forth. Times like these made Lee miss his dad. If he had lived, how would his life have changed? Lee rolled his eyes. His padre had been the definition of a dead beat. No use wondering that, better to wish Santa would visit.

"Congratulations, Lee." His Tia Leah gave him a hug. "We couldn't stay away when we found out you were graduating."

"Congrats Lee!"

Lee heard his sister's voice and looked around. He could have sworn she was right there. He looked at his family and they wore big grins. His prima held up her phone.

"Skype."

Lee looked into it and couldn't help the grin that broke out over his face.

"Hi, flakita. Thanks."

"Are you coming back home on leave?"

"No, I'm heading to A school in Florida. I'll be there for the next six months."

"I'll miss you."

Lee's heart swelled. He did love his hermana. "I'll be back at some point, brat."

Jacinta laughed, then turned her head. Something had caught her attention. Lee heard a voice he'd dreamed of hearing. He pressed a hand to his chest. Isabelle. Jacinta's conversation with her was too low for him to hear. His view turned and he heard a gasp and saw a tear stained face.

Jacinta's face popped back in. "Gotta go, Lee. TTYL."

"Wait…"

"Love you. Bye."

The screen went black. Lee cursed. He realized his uncle and aunt were still talking. Damn it. Why was Isabelle crying?

"It brings back memories." Tio Esteban looked around the drill hall.

He needed to find out what was wrong. Not that he had the right. He'd lost that when he didn't call back. His aunt's voice brought his attention back to them.

"If we'd have known that you'd enlisted I'd have sent letters and care packages. We just found out you were graduating from Mama Rosa. Surprised the heck out of us. No one bothered to tell us you had joined." She gave Nico an evil eye. "Boot camp can be very lonely." His aunt sighed, then perked up. "But the rest of your time will be a blast. I loved being in the Navy."

Lee had forgotten about that. His aunt looked around the building filled with recruits and their families. She had a smile filled with memories.

"My graduation was in Orlando. When I was in, the only boot camp for women was in Orlando Florida. Our Pass in Review took us around the parade grounds, outside." She sighed. "It makes sense to have it in here, as cold as it is out."

Lee nodded. "It would be way too cold." He shivered. "I swear I haven't been warm once since I've been here."

Nico laughed. "That's what happens when you choose to join the big blue team. Pendleton was warm."

Lee shoulder bumped him. "Yeah, but maybe I didn't want to be a Jarhead."

Nico snorted. "Better than being the Marine's taxi service."

Lee chuckled. "Don't forget who patches up your dumb asses."

"Enough boys." Tio Esteban stopped them with a smile. "You're still family." He elbowed Nico. "And you're both part of the Department of the Navy."

Lee snorted while Nico rolled his eyes.

Lee's cousin Savina came up and hugged him.

"I'm so glad to see you. Congratulations." She stepped back and looked at her parents. "I'm hungry. When can we eat?"

"I need to check out at my barracks. We can head over there and then I should be free to go for a while."

"What's your curfew?"

"Nine o'clock. We have muster at twenty-one fifty. Then I fly out tomorrow for Pensacola."

"What rating did you choose? Some type of airman?" His uncle asked.

"No. Information technical systems."

"Awesome dude! Now I know who to contact when my shit breaks." Nico clapped him on his shoulder.

"Where's your girl, Nico?"

"She's still doing rehab in San Diego. I'm only in town for your graduation. I fly back out tomorrow for Pendleton."

Lee's heart swelled. Not that he was about to show it. He would totally play it cool.

"How's Alejandro? Have you seen him?"

Nico snorted. "Probably wimping out. He looked beat, like every other recruit when I saw him. He's at a real boot camp." Nico grinned at Lee who just shook his head. His primo loved to tease. Sometimes to the point he'd get smacked, but he'd just laugh and finally behave. Maybe.

"Food guys, I'm starving here." Savina grabbed her stomach. "Can't you hear it protesting?"

His aunt laughed. "She's right. Time to eat. You two can poke at each other over food. Move it Nick." She grabbed his primo's arm, tugging at him as she headed out the door, following the rest of the recruits. "Lee, you better lead the way."

Lee hooked his arm into his prima's and listened. He loved his aunt, but you sure didn't want to make her mad. His uncle on the other hand was laid back, almost to the point you'd think he was asleep.

"Thanks for coming to watch me graduate."

"We wouldn't miss it for the world. Especially when we found out no one else could make it." Esteban shook his head, a frown on his face. "I'm glad we found out and could come."

Lee was speechless. He thought no one would show and to see that his uncle was upset that none of the rest of the familia had bothered to come choked him up. His tangled emotions had eased to see part of his familia there. Seeing Nico and knowing he had made the trip out here just to see him graduate warmed him despite the freezing weather.

Lee arrived at his barracks, his family chattering away around him.

"Here we are. Let me sign out and then we can go."

"We'll wait right here."

"Don't take long, I'm hungry." Savina's whine overrode anyone else's response.

"Brat. I'll be as fast as I can."

Lee headed into his barracks with a wide smile on his face. Being with his aunt and uncle and his cousins made him feel at home. Nico, the same age as his hermano, and Savina, the same age as Jacinta, catapulted him into his comfort zone. When they all came to visit, the casa became a beehive of activity. The girls, Jacinta, Savina and Isabelle hit it off, too well in his opinion. The house would echo with giggles.

Thinking of Isabelle made his stomach drop. Why was she crying? Usually she could be found smiling away and causing trouble when she and Jacinta got together. He wanted to comfort her, but he'd lost that right when he left.

Nico and Alejandro were two peas in a pod. Nico always included Lee. The three of them always managed to find some sort of trouble when they were together. Nico and Savina being there eased away the loneliness Lee had been feeling.

"So, where shall we go?"

His familia's heads turned toward him.

"I haven't been outside these gates in eight weeks, since I arrived." Lee looked over at his uncle. "Isn't this your old stomping ground?"

"More Leah's than mine. She grew up near here."

"We could go to the Lake Forest Mall and eat. There's a theatre there if you'd like to see a movie after. If, of course, it will give you plenty of time to return for curfew."

A spark of excitement lit him up. He loved going to the movies. Guess his aunt remembered that. Real food would be good too. Something not made with lots of grease and questionable ingredients in the mess hall. There should be a major electronics store, too. He could see about getting a phone.

"That should give us plenty of time. I have to be back by twenty-one hundred." Lee couldn't hold back his glee. He slapped Nico on the back and hugged Savina. One thing he'd missed while at boot camp, was going to the movies.

Esteban laughed. "We'll make sure we go then. I have no idea what's playing but I'm sure it's nothing you've seen."

"Food, first." Savina grabbed Lee's hand and started pulling him to the car. "Then movies. Let's move."

They walked to the car. Lee's uncle had parked away from the area surrounding the graduation ceremony. Esteban walked toward it, looking around the grounds.

"This place has really changed."

"Not that much." Leah answered.

Lee and Nico exchanged glances.

Nico rolled his eyes and whispered. "Every time they come here they say the same thing."

Lee frowned. "How often do they come here? And why?"

Nico chuckled. "They both went to school here on base. Why do they come back?" Nico shrugged. "Who knows?

They're old."

"I heard that Nick. If you weren't in uniform, I'd Gibb's slap you." Leah laughed, swatting the air near Nico's head.

Nico grinned and ducked. "Mom, behave."

Lee always forgot that Nico and Savina hadn't grown up speaking Spanish. Nico was Nick to his mom and dad. Mama Rosa was the one that called him Nico and it stuck. Of course his Tio Esteban was called Benny at home. It wasn't a name he'd ever heard his aunt call him.

Hanging with all of them for the afternoon would be fun. He wouldn't sit in the barracks alone, thinking about Lenny and longing for Isabelle, worrying why she was upset.

He'd make sure he got a phone. Hopefully he'd be able to get a California number. He wasn't sure how it would work, buying a phone here and setting up service. He'd probably have to buy one of those pay as you go plans, regardless of the number, just so he could call Isabelle.

Lee could admit now that he wished he'd lived his life differently. He had a chance to start over, a chance Lenny would never have. Maybe it would make him into the kind of man that could maybe, just maybe, deserve her. He knew Isabelle had a crush on him when she was younger. It wasn't beyond the realm of possibility that it could be rekindled, or so he hoped.

* * * *

Isabelle eased her way up, leaning against the vanity until she had her balance. Her stomach still churning, she rinsed out her mouth. Just looking at the toothpaste had her belly twisting. But what would be worse? The smell coming from her mouth or the chance she'd lose it again? Isabelle swallowed and decided to brush her teeth.

It would delay the inevitable. She knew her father had found the pregnancy pamphlets and prenatal vitamins. Isabelle didn't want to go out there and face him. She had no idea what to say. Honestly, what could she say?

Isabelle had no idea of how her father would react. He sounded calm when he spoke to her. Somehow, she knew that wasn't how he felt. Isabelle leaned over and rinsed her mouth and face, then patted her face dry. It used up a bit more time. She stood up, time to face the music.

Isabelle moved slowly toward the kitchen, a hand across her belly. The swirling sensation had her swallowing. Whether morning sickness or apprehension, she didn't know.

"Sit down." Her dad swung a chair around for her to sit. He pulled out another and sat. His face grim. Grimmer than normal. He spread out the pamphlets on the table. "I think you have something to tell me."

Isabelle closed her eyes, swallowed, and opened them again. She opened her mouth to speak and started sobbing instead. Isabelle could feel her nose swell shut. Her breathing constricted with each deep cry. Her body shook as she wrapped her arms around herself.

"Shit."

Her father's arms pulled her close, sliding the chair along

the floor until Isabelle wet the shoulder of his shirt. His warmth soothing and familiar. Isabelle gulped, her harsh cries tapering off.

"I gather the fliers were in your purse for a reason."

Isabelle nodded against his chest.

"Who's the father?"

Isabelle stilled. She didn't want to say. Lee obviously wanted nothing to do with her. He hadn't made an attempt to see her or even talk to her before he left. She didn't know what to do. But she didn't want to tell her dad the name of the father of her baby.

Isabelle ignored his question. "Maybe it's wrong."

"Maybe what's wrong?"

"The tests the doctor did. Maybe she is wrong."

"I doubt it. Did she do a urine test?"

"Yes." Isabelle's reply almost inaudible.

"Then it's not wrong." He eased back, releasing Isabelle from his embrace. "Do you know how far along you are?"

Isabelle's lips trembled. She could feel the buildup of tears in her eyes again.

"About two months." Isabelle wiped her eyes on her arm.

"Do you know what you're going to do?" He poked at the pamphlets in front of him. "I see information about adoption. Is that what you're planning on?"

Her hand crept to cover her non-existent belly. "I don't know. I still don't believe it."

Her dad sat back, rubbing his hands over his face. "I tried to instill morals and values in you girls. I know I've failed with Caroline. I thought you knew better."

Isabelle's cheeks burned. She ducked her head, tears rising again. "I didn't mean for this to happen."

"I'm sure you didn't." Her dad ran his hands through his hair, tugging on the ends. "But your actions obviously didn't prevent it." He looked Isabelle over, staring at her belly. "You could get rid of it but that would be murder in the eyes of the Lord."

"No."

"I'll have to send you away before you start showing until you have the child." He picked up the pamphlet on adoption. "I'll look over this. You should follow the guidelines the doctor gave you. You can give the couple that adopts it a healthy happy child."

"I don't know if I want to give my baby up for adoption. I haven't decided."

"Having a pregnant unmarried daughter will look bad for me." Her dad stood up and paced. He continued to read, ignoring her. "It says the couples that adopt will cover the cost of the birth in most cases."

Isabelle tightened her lips. Protectiveness washed over her. "You can't decide what will happen. It is my decision."

"Think of what's better for the baby. A warm loving family for it, and you can go on to whatever career you decide without anything holding you back."

Isabelle stood up carefully. Her tears left her eyes sore

and the drying tracks tightened her skin. She didn't feel like crying anymore though. Anger dried her tears. Isabelle wouldn't let her father make this decision. It was too important. She lightly touched her belly.

"I'm going to lay down for a bit. I don't feel well." Isabelle grabbed the pamphlets still on the table, the prenatal vitamins on the counter, and her purse. She clumsily shoved the paper and pills in her purse. Isabelle just wanted to leave the room. Her dad ignored her, reading aloud some of the points on the pamphlet.

Isabelle could see the determined look in his eyes. His singlemindedness had helped him achieve his goals in life. He always told her and Caroline that. Isabelle just never expected to have that determination turned on her and her life, at least not in this way.

She left the kitchen, shoulders stiff and back straight. Her nausea had receded and her stomach started to growl. Isabelle headed upstairs. She wouldn't stay in the kitchen with her father. He pissed her off, and she didn't want to say something she couldn't take back. Isabelle opened her bedroom door, and slammed it with a bang, flinging herself across the bed.

Isabelle rolled over, staring at the ceiling. She placed her hands on her belly. Still flat, well as flat as normal. It didn't seem possible. Isabelle glanced at the clock. Study hall was coming and lunch period would be starting soon.

Isabelle sat up. She needed to talk to someone. Who better than her best friend? She could go to school for the last half of the day. They had study hall together and should be able to talk then and through lunch. Isabelle sat up and yawned. Her jaw cracked, popping her ears. She debated whether to eat or just go to sleep. The loud growl settled it. Isabelle would grab Jacinta and they could go somewhere off campus for lunch.

She grabbed her backpack and purse, making sure to dump out the literature from the doctor and the vitamins. Isabelle didn't want any rumors to start if they fell out. Until she knew for sure what she wanted to do, no one but her best friend needed to know. Dumping them on the bed, Isabelle headed into the bathroom.

She couldn't go to school with red eyes and a dirty face, not to mention without her war paint. She set about fixing herself up. Another protest from her stomach had her hurrying through her normal routine.

Done, Isabelle scooped up her purse, backpack, and tiptoed down the stairs. She didn't want her father to hear her leaving. She didn't want to hear any more about adoption. Heck, she wasn't sure she even wanted to give her baby up. The only thing she knew? She needed to talk to her best friend.

Isabelle escaped out the front door and quickly slipped in the car. Starting it up, she glanced over to see her father standing in the window watching as she pulled away. He hadn't come running after her. Good. His changing moods lately were driving her crazy. From indifferent to affectionate to trying to manage her life without her input, Isabelle's world turned upside down on a daily basis. Adding today's news would make it even crazier. She was sure of that.

Swallowing, Isabelle wondered if her day could get any

worse. A short trip to school and Isabelle found her day could get worse. Jacinta wasn't in school today. Isabelle's eyes welled up and she scrubbed away the tears on her sleeve.

Glad she hadn't checked in with the school, Isabelle slipped back out to the car before the bell rang. She didn't know why Jacinta wasn't in school, but that wouldn't stop her from going over to her house. Blinking to clear her eyes she slid behind the wheel and started the car.

Seeing the parking lot clear of teachers, Isabelle left. The few minutes it took to arrive at Jacinta's seemed to take forever. The road stayed clear, and there were even parking spots available in front of the house. Isabelle pulled in and parked. Taking a deep breath, ignoring her swollen nose and glancing in the rear view mirror, and yup, definitely pink rimmed eyes, Isabelle got out.

She knocked on the door and turned the handle, going inside. The door was locked only at night. Isabelle heard Jacinta say 'congrats Lee' but didn't see him anywhere. Could he be home?

Isabelle walked through the living room and into her bedroom. "Jaci?"

Jacinta turned her head and looked at Isabelle. "What's wrong?"

"What are you doing?"

"Talking to Lee. See?" Jacinta flashed her phone at Isabelle and she stared in shock. Lee stood there, dressed to the nines in a navy uniform looking back at her.

Isabelle burst into tears.

"Gotta go, Lee. TTYL." She took a breath. "Love you. Bye."

Jacinta shoved her phone in her pocket. Her arms encircled Isabelle, a mix of Spanish and English spilling from her lips.

Isabelle hugged her back, crying into her shoulder. All just too much to take in in one day. She guessed she'd hoped that Lee would be there and she could turn to him. Now, she knew it wasn't possible. She'd have to face this on her own.

Finally her tears slowed. Her face wet, nose swollen and running. Isabelle took a couple of deep breathes. Her eyes were sore and her head was pounding.

"What's the matter, Izzy?"

Isabelle started to speak, her voice hoarse and scratchy.

Jacinta shook her head. "C'mon. This is obviously a kitchen discussion." She grabbed Isabelle and pulled her behind her.

"Yeah, it is." Food was the great comforter, even if she couldn't keep it down.

"Here, sit. Let me get you a glass of juice and we'll talk." Jacinta grabbed a glass from the drainer and poured a tall glass of orange juice and placed it in front of Isabelle. "Drink some of this then spill. We're actually alone in the house for the first time in like forever." Jacinta grinned. "A perfect time to tell me what's bothering you. Absolutely no one to over hear you."

Isabelle took a sip of juice. This sucked, and it hurt. Jacinta knew she'd been with Lee. She'd easily be able to figure out Isabelle was pregnant with Lee's baby. Maybe she should have thought this through.

"Now I don't know if I can tell you." Isabelle laid her head on the table in her arms. "Oh God, I don't know what to do." Her head pounded, the blood rushing through her temples with each racing beat of her heart. "I'm pregnant."

"What? You're mumbling. I could have sworn you said you were preggers." Jacinta grabbed Isabelle's arm and shook it. "Repeat that."

Isabelle raised her head, swallowing back another rush of tears. "I'm pregnant, knocked up, and I don't know what to do." She ended on a wail. If she couldn't break down in front of her best friend, who could she?

"Crap." Jacinta scraped her chair across the floor and embraced her. "We'll figure out something."

Isabelle turned into her embrace and cried. She couldn't help but giggle when Jacinta joined her. Her tears flowing freely.

"Why are you crying?" Isabelle hiccupped trying to stop. She grabbed a paper towel and wiped her eyes.

"Don't know."

Isabelle gave a watery giggle. "You're crazy."

Jacinta giggled and sat back wiping her face and blowing her nose on a napkin. "Hey, if you're pregnant that means it's my sobrino." She smiled widely. "That's awesome."

"What the heck is a sobrino?" Isabelle hadn't heard that term. Tio and tia meant uncle and aunt, primo was cousin. Abuela and the more affectionate abuelita was grandma. Sobrino? Not a clue.

"Nephew. Or niece if it's a girl, but the Santiago's seem to shoot boy sperm most of the time."

Isabelle snorted and rolled her eyes. "Lee only called me once after that night. I haven't heard from him since Lenny's funeral. So this baby is all mine."

"That ass!" Jacinta mumbled about torture under her breath. "Doesn't change the fact that it's Lee's just because the ass hasn't called."

"Why was Lee in a uniform?"

"If you had let me talk about him the last couple of months, you'd know."

Isabelle's face flushed. "Sorry."

"After that morning when Mama Rosa saw you sneaking out, then the police looking for Lee about Lenny's death, Tio Mateo put his foot down. They forced Lee to join the military."

Isabelle gasped. "Oh my God."

"I know, right?" Jacinta nodded. "Today he graduated from boot camp. Savina Skyped it for me so I could see it."

"I thought he'd just taken off to get away from here."

Jacinta was shaking her head. "No. He didn't have a choice. Mama Rosa said he had to leave. It seems to agree with him though. He looks a lot better, now."

Isabelle could only nod vigorously in agreement. Lee had looked really hot in his uniform. He looked like he'd lost weight. Isabelle almost didn't recognize him. His over long curls were gone, his hair hidden beneath his sailor hat. It drew attention to his blue eyes. Before, his curls had covered them.

"Is he coming home?" Isabelle couldn't help being hopeful. If Lee had managed to change, maybe there was hope for her.

Jacinta looked stricken. "No."

Isabelle froze. "No?" Her throat so tight she was surprised she'd been able to speak.

"He's going to Florida. He has to go to school."

"How long will he be there?"

"Six months." Jacinta looked at her with a look of pity. "That sucks."

Isabelle's lips trembled. That would bring it almost to her due date. If the baby came early, she'd be alone. Not that he wanted anything to do with her anyhow. If he did, he'd have called.

"What am I going to do?" Isabelle frowned, tears once again ready to spill. She could hardly breathe through her nose, her throat sore from all of her crying. "Jacinta, what am I going to do? The doctor talked about abortion, adoption, and keeping my baby."

Jacinta drew in a breath. "Oh God. You're not thinking about abortion are you? It's against my religion."

Isabelle giggled through her tears. This time a bit more

hysterical. Her hand once again covered her belly when Jacinta mentioned abortion. She needed to calm down. Certain this much crying couldn't be good for the baby.

"Against your religion?" Another giggle escaped. "Really? That's all you have? And no, not abortion." Her hands smoothed over her nonexistent bump. "When the doctor said that, it practically made my hair stand up. I just couldn't."

"Good." Jacinta laughed. "And it is against my religion. I'm Catholic, unlike you."

"Pfft. I can't help what I am. My dad is a minister. Try going against that." Her reality hit her again. Isabelle drooped. "My dad is talking about adoption. He read the pamphlet the doctor sent home with me. I haven't even had a chance to think about it."

"Oh wow." Jacinta sat back. "Is that what you want?"

"I don't know what I want!" Isabelle stood up and started pacing. "I still can't believe it."

"It's part of you, and part of Lee."

Isabelle leaned against the counter. She stared down at her stomach. "I know." Isabelle looked at Jacinta. "How am I supposed to decide? What am I going to do? My dad is dead set against me keeping the baby. I wish Lee were here."

"Lee has the right to know."

"I know. What's he going to think? I didn't even know that he'd joined the Navy."

"You would have if you'd have let me talk about him."

Isabelle stuck her tongue out at her. "You had to go there."

"I think he needs to know."

"D'uh! I don't know how to tell him." She scuffed her foot on the floor. "I tried to call him when I left the doctors. His phone number was disconnected."

"Tio Mateo cancelled his phone. He couldn't have one, anyway, in boot camp." Jacinta shrugged. "I'm sure he'll get one now that he's going to school. I'll give it to you when he does."

"I guess he really couldn't call me. What if he still doesn't? Maybe he won't get a phone."

Jacinta laughed. "He loves gadgets. Plus he's going to some kind of techy training. He'll get one."

Isabelle nodded. What could she say? Jacinta was probably right. It didn't mean he would call her though.

Jacinta sighed and cocked her head, looking at the ceiling. Her 'I'm thinking really, really hard about it' look. Isabelle had seen it often, but it usually ended up with them in trouble.

It made Isabelle antsy. She turned and opened the fridge, suddenly starving. "I'm hungry."

"Jeez, get out of the fridge. Let's go get something to eat."

Isabelle slammed the door shut. She felt energized at the thought of going out and just being normal. This day had been too much. She wanted to go back to being a high school senior and not a future mom. Isabelle wanted a redo.

But, if she had a redo she wouldn't have had that one night with Lee. Isabelle had to fan herself just thinking about it. Remembering the feel of his hands on her body had her shivering.

"Come on, let's get moving before everyone gets home." Jacinta grabbed her arm, dragging her out of the moment, and the door. "I'm hungry, too."

"I've got the car, so we can go anywhere." Isabelle pulled the door shut behind them.

"How about the mall?" Jacinta said, crawling into the car. "Hopefully we won't run into anyone we know."

"Sounds good." Isabelle checked the road and pulled out. "Montebello or Las Puentes?"

"Oh, let's go to Las Puentes, less chance of running into any muchachos we know. Plus we can go to the Souplantation."

"You always want to go there."

"It's good, so why not?"

Isabelle couldn't argue with that. "Fine. Souplantation it is."

Her mind wasn't really on what to have for lunch. Instead Isabelle kept thinking of the choices she faced. Her body went from hot to cold. Scared of her future when she had been looking forward to life after graduation. Never once did she see herself pregnant and alone. She rubbed her belly.

The thought of giving her baby away stressed her out.

Maybe an answer in itself.

How would she tell her father? He already planned on sending her God knows where and pretending her baby didn't exist. Sure, some couple would get her baby, but how would she know they would love it? Who says that her baby would be better off? She'd heard the horror stories. What if he ended up in foster care instead? How could she deny her baby the family that he already had?

Isabelle's head whirled. Maybe her baby would have every advantage in life if she gave it up for adoption. If she kept the baby, she'd be struggling for years to support the two of them. Maybe Lee would want nothing to do with her when he found out she was pregnant. He had his life on track. How could she disrupt it?

"Hey, don't miss the turn."

Isabelle slid into the turn lane, squeaking in between a beater, blasting his music so loud Isabelle could see the car vibrating to it, and an old lady driving a beamer.

"Want to walk around the mall after we eat?"

"Sure thing."

Isabelle parked outside Souplantation, between the mall and the restaurant.

"Hey, you could have parked a little closer."

"I won't have to move the car here. It's between the restaurant and the mall."

"So what? That means we have to walk from here to the mall."

"Lazy."

"Yup."

Shaking her head, Isabelle laughed, hooked arms with Jacinta and headed in to eat.

They joked and stayed off any serious subject while they ate. Grateful, Isabelle just wanted to ignore the whole thing. For a while. She hadn't had time to process the news she'd gotten.

Isabelle stretched in her seat, sleepy now that her belly was full.

"Hey sleepy head, let's go window shopping." Jacinta slid out of the booth and stood up. "I'm ready to start moving."

"Okay, give me a minute. I have to head to the ladies room."

Jacinta snorted. "Get used to that amiga. It only gets worse as your bladder gets squished into a tiny pea shaped size."

Isabelle giggled. "Good heavens, I don't know about you, girl." She grabbed a bill from her purse. "Here's money for my lunch. Go pay and I'll be right back."

"Fine, just remember I told you first." Jacinta grinned and headed to the cash register.

They leisurely walked to the mall, neither of the girls in a rush. They chatted about nonsense, the teachers they hated, the cute boys in class.

Isabelle relaxed, happy until they opened the doors to the nearest store and stepped inside. She looked around, and drew a deep breath. All around her were toys, baby clothes, and little children of various ages. Toys 'R Us, what were the odds?

Isabelle looked around. She'd never noticed so many babies before. Some sleeping and some screaming as they were pushed or held by their parents and, in some cases, siblings.

"Move it, they won't bite."

"Hmm. I wouldn't be too sure."

Jacinta's gaze followed Isabelle's finger and they both giggled. A little boy bit his sister while she screamed. A harried mother pulled them apart to separate them.

"Crazy."

Isabelle snorted then laughed. It did seem surreal.

"Can we look around?" Isabelle wasn't sure why she'd asked. Her stomach churned. "Never mind."

"No, no. Let's. I have to find a birthday gift for my primito anyhow."

"Fine."

"He likes trucks."

They headed down the aisles, looking over everything. They turned and ahead of them were cribs, blankets, and baby clothes. Isabelle walked forward, gaze locked on the itty bitty clothing.

"It's so tiny." She could hear the awe in her voice. She fingered the little outfit, imagining a little boy with Lee's curly hair and bright blue eyes. Isabelle turned away and saw a crib, the sheets and mobile in a sailor motif. She looked around, her hand sliding across her stomach.

Jacinta stood back and watched her. Her lip between her teeth.

Isabelle wandered forward, going deeper into unknown territory. On all sides were things for the baby. Cribs, strollers, high chairs, swings, sheets, and car seats surrounded her. Isabelle had no idea babies needed so much stuff.

"Maybe my baby would be better off if he had parents that could afford all this." Isabelle looked around. "Not to mention a house to put all of this in."

Jacinta snorted. "Babies don't need all of this crap." She walked over and gestured around her. "How much of this junk do you see at my casa? Hardly any of it, and you know how happy those babies are."

Isabelle looked around, wandering aimlessly down the aisles, a tiny frown between her brows. She ran her hands along the edges of a bassinette, pushed a swing and watched it rock. Biting her lip, Isabelle picked up a little stuffed bear and set it back down. She sighed and glanced at Jacinta from the corner of her eye.

"I'd need some of it, though." Isabelle turned and looked at Jacinta. "Some of it is necessary."

"Si. Some is. Diapers. A car seat."

"If I had a car."

"Hey someone might take you somewhere. Or you can call a taxi."

Isabelle rolled her eyes.

"Don't be doing that. I'm just saying. A car seat is

necessary."

"Okay, fine." Isabelle walked over to the car seats. "Look, over a hundred dollars. Where do you think I'd get that from?"

"You find work."

"My dad doesn't want me to work while I'm in school. He says the allowance I get for cleaning the house is all I need."

"I don't suppose he pays when you work at the church? He pays everyone else."

"No, he says that is part of the obligation of our family."

Jacinta shook her head. "That's a bunch of BS."

"Jeez, just say how you feel."

"I did. You work there so much you can't work anywhere else. That's slave labor, amiga."

"He keeps a roof over my head and food in my belly. Pays for car insurance and gas."

"Again, BS. That's what a parent does. You don't charge your kid for stuff they should be providing. Besides, Caroline usually has the car." Jacinta frowned. "If that is what you think parenting is maybe you should give the baby up for adoption."

Isabelle sucked in a deep breath, clenching her hands. Her heart squeezed at those words. She'd *never* do that. She'd never treat her baby that way. Swallowing, Isabelle realized she didn't want to give up her baby. She let out her breath in a sob.

"Fuck you!"

Jacinta chuckled. "Finally realized something?"

Isabelle wiped her eyes. "That you're a psycho bitch? I've always known that." She let out a watery chuckle. "What am I going to do? My dad is going to have a cow."

"Well, you're familia now. La pequena is a Santiago. You can always come to us. We can share a room." Jacinta squealed, making Isabelle wince. "That would be awesome."

"After I puked all over, not so much."

"C'mon girlfriend, it would be."

Isabelle shook her head, smiling. "Let's hope not. I've got to tell my dad I'm keeping my baby. Eventually."

Wandering around the mall, they seemed to gravitate toward the baby sections. Ooh'd and ah'd over cribs at Toys 'R Us, Burlington Coat Factory, and Sears. Isabelle realized Jacinta was right, she'd have to get a job. At least until the baby was born. Baby stuff was really expensive.

"Think Burlington is hiring?"

They had the cheapest, cutest stuff and she bet they had an employee discount.

"Only one way to find out." Jacinta grabbed her hand and pulled her along.

"I can get there without being dragged, you know."

Jacinta laughed and let go. "I didn't want you changing your mind."

Isabelle smiled. "You were right. I need a job."

Jacinta crowed. "I told you so."

"That is so not attractive, you know."

"Don't care." She grinned, waggling her brows. "I love being right. Maybe I should apply too. I need a job over the summer anyhow. Might as well apply now."

They talked to one of the sales women, who pointed them to the customer service desk. They were looking for one associate.

"Go for it. And then we can check Toys 'R Us. Think if we had a discount to both places? That would be awesome."

Isabelle smiled. "You're right. Hopefully they are hiring too."

She filled out the application, turning it in to the clerk.

"The manager will be in tomorrow. He'll look your application over then." She put it under the counter.

"He'll call me?"

She shrugged. "I guess." She turned away to answer a customer's question.

Jacinta decided she'd call just to make sure he got it. The sooner she was employed the better. "Let's go. See who else is hiring."

"Sounds good."

They both filled out applications at Toys 'R Us, Sears, and Ross's. They had circled back to the food court. Isabelle's stomach growled at the scent of cinnamon in the air.

"Oh, God. I need a cinnamon roll."

The gooey goodness was placed in front of them, warm from the oven. Isabelle grabbed a carton of milk to go with hers, while Jacinta got a coffee. She was addicted. Isabelle loved the smell but she thought the taste was horrible.

Sitting down, she groaned. "My feet ache."

"Mine too." Jacinta's reply was garbled. She'd already filled her mouth, moaning while she talked.

Isabelle moaned too at her first bite. She saw a help wanted sign in the window. "Maybe I should apply here."

"Sure and be round as a pig by the time you had the baby. And it would all be Cinnabon, not baby." Jacinta cracked up, arms out impossibly huge.

Isabelle laughed. "True. Maybe not."

Her phone rang. She glanced at it. Didn't recognize the number. She turned her phone to Jacinta. "Do you recognize this number?"

"No. Just ignore it."

Shrugging, she let it ring. They could leave a message. She had more important things to do, like finish her cinnamon rolls.

Jacinta's phone rang. She glanced at it and ignored it.

"What was that number that called you?"

Isabelle shrugged. "I don't know. It was an out of state number."

"Huh."

Isabelle's phone rang again. Isabelle shook her head. "Same number." She put her phone on vibrate.

"Totally a pest."

"Yeah, persistent for a wrong number." Isabelle shrugged, licking the icing from her fingers. "So good." She popped the last roll in her mouth. She finished off her milk, washing it down. Her phone beeped. "This time they left a message."

"Now you'll find out who it is, at least."

"Yup." It rang again. "This is ridiculous. I'm going to find out who this is." She swiped at her screen. "Hello?"

CHAPTER SIX

Lee growled. She didn't pick up. He paced the airport. He'd tried calling but Izzy never picked up. Time to call his hermana. Since Jacinta was Izzy's best friend she could tell him what was going on. He hadn't left a message. Lee didn't really know what to say. He was more and more convinced that it was Izzy he'd tossed out of bed.

He'd tried calling both Isabelle and Jacinta, but neither picked up his calls. Frustrated Lee tried Izzy again. He looked at his watch. His flight was scheduled to leave in thirty minutes.

He'd waved his aunt and uncle good-bye. They had insisted on taking him to the airport. They said that since Nick had to fly out anyhow, they would take both of them. He'd insisted they didn't need to go to the gate with him. Tight hugs left him in no doubt that they'd enjoyed seeing him. Nick gave him a slap on the back and headed to a different terminal. He was anxious to get back to his girl.

Isabelle's phone rang and rang. He knew that she might be busy, but enough was enough.

"Izzy. Pick up the phone, damn it."

Lee hung up. Maybe now she'd call him back. He rolled his eyes. Or now she never would. He had a few minutes so decided to call home. Maybe Jacinta would answer. He could ask about Isabelle then.

The phone rang and rang. Lee sighed. His abuelita didn't like answering the phone. He'd have to leave a message. It clicked and he listened as the message ran.

"Hey. It's me. Lee." He waited to see if someone would answer. "Just wanted to call home and say hi. Here's my new number." Lee recited it slowly so someone could call him back. "Okay. Bye."

Lee hung up. Debating, he grimaced and called Isabelle again. Her phone rang and rang before it clicked to voice mail. She probably didn't get his earlier call. "Shit. Isabelle. It's Lee. I just wanted to talk to you. I know you probably don't want to talk to me." He was silent, thinking of what to say next, when it dawned on him. He had to leave his number for his family, how the hell would Isabelle know it was him calling. "Crap, how would you even know it's me? I'm an idiot. Izzy, I miss you. I'm going to call again. Hopefully you'll answer once you know it's me. Or call me."

Lee stared at his phone and hung up. His flight was called for boarding. One more try. Before he had to turn it off on the plane.

"Hello?"

"Izzy?"

"Yes."

"It's Lee."

"Hi, Lee." She sounded shy. "How are you doing?"

"Fine."

Lee could hear shouting in the background. "What's going on?"

"Just some idiots at the mall."

"Oh." Lee didn't quite know what to say. "How are you doing?"

"Okay. So, you're in the Navy?"

"Yeah, I enjoy it. I didn't really expect to." He looked at his watch. "Crap, I have to go. I'll call you tomorrow, okay? My plane is boarding."

"Okay. Bye, Lee."

"Bye, Izzy." Lee swallowed. "I miss you." He hung up, not waiting to hear her response.

Lee grabbed his carryon and hurried over to board. It was a full plane. It was going to be a long flight. Luckily the person next to him looked like they were sleeping. He sat and flipped through the magazine in the seat pocket.

Lee grinned. Gadgets galore. If he took his time, he'd be able to occupy his whole flight. The Sky Mall magazine was huge.

Base was a shock after boot camp. He was brought to base, shown his barracks and given until Monday to acclimate himself. No civvies and no leaving base. He had two weeks to earn wearing civvies by completing a watch assignment.

He had one roommate for now. Lee chose the open bottom rack. He only could use the closet and desk assigned to him. No personal gear sitting out. Monday he had muster and would be given assignments until his class would form.

Lee unpacked his gear, stowing it all away neatly. His dresser consisted of two drawers built into his bunk, below his mattress. Next he checked out the head. Neat and clean with baskets for each rack. His room shared the head with the room next door. Putting his toiletries in the basket marked with his bunk number, Lee went back and sat at his desk.

Debating, he pulled out his phone.

No calls.

He did say he'd call her tomorrow. Lee didn't figure that he'd be free so soon. He probably should leave it. No use scaring her off.

He changed from his dress uniform to his digital cammies. He'd been watched and surrounded by people for the last two months. Going out and walking around at his own pace was appealing. He could start watch tomorrow. He had the information. The sooner he completed it, the better.

Lee put his phone and wallet in his pants and grabbed his hat. *Shit, cover*, he had to remember that, and quickly headed out the door, taking the stairs two at a time.

He said tomorrow. He'd be patient. He didn't want Isabelle to not take his calls if he was a pest.

Lee scoped out the chow hall, the PT grounds, the

building where his classes would be held, and the Exchange.

He couldn't wear civvies, but he could buy them. Grabbing a couple of pairs of jeans and shirts, and some real shaving cream, Lee found the magazines. He grabbed a few he liked. Wired and Popular Science were good for gadgets and projects, Entertainment to get him back up to date with new movies and Hollywood gossip, his secret vice.

Lee eyed Cosmopolitan, checking out the headline about relationship advice. Lee shook his head. No, he wouldn't stoop that low. A bunch of crap to get women to buy it. He walked away.

"Shit."

Lee gritted his teeth. He turned back and grabbed it, tucking it between the others so no one saw him carrying it. It didn't matter if he didn't know anyone yet. He didn't want anyone seeing him with it.

He debated grabbing a cart. He was allotted a shelf in the refrigerator in his room. Plus there was a microwave. He could grab some quick food for himself if he was too lazy to go to the chow hall over the weekend.

Why not? He didn't have anything else to do. Lee piled what was in his arms in the cart, careful to keep Cosmo hidden.

He eventually found the electronics section. He'd wandered around for a couple of hours, poking throughout the Exchange. Lee grinned, heading to the laptops. His old one was at home and he shared it with his sister. This one would be all his.

Finally, Lee decided on the one he wanted. Plenty powerful enough for online gaming and Netflix. He then checked out the XBOX One and the PS4, debating if he should get one.

"Can I help you?"

Lee looked up.

A young man hovered over him. He looked longer than Lee. Not a Navy man with his long on top and shaved sides. Lee rolled his eyes at the hair reaching to his chin. His name tag read Marvin. Lee snickered.

"No thanks, I was just looking."

"Okay. If I can help you with anything let me know." Marvin turned away, flipping his hair back from his eyes.

"I did want to get a laptop."

Marvin turned back eagerly. "Sure thing. We have a lot of them. Did you want it for gaming, skyping or just surfing the net?"

"All of those."

Marvin headed to the laptops. "Follow me. We can find one, for sure."

"I already know which one I want."

He stopped. "Oh, okay. I can get it for you. Show me which one it is and I can ring you up at the counter."

"Sounds good. Can I pay for all my stuff here?"

He looked around. "Sure. We're not that busy."

Lee pointed out the laptop he wanted and watched Marvin head to the back room. Lee went to the cash register, setting his stuff on the counter.

"This is a great model. Picture quality is excellent. It has a special graphics card just for gaming, a built in webcam and the speaker is right in front. It works great for skyping. I have the same model." Marvin smiled sheepishly. "I bought it with my first pay check."

Lee laughed. Marvin may look silly but he was as geeky as Lee. "This is all my first check, too. I just got out of boot camp, graduated yesterday."

"Did you want the extended warranty?"

"Sure. You never know where I'll end up."

Marvin nodded. "Yeah, my dad was on board ship and his slipped off a table and cracked the screen. Lucky he had the warranty, it replaced it."

"Good to know."

Marvin finished ringing up electronics and started scanning up the rest of Lee's stuff. He grabbed the magazines and snickered.

"Girl trouble?"

Lee groaned. He'd forgotten he had the Cosmopolitan magazine in the pile. "Yeah. Hide that in the bag."

"We sell that one to a lot of guys. Especially when they do something stupid."

"Like go off to join the Navy and not tell their girl?"

"Dude. No." Marvin shook his head. "I'm not sure this will help you. Not sure anything will."

Lee gut twisted. "Well, it's worth a try." Maybe since

Izzy wasn't technically his girl, he'd be okay. Maybe.

Marvin totaled the bill and Lee swiped his card. He'd never spent so much in one shot. He liked having money to spend again. Money that wasn't mooched from his mom or brother.

"Thanks, Marvin."

"Good luck. I think you're going to need it."

"Yeah." Lee grabbed his stuff. Marvin had stuffed everything but the computer in one large bag.

It was dark by the time he left. After putting his stuff away in his room, Lee headed to the chow hall then back to the barracks. Didn't matter if it was early. It had been a long two months.

Lee grumbled, turning over. The warmth of the beam streaming across his face was great, but it was too damn early. He didn't have a damn thing to do today but try to reach Isabelle. Lee glanced at his watch. Six a.m. That would make it three a.m. California time. Izzy would never talk to him again if he woke her up on a Saturday.

"You might as well get up. Chow's only served for another couple of hours."

Lee peeked out of his covers. "Hey."

"I'm Jameson."

"Santiago."

"Make sure you make your rack every day. They do surprise inspections. I don't want to have to pull extra duty or lose privileges if we fail inspection."

"Sure thing." Lee watched his roommate tuck in his

sheets and make his bed. Not a smile from him. He was dressed in jeans and a t-shirt. Burrowing back under the covers, Lee decided to wait until he was done before getting up.

The closing of the door woke him up again. Lee yawned, glancing at his watch. He'd slept for another hour. Still too early to call.

Lee rolled out of bed, stretching his spine. At a pop, he straightened up, scratching his groin. Time for a shower.

Lee caught the tail end of breakfast. He grinned. He'd been able to have an omelet made to order. Lots of fruit too, and he walked out hurting he was so full. It was good. He had time to get ready for watch. He had two weeks to complete his qualifications. He started at noon and ended at four today. By then Izzy should be awake, and probably with his sister.

To fill in the time until then, Lee hit the gym. He ran his hand down his abs. Lee smirked. He was looking fine. He could actually feel muscle instead of the beer gut he'd been getting. Lee only hoped Izzy liked the change.

Workout and watch came and went. Lee's gut churned. He gripped his phone and taking a deep breath, dialed.

"Hello."

"Hi, Izzy."

"Hi."

"How's the weather there?" Was he so idiotic that he could only talk about the weather?

"Hot. How is it by you?"

"Hot and humid." Yup, the weather. His lips tightened.

God this was stilted. He could hear his sister in the background. Jacinta and Isabelle were nearly inseparable, no surprise she was there. Lee heard her moan. "Izzy?"

"Bye."

Lee's mouth dropped. Isabelle hung up on him.

His phone beeped. Glancing over Lee saw it was his hermana and answered it.

"Hey, flakita!"

"How's it hanging dude?"

"Good. How's it going there?"

"Same old thing. How about you?"

"Classes are kind of boring. A lot of reading."

"Poor Lee."

He could hear the laughter in her voice, his hermana had no sympathy, a huge bookworm when she wasn't causing trouble.

"Izzy just hung up on me. She didn't sound too good." Lee could hear what sounded like someone being sick. "She okay? Jacinta?"

"It's just morning sickness. Gotta go."

"What the fuck?"

He swore he heard her laughing as she hung up.

The click and Jacinta's words stole his breath. Fuck. His hand clenched. Isabelle? Pregnant. Lee could feel his ears burn. She was his, damn it. Who the hell had gotten to her? He froze while his stomach crawled up into his throat. Lee did something he normally didn't. He prayed she hadn't been raped.

He plopped on his bunk, head in his hands. Jacinta would surely have told him if that happened. Regardless, he had to find out the truth. Lee sat up and dialed Jacinta back. Then he started to count with each ring. Fuck. Shit. Damn. Plenty of pregnant aunts and he knew the answer. It could only be his.

He knew his hermana. That stubborn perrita wouldn't answer. She took joy in tormenting him. It was definitely his baby.

Lee jumped up, still gripping his phone. He called Jacinta again. No answer. He paced back and forth. Damn it! There wasn't a thing he could do from here, and he couldn't go home. He would be AWOL. Not the way Lee wanted to start the best thing that had happened to him in a long time. He needed the Navy. The discipline and rules, much as he didn't like them, centered him.

Gaining a sense of self, the Navy taught Lee he was worth more than he thought. He could be more than he thought. His goal, originally, was to become worthy of Isabelle. Now it was even more important.

He called Isabelle. She probably wouldn't answer if she was puking. He'd try though. Her phone rang and rang. Voice mail again.

"Izzy. Call me." What else could he say? His heart felt ready to burst. He was going to have a baby. He was sure of it. With Isabelle.

Now he had a chance to make her his. He paced across

his room. What if she didn't want him?

"Santiago, go to the lounge. I'm trying to sleep."

Lee forgot his roommate had been in bed when he came back. "Sorry dude. Shit's fucked up at home." He snagged his keys as he left the room.

"Whatever. I need my shuteye."

Lee closed the door, resisting the urge to slam it.

He dialed Isabelle again. His heart pounded. Nothing. Maybe someone else be home. Lee tried the house. It rang and went to the answering machine. Damn it.

Lee paced around the lounge. He had the place to himself. Good. He wouldn't have to worry about explaining himself.

He dialed Isabelle again.

"Let her puke in peace why don't you?"

"Is she okay? Let me talk to her."

"Jeez." Jacinta heaved a huge sigh. "Give her a minute."

Lee rolled his eyes. His hermana should go be in the movies. She had the drama queen role down to a T.

"Here she is."

Lee could hear his hermana telling Izzy that she didn't have to talk to him. "Give her the phone!" Both the girls snickered at his roar.

"Fine, I've got the phone."

"You hung up on me." Silence. Damn it that was the wrong thing to say. "Izzy is it true?"

"Are you mad?"

It wasn't really an answer but it was.

"No." He heard the phone hit something hard.

"She'll talk to you later, okay?"

Lee could hear Izzy getting sick again. His stomach heaved. Lee swallowed down bile. "Okay. I'll call tomorrow."

Lee hung up. Dropping on the couch Lee ran his hands through his hair. What the hell was he going to do? Izzy. Pregnant with his baby.

Lee shook his head and stood up. His blood was pumping. Knowing he wouldn't be able to talk to Izzy again tonight, he headed outside.

His phone buzzed. Jacinta.

His phone rang. He grabbed it, hoping Izzy was calling. It was his hermana. "Hey, sis. What's happening? How is Izzy?"

"Mama Rosa is pissed at you."

Lee sighed. "She's been pissed at me for months."

Jacinta laughed. "Yeah, well I thought you should know. Izzy's good. Gotta go, daddy."

Lee didn't think he'd get used to hearing that.

He walked around for a bit. A line was forming at the chow hall. He might as well eat. Unfortunately all he did was pick at his food.

Back at the barracks, Lee debated. He wasn't really tired, but he was homesick. Lee sighed and decided he had better call his abuelita. There was no doubt Jacinta had told everyone he'd talked to her. That's probably why she was mad at him.

Lee called and to his surprise his abuela answered.

"Hi, Mama Rosa."

No sooner than he spoke she began a torrent of words. He clamped his mouth together, biting his tongue. Lee didn't like what she said, couldn't refute any of it, but hated to hear it. He learned why he hadn't been arrested. Learned how sick Isabelle was and that his abuelita would skin him like a dog if he didn't do what was right.

Lee swore under his breath. Not low enough, his abuela yelled at him again. He'd have to clean his language up, with the baby coming. She finally ran out of words and hung up. Lee stood slack jawed. Jacinta was right. Mama Rosa was pissed.

He kept thinking about Isabelle. She really was having his baby. A horn blew. Lee stepped back from the curb. He almost walked in front of a car. He was definitely distracted. Spying a bench, Lee sat.

Remembering the scent of honeysuckle trapped in his blankets, Lee groaned. He shifted uncomfortably flashes of soft skin, and desperate kisses teasing him. His memories too real not to be true.

Fuck.

"Hey, Santiago. Didn't know you were headed to Pensacola."

Lee looked up and smiled. Smyth and Groves from his boot camp company were standing around outside the

Exchange.

"Hey."

"What you up to tonight?" Smyth was always the first to talk.

"Want to go to Portside? The townies manage to get in." Groves winked. "There's some hot babes that come, I hear. Totally into Sailors."

"Sure. I can't drink though." Lee didn't wonder how he heard. Groves always knew what was going on in boot camp too. He always claimed to have his ears to the ground.

"Why not?"

"I do stupid shit."

Groves laughed. "Don't we all?" He slapped a hand on Lee's shoulder. "Don't let that stop you."

Lee shook his head. Even after three months his gut clenched thinking about Lenny. If Lee drank less that night, Lenny might still be alive. Hell, Isabelle wouldn't be pregnant. He'd fucked up their lives that night without a care in the world.

"We're getting dinner first. Join us." Smyth seemed to get what Lee couldn't say. "You don't have to stay, but you do have to eat."

Lee waved at the chow hall. "Already have."

Groves clapped a hand on his shoulder. "Join us anyhow."

"Fine." Maybe their company would stop him from thinking about Isabelle.

"All right, man." Smyth high fived him and Lee rolled his eyes. "Way to leave a guy hanging." Smyth laughed.

They headed to Portside. The line moved slowly forward, letting more people in.

"Hey, we'll tell them we're here for dinner. Maybe we'll get in faster."

"We are here for dinner idiot." Smyth shook his head.

"Yeah, sure. But party time too." Groves winked at the young ladies behind them. He'd been flirting with them since they got in line. It was just what he did. The giggles told him that they were on board with his idea.

"Three for dinner."

"That way." The guard at the door waved them toward the dining room. When they finished they could go straight to the bar.

"Thanks." Smyth always had manners.

"Bye ladies." Groves blew a kiss toward them, setting off more giggles. "See you later."

They headed into the dining room. It looked like any other sit down restaurant, but a bit faded. Clean enough, though. They sat down at an open table. Menus already at each setting.

The waitress headed over.

"Would you like drinks while you look over the menu?"

Groves spoke up. "Beers all around." He glanced over at Santiago. "One won't kill you."

Lee wasn't too sure about having a beer, but thinking

about Isabelle and his baby had him nodding. He could use a beer. He was still reeling from the news.

"ID's please."

Lee pulled his out, flashing it. Groves grumbled but showed his, while Smyth flashed his with a smile. They'd been the oldest in their company and tended to gravitate to each other. The other boots made him feel old. Wet behind the ears and fresh out of high school, their whining had him gripping his hands and gritting his teeth to keep from slapping them.

Groves had dropped out of college to join against his parents' protests. Said he felt he had to do his part. He only had one year left so figured he could easily finish it when his enlistment was up.

Smyth lost his job, didn't want to go to college so headed into the recruiters' one day.

Lee didn't share his story. He grunted anytime Groves asked. And it was always Groves who asked.

The waitress brought their beers over and they placed their orders. Pregnant. What. The. Hell. Lee tipped back his beer, chugging most of the bottle. The cool slide of the slightly bitter taste slid down his throat. It hit his stomach and spread over his body. The fuzzy euphoria mellowing him. Lee needed it. Pregnant. Jesus.

* * * *

Isabelle groaned. It figures. Lee calls and all she could do was puke and hang up on him. Fat chance he'd call again.

Jacinta walked in the bathroom announcing Isabelle had morning sickness and hung up to whoever she was talking to.

"What the hell?" Isabelle's temples pounded. "Who the hell did you tell I was pregnant?" The screechiness in her voice had her wincing. "Jacinta! I don't want it all over school!"

"It won't be." Jacinta turned on the sink, wet a washcloth and handed it over to Isabelle. "You might want to wipe your face."

"Jacinta!" Isabelle tore the cloth from her hand and rubbed her face. "Who?"

"Just Lee."

"What?" Isabelle turned on the floor and propped herself against the side of the tub. Her hand closed convulsively on the cloth, water dripping from her hand. "Why?"

"Don't you think he ought to know?"

"Don't you think he ought to be here?" God, Isabelle knew she sounded bitchy. Scared of the future. Her dad constantly talking about adoption. He wouldn't even give her a chance to tell him she wanted to keep the baby.

"He had to go Izzy. You weren't here. Tio gave him no choice. Hell Mama Rosa even wanted him gone. She wanted him to live, not die. I heard it by accident."

Isabelle snorted. Jacinta eavesdropped constantly. No one could keep anything from her. Isabelle wondered why her family even tried.

Jacinta's phone rang. She ignored it.

"What do you think he's going to do?" Isabelle swallowed, the lump in her throat and burning of her eyes making her voice gruff. "I don't think he remembers Jaci." Isabelle swallowed a sob. "If I hadn't woke up in his room I'd have thought it a dream."

Jacinta slid down and put her arm around Isabelle. Isabelle leaned into her shoulder and let the tears go.

"Shh. It will all work out, you'll see."

Isabelle's phone rang. She glanced at it. It was laying on the floor next to the tub. Lee. She let it ring.

Jacinta grabbed it while Isabelle leaned over the porcelain god once more. You think God would have pity on one little mistake.

Isabelle's shoulders heaved. Wiping her mouth, she sat back. Her arms crept around Jacinta, holding tight. She ignored the phone waving in her face. Her nose clogged making it hard to breathe. It had been too long since she'd been able to let her emotions out.

"You don't have to talk to him."

"Give her the phone!" Lee's roar came through loud and clear.

Isabelle looked at Jacinta and they both laughed. Wiping her face with the still damp washcloth, Isabelle grabbed the phone. "Are you mad?"

"No."

Her heart fluttered then the tinny taste rose up her throat again. Isabelle dropped the phone, leaning again over the toilet. She heaved, her throat stinging and sore. Her abdomen twisted in knots. She had nothing left to give, but her body didn't seem to get the message. Her knees ached. Her arms surrounded the seat and Isabelle rested her forehead against them. God knows if Lee was still on the phone. Isabelle was pretty sure she'd hung up. Hopefully.

She took a breath, the pain easing. "This sucks." Isabelle slid down, moving to rest against the tub.

Jacinta's arms came around her, hugging her. "Yeah."

"Now what?"

"I think that's up to you and Lee."

A noise at the door had both girls looking up. "Mi hija, que pasa?" Mama Rosa asked what was happening. She sounded worried, wanting to know what was wrong.

Isabelle stiffened, keeping her face hidden in Jacinta's hair. Isabelle sniffed and reared back. "What is in your hair? It stinks."

"Pfft. Nasty." Jacinta grabbed the washcloth from Isabelle's hand and tossed it over her head into the tub. "I'm trying a new hair treatment."

"It smells awful." Surprisingly the smell didn't make Isabelle's stomach roll.

"Chicas…"

"Nothing, mama. Just, you know, girl talk."

Mama Rosa shook her head, a disbelieving look on her face.

"Eat some crackers mi hija. It will settle your stomach."

She turned to leave and looked back at them over her shoulder. "We will talk about this later."

Mama Rosa left, closing the door behind her.

"Oh God, do you think she knows?"

"Probably." Jacinta let out a big sigh. "Maybe it's better?"

"I don't know. I just don't know."

"Mama Rosa ought to know a pregnancy. She's seen enough of them."

Isabelle gave a halfhearted chuckle. "Had enough of them, you mean."

"Hey, don't hate." Jacinta grinned. "Just because you don't have a huge family."

"Don't want a huge family." Isabelle stuck her tongue out. "Gah, I need to brush my teeth. Can you get my purse?"

"Why?"

"Cause I've started carrying a toothbrush in there. I've been puking so much that without it, my breath stinks to high heaven."

Jacinta laughed and got up. "No problem, amiga. I'll go grab it." She exited the bathroom.

Isabelle rested her head on her knees. She filled her lungs with air and let it out slowly. Sitting back she grabbed the toilet seat and the edge of the tub, pulling herself up slowly. Her tummy ached and her tongue was fuzzy. The smell of her own vomit had her swallowing convulsively.

"Here you go." Jacinta tossed her purse on the vanity. "Man, it stinks in here girl." She climbed in the tub and opened the window. "Need some fresh air."

Isabelle grabbed her purse and pulled out her toothbrush and paste. It sat right on top when she opened it. She used it a lot. Leaning against the vanity she unwrapped it and rinsed her mouth before brushing.

"How often are you getting sick?"

Isabelle shrugged. She needed to brush her tongue too. Jacinta's questions could wait. If she talked, the chance of her accidentally swallowing the paste was good. She knew she'd be sick again if she did. Her stomach churned just from the minty smell.

She leaned over and rinsed her mouth, careful not to swallow any as she did.

"Constantly, it feels like." She flipped down the toilet lid and sat. "I wish it would end."

Jacinta laughed. "It will, you're like, what? Three, three and a half months? It should stop soon."

Isabelle rolled her eyes. "Jeez, I thought you were a wiz at math! I wish. I hope it stops soon."

Isabelle sat back, the toilet creaking from her leaning on the tank. She let out a puff of air. Isabelle rubbed her belly. The soothing motion helped her relax. Her stomach let out a growl. Isabelle's cheeks heated.

Jacinta laughed. "How about we finally leave the bathroom and hit the kitchen? There's always soup on and enchiladas in the fridge we can heat up."

"Sounds good." Isabelle stood up shakily. "My legs feel like noodles."

"You've spent too much time in front of the porcelain god." Jacinta slid her arm around Isabelle's waist. "C'mon, let's get some food into you."

"You know, I'd just like to relax for a bit. Maybe listen to some music."

"How 'bout we go sunbathe in the park?"

"That sounds like fun."

Mama Rosa looked up and shook her head.

"We're going to the park, Abuela." Jacinta waved as she grabbed a couple of bottles of water from the fridge.

"Be careful, mi hija."

Isabelle pulled a couple of beach towels from the hall closet and stuffed them into a bag. Routine felt good. Jacinta and she spent most of their time at the park when they weren't in school. The warm spring day begged for them to relax. If they were lucky, there'd be a game of soccer going on. Shirts and skins if they were really lucky.

They were. Isabelle and Jacinta spread out the towels, far enough away to not get kicked or a ball in the face, but close enough to admire the view.

"Do you really think Lee is okay with this? What if he wants to give the baby away?"

"You're going to have to figure that out together."

"I know." Isabelle couldn't help the wail in her voice. "But how?" She sat up and crossed her legs. Isabelle lowered her head into her hands, her elbows sharp against her knees. "He's not even here. How can he not help but hate me? I've ruined his life."

"Nah, I doubt it." Jacinta shook her head. "Hell, it's not like Lee had much of a life here. Too much drinking and partying. He'd end up like Lenny if he stayed."

The thought made her stomach turn. Not in a puke up lunch kind of way. Isabelle took a deep breath. "Let's talk about something else. Have you heard back from any of the college's you've applied for?"

Jacinta looked at her and rolled her eyes. "No. I'll probably go to Rio Hondo or LB city. Get my requirements out of the way on the cheap."

"Yeah, me too."

Jacinta sighed. "I hate how life is changing. Both mi hermanos gone. Tio Mateo is moving."

"What? When did that happen?"

"I dunno. He's been looking for years. I kind of think he stayed here because of us."

"What do you mean?" Isabelle grabbed a bottle of water and stretched out, laying down. She turned to face Jacinta. She watched a frown cross her best friend's brow as she sighed.

"With no dad in the picture, I think he stayed around to help mom raise us. Now that mi hermanos are gone and I'm graduating, I think he is starting his life again." She rolled to face Isabelle. "Do you think we ruined his life?"

"No! Why would you even think that?"

"He's not married and he did more to raise us than my mom."

"That would be your mom ruining his life not you."

Isabelle snorted. "Like that helps."

"Look, your tio could have still helped raise you even if he didn't live here."

"I suppose."

"Really, it was Mama Rosa that raised you. Your uncle just paddled your behinds."

Jacinta laughed. "Especially los muchachos! They were the trouble makers."

"Keep thinking that." Isabelle laughed. She knew what trouble Jacinta had gotten into. Most of the time, it was the two of them.

"Do you think he regrets it?"

"Paddling you three? Nope. I bet he wished he did more of it."

Jacinta snorted. "Nice. Bitch."

Isabelle laughed. Both of them laid back, staring at the sky. Isabelle gulped a drink from her water bottle.

"It's peaceful here." If Isabelle ignored the yells and cheers at the soccer field. Which she did.

"Yup."

They let the silence stretch peacefully around them.

"Do you think I'm making the wrong decision?"

"Can't read your mind, amiga. Which one now?"

"Puta. Keeping my baby."

Jacinta laughed. "Nope. Only if you think it is."

Isabelle sighed and stretched, rolling back to her side. "I'm scared. My dad is totally against me keeping the baby."

"You're eighteen. He can't force you to give it up."

"No, but he can make my life a living hell."

"He already does that."

"No, I mean it. Dad's not so bad. He just knows his own mind."

"And thinks he knows yours too."

Isabelle couldn't even answer her back in the negative. Her dad did always think his was the only opinion. Not that he knew her mind, just that her opinions didn't matter.

"You'll see. It will all work out. You worry too much."

Jacinta sounded so sure. Isabelle decided that she was right. Her main problem was Lee's reaction. He just found out. If it was anything like hers, he was still in a daze about it. Heck, she still was.

The shouts from the game were getting louder. Isabelle sat up, Jacinta following to do the same. A fight had broken out on the field.

"You think we ought to leave?" The sky had turned into dusk and the sun headed down. They'd laid around, watching one game end and another begin. Relaxing the evening away.

"Probably. We don't want to be here if someone pulls a gun."

"That doesn't happen a lot does it? There are kids here."

"Look, not so much anymore." Jacinta waved her arm at the playground.

Isabelle could see a couple of parents, pulling their kids away while they cried.

"Shit."

"Yeah. We've called in gun shots before. It's getting really bad. Abuela wants to get security doors."

"Jeez." Isabelle stood, grabbing her towel and bundling it up under her arm. "Let's go then."

They headed out of the park. Isabelle looked back, the fight grew, more of the players getting involved. She could see why Mama Rosa wanted security doors. No telling what could happen if this happened a lot.

Jacinta opened the door, both girls entering in a hurry. They tossed their towels into the dirty hamper.

"I've got to pee." Isabelle shoved Jacinta out of the room. She could hear her laugh as she left.

"Mama, there's a fight at the park."

Isabelle winced. Jacinta rarely spoke quietly. When she shouted you couldn't not hear her. Jacinta wasn't born with a low volume switch.

Finished, Isabelle washed her hands and headed into the kitchen. It's where they always hung out, sitting around the table.

Isabelle could hear Jacinta's voice. Isabelle stepped into the kitchen.

Jacinta set her phone down on the table, one of her mischievous grins on her face.

Isabelle didn't even want to know. Her stomach growled. Isabelle pressed her hands against her heated cheeks. Jacinta laughed and Mama Rosa shook her head.

"Sit." She started bustling around the kitchen, muttering to herself.

Isabelle winced when she started slamming pans around. She wondered what had upset her.

"What did you do to make her mad?"

"Nothing. Told her about the fight is all."

"Do you think she's scared?"

"Nope. She's definitely pissed about something."

Isabelle frowned. "I don't want her to feel like she has to feed me. I can pick up something on the way home."

"Why don't you spend the night?" Jacinta laughed. "Take a night and relax."

The pans smashing together got louder. Isabelle shook her head. "It's okay, Mama Rosa. I don't need anything to eat." Isabelle started to get up, ignoring Jacinta, shaking her head in warning.

"Sit."

Mama Rosa's sharp bark had Isabelle plopping back in her chair.

"Don't ever try to get Mama to stop when she's planning

on feeding you." Jacinta's whisper wasn't low enough. "She's not mad at you. I don't think."

Mama Rosa glared and began mumbling again. The phone rang, Jacinta started to get up again and Mama aimed her spoon at her.

"Sit." She turned and picked up the phone. "Hola. Como esta?" She listened and started speaking rapidly into the phone.

Her Spanish so fast Isabelle couldn't keep up. Her Spanish class hadn't in any way prepared her for everyday usage. Isabelle just knew she didn't want to be on the other end of the call. Mama Rosa was pissed.

"Fuck. Mama knows you're pregnant." Jacinta scraped her chair closer to Isabelle. Her voice was a low whisper.

"How do you know?"

"I just heard her." Jacinta shook her head. "She's reaming Lee."

"Crap." Isabelle bent her head. Her eyes ached and her nose stuffed up. "He'll hate me!"

"Well, at least he knew before abuela told him." Jacinta sounded way too cheerful to be her best friend.

"Some friend you are." Isabelle wiped her eyes on her arm, glaring at her.

"Aren't you glad he knows?" Jacinta sat back. "How do you think he'd feel if you handed him a baby the next time he came home?"

Isabelle dropped her head on the table. She'd just ignore that last comment. She knew Lee loved kids but who said he wanted any of his own? And with her?

"Not much I can do about it now." The past two days had her head whirling. Isabelle had to remember Lee had called her before he knew she was pregnant.

"You're just hungry." Jacinta leaned forward. "Don't think I didn't know about the crush you've had on him for forever."

Isabelle hoped Mama Rosa hadn't heard. She thought she'd hidden it well. Even from her best friend, though she had her doubts. But Jacinta hadn't ever called her out on it before. Isabelle squirmed wishing Jacinta hadn't mentioned anything.

"He has to like you too, or you wouldn't be in the condition you are now."

"Shut up."

"Lee and Isabelle, sitting in a tree. K I S S I N G."

Her singsong had Isabelle grimacing. "Shut up!"

Jacinta laughed. "Okay, so it was obviously more than kissing."

"Shut up." Isabelle giggled at the kissy noises Jacinta made. Her mood swings were ridiculous. "I hate you."

Jacinta laughed. "Good thing I love you."

The phone slammed down and both girls stopped laughing. No one spoke as Mama Rosa went back to banging pots and pans. The hiss of the gas stove ended all but the sound of the spoon hitting the pan. She wasn't even muttering anymore. No telltale humming expressing her happiness, either. Not a good sign.

Isabelle sat up, and exchanged glances with Jacinta. Nope, not saying a word.

Mama Rosa filled plates and served them, still not talking. Even Jacinta was quiet while they ate.

"I'm going to get going, Jaci." Isabelle got up and put her plate in the sink.

"Okay, I'll see you tomorrow."

"Thank you for dinner, Mama." Isabelle grabbed her purse from the bathroom, making sure she had her toothbrush and phone. Glancing at it, she saw she had a message.

"Bye." Isabelle left, waving.

She called her voice mail, hoping it wasn't a message from her dad. He wasn't happy with her right now. Pregnant and applying for jobs outside of the church. She wasn't doing anything he approved of.

Lee's voice almost had her dropping her phone. She listened to his message, both of them on the way home. She'd forgotten he'd left a message yesterday. Isabelle couldn't stop the smile on her face. Lee had called. Said he missed her. Before he'd known about the baby. She floated the rest of the way home. Happiness bursting from her pores.

Isabelle hurried into the house waving at her dad. He was watching the news in the living room. His normal frown on his face. In Isabelle's opinion, there was never anything good on the news, so why bother to watch it?

She took the stairs two at a time, in a rush to reach her bedroom.

She sat on the bed and listened to Lee's message again. Taking a deep breath, she dialed.

"Izzy?"

"Lee, I'm sorry."

"What for?"

"Being pregnant."

"Did you do it on purpose?"

"No! I barely remember anything."

Lee chuckled. "That's not what I wanted to hear."

Lee's voice was smooth, lower in tone than Isabelle was used to. Isabelle shivered, her body tingling. "You don't remember anything either. You said so."

"Izzy. I do. I just didn't want to believe that I was so stupid."

Isabelle shoved her hand in her mouth, hoping Lee hadn't heard her cry out. Her heart ached. He did regret it.

"I always liked you. More than liked you. I never wanted to hurt you. I know I fucked up. I just... I just wish I remembered it all Izzy. Not bits and pieces." He was silent. "That's all. I don't regret it. I just want all the memories."

Isabelle swallowed, and wiped her eyes. "Are you sure you don't regret it?"

"Fuck no. I always wanted to make you mine. But you know your dad hates me. Plus, you had such big plans after high school. Me, I had none. Three years I sat and pickled myself. I miss Lenny, but..."

Isabelle heard Lee sigh.

"But?"

"If I stayed, I don't think my life would have gone any different than his." Lee's words came out in a rush. "Me leaving was for the best."

Isabelle shook her head. "Don't say that."

"Izzy, you know it's true. I'm changing. I really am. The Navy is good so far."

She sniffed and wiped her tears away, again. Damn hormones. "What does that mean for me? For our baby?"

"Would you consider me, as a boyfriend? I know I'm not there. I can't be yet. But I want you in my life, Izzy. You and my baby."

Isabelle heard Lee's knuckles crack. He wasn't as calm as he was trying to sound. He did that when he was nervous or upset.

"I listened to your messages."

"You did?"

Isabelle smiled. "You said you missed me."

"Yeah, I did. I do."

"Before you found out about the baby."

"Is that a good thing?" His question was tentative. Lee was just as unsure as she was.

It eased her mind. Isabelle exhaled thinking about it. Her heart beat just a bit faster. "Yeah, Lee, it is." She nibbled on her fingertip. "Do you want the baby?"

"Yes! Of course I do." Lee was silent. "Izzy, do you?"

"Yes. But I don't want you to be sorry."

"I could never be sorry about that. Just think, in a few months we'll have a little mini-me."

Isabelle snorted. "It might be a little girl."

"That would be okay with me too. Daddy's little princess."

"My dad wants me to put the baby up for adoption." Isabelle bit her lip, waiting for Lee's reply. She wasn't sure she should bring it up, but he needed to know.

"Is that what you want, Izzy? You want to give up my baby?" Lee sounded wounded.

"No, God no."

"Good. That's my baby. You can't fucking get rid of it. You don't want it, I'll keep the baby."

"I do want our baby. I just wanted to make sure you did too." Isabelle swallowed, happiness blossoming. "You're sure?"

"Absofuckinglutely."

Isabelle heard a voice in the background and a muffled reply from Lee.

"Izzy, I have to go. I'll call you when I can, okay? My roommate is grumbling."

"Okay, Bye Lee."

"Bye, Izzy."

Isabelle hugged her pillow to her chest. She just knew everything would be okay.

CHAPTER SEVEN

Pregnant. God, Isabelle, pregnant, with his baby. It was… Lee didn't know what to think. He was ready to beat his chest in pride then curl up in shame for not protecting her.

The need to find out more had him calling back home again. To his surprise, Mama Rosa answered. Then she started reaming him out. That wasn't a surprise. He always did have a knack of making her mad.

She was so upset that he could barely follow her words. But he did, just enough to know she would have tied his balls in a knot if he were home. Stunned at her words, he wasn't sure how he even answered her. Not the way she wanted if the slamming of the phone echoing in his ears gave any indication.

The beer brought images of a soft armful. Isabelle. Him drunk on too many beers. Her telling him she was celebrating her birthday, her eighteenth birthday. His drunk ass brain thinking "no more jail bait."

He thought back to that morning. Imagining Isabelle's soft sexy scent. Pushing her out of bed. He groaned. How could he have done that?

Leaving Groves and Smyth flirting, Lee made his way back to the barracks. Stripped, remembering to toss his clothes into the hamper, Lee left his boxers and crawled into bed.

His phone rang.

The conversation with Izzy sent his heart rate flying. She forgave him. At least he thought she did. Lee swore he could see her smile through the phone. Of course he could picture her crying when she got really silent.

Hell, it was all he could do not to tell her he loved her. He choked it back, letting her go when Jameson started bitching about him talking on the phone. So far his roommate was a real stick in the mud.

At muster on Monday he found out his classes started that day. He was definitely one of the lucky ones. One of the guys had been there for a month. Lee hoped that meant he would be home on leave to see his baby born. Lee could hardly wait. Izzy was just over two months. With the six months of classes in front of him, Lee knew that was cutting it close. But there wasn't much he could do about it.

He and Izzy talked during his lunch each day. He called her before she left for school. Warmth spread from his heart. It was the best time to reach each other. Her dad gone to work and his sister not there to butt in. They'd been discussing baby names last night. Lee had Izzy giggling after telling her he wanted to name the baby Alfredo. She said she wasn't naming her baby after noodles. Lee swore it was his favorite dish and a fitting name.

After class he had watch. He wanted to get qualified as soon as possible. Then he'd be on rotating duty so they'd be able to set up times to Skype. Once she got it set up. Lee had set up his computer and tonight planned on walking Izzy through setting up hers.

He didn't want to miss any more of her pregnancy. He wanted to see her blush when he teased her. Her and Alfredo. Lee chuckled.

"Santiago." A fist rapped on his desk. "Class is dismissed."

His instructor walked back to the front of the classroom and sat down.

Lee stood up, gathering his books. Lee set them back down and straightened his shoulders. With a deep breath he approached his instructor.

"What do you need, Santiago?"

"Chief, can I ask you a question?"

"Sure."

"If I'm not on duty, can I go home over the weekend?"

"Home being where?"

"California."

He grunted. "I wouldn't recommend it. You haven't been here long enough to even leave the base."

Lee slouched and turned away. What the hell was he going to do?

"Seaman, what's the problem?"

The hand on his shoulder had him jumping. Lee hadn't

even heard the chief move. He turned back around to face him.

"I talked to mi abuela, my grandma last night."

"Is she okay?"

Lee nodded. "Yeah, but I found out my girl is pregnant." He stared down at his boots. They needed a shine. Isabelle pregnant, with his baby. It still blew his mind.

"Your grandma told you."

Lee nodded. He clenched his fists. "Yeah. No. Mi hermana spilled the beans first. Then Izzy told me." He sighed. "My abuela is ready to kill me. I've never heard her so mad. I hooked up with Isabelle over Christmas. She's not really my girl, but I want her to be. She's mi hermana's best friend. Now she's going to have my baby. Her dad is a minister and, and…" Lee didn't know what else to say. Heat crept up his neck.

"Sounds like you fucked up, sailor."

Lee nodded. He really had. Over and over he had.

"You're going to have to fix that shit storm."

Lee nodded. He just didn't know how. "I know."

"You need to think about what you're going to do." The chief leaned back against a desk. "How serious are you? Do you want the baby? Does she want the baby? Should she have an abortion? Should she give it up for adoption? Are you going to try to make it work with her or are you going to ask for custody, joint custody or give up custody if she wants that?"

Lee's ears burned and each question had his heart

squeezing. His fists clenched. How could he not want his baby? The thought of Isabelle round with his child made his dick hard. If only he could remember more than drunken snippets.

"Of course I want my baby. And Isabelle. So does she." Lee sighed. "I want to go home and talk to her." He paced away from the chief. "And not just on the phone."

"We don't have any ninety-sixes coming. Not until Memorial Day and you might not be allowed to go then either."

"I just need to talk to her, see her."

The chief was shaking his head. "I suggest you Skype. It's the easiest way."

"She's graduates high school in June." His gut sank. He couldn't jeopardize his enlistment. The chief was right even if he had been hoping to get a different answer.

"Santiago. Is she under age?"

He shook his head quickly. "No Chief. We celebrated her eighteenth birthday that night." Lee rubbed his head. "I remember that much. Both her and my sister graduate in June. Do you think I might be able to go home then?"

"You might be able to get off for your sister's graduation. Put in a request and see if it is approved."

"Okay." Lee swallowed. "What should I do next? I don't know what I can do to help Izzy,"

"Contact Military Personnel about dependents. You will also have to pay child support if you don't get married."

"Okay. Thanks Chief. And just so you know, I may have

been a fuck up most of my life, but I joined so I could change. I wanted to be someone mi familia and Izzy could be proud of. I'd never not pay child support if that's what Izzy wanted. I don't want to be a dead beat like my dad."

"Good to know, sailor. This will give you extra incentive to excel at your training."

Lee wanted to roll his eyes, he really did. But the chief was right. He needed to be all he could be, even if that was the Army's motto.

"Thank you, Chief."

"You know, you just might want to call to talk to her."

"Thanks. I have been." Lee smiled despite his frustration. "There's a lot I still need to ask though. I appreciate your help."

"No problem. The Navy needs all of her sailors alert. Keeping the home front happy helps. Dismissed."

The chief stood and turned back to his desk.

Lee grabbed his books and headed out. He grunted in relief when the entryway was clear of his classmates. In no mood for polite chitchat. He'd eat at the chow hall and go back to his room. Hopefully his roommate would be quiet, if he wasn't out somewhere.

Glancing at his watch, Lee headed over. Dinner was being served. He got in line, his mind a thousand miles away. Maybe, what he thought his wishful thinking were memories. Hard to believe that Isabelle had succumbed to him. He knew he never would have even pressed his luck with Isabelle if he wasn't drunk off his ass. The same party and both blitzed, was evidently a dangerous combination.

Lee frowned. He didn't like that idea. He'd rather that Isabelle had knowingly chosen him. The only problem? Lee couldn't remember. Maybe she did. He shuffled forward, the line moving into the chow hall.

"Hey, Santiago. Forget the chow hall, why don't you eat with us? We're going to the club."

Lee looked up. Groves, Smyth, and a bunch of guys from class stopped in front of him. Groves as usual, the spokesperson.

"No thanks, Groves. I have to call home tonight."

"Didn't you talk to someone yesterday?" Smyth piped in.

"You call home every day. Are your apron strings that tight?" Groves laughed.

"Yes, I did. I promised to help set up Skype."

Groves shook his head. "You're not a lot of fun, Santiago." He laughed. "Your loss dude, your loss."

Lee had never had that said about him before. But his whole purpose in joining, to learn responsibility, to change from the fuck up looking at an early grave. Fate decided to definitely hand that to him in spades.

"I know. Thanks for asking, maybe another time."

Smyth shrugged. "Yeah maybe. Have a good night."

Lee watched as they walked away joking and hamming it up. Their antics brought a reluctant smile to his face. Going out with them probably would make his evening more enjoyable, but he had some serious issues to face.

Running away and drinking his troubles away never had worked for him. The situation with Isabelle spelled that out plainly.

Lee headed into the chow hall and grabbed a tray. The food was tasty and surprisingly good. He wondered if he shouldn't have gone for MS, Mess Management Specialist. He loved to cook. He used to follow Mama Rosa around the kitchen, learning all he could. He'd never starve.

Being inside all day just wasn't his thing though. Lee grabbed his choices and headed toward a table away from everybody. He didn't really want to talk to anyone. He had too much on his mind. Lee thought about the conversation they'd had earlier in the week. His gut clenched, remembering. He really was going to be a father. He couldn't resist calling Izzy the next day.

"Hello?"

"Hola Izzy."

"Morning, Lee."

"It's really true?"

Isabelle giggled. "Are you going to ask me every time you call?"

"Si." It was silent. Still awkward, but they'd get there, Lee hoped. "You didn't answer."

"Yes, you know it's true."

Lee bet anything Izzy was rolling her eyes.

"I can't wait. Thank you Izzy."

"You're happy?"

"I'm happy. I can't wait to hold you and our baby."

"You're sure?"

"Yes. I've never wanted anything more." Lee was surprised how good it sounded to him. He could just imagine Izzy holding his baby, standing in his arms.

"That's good."

Lee heard the sound of a bell ringing. He hadn't meant to call her at school. "That the school bell?"

"Yeah, I have to go. I don't want to be late to class."

"Sure, I'll call you tomorrow, Izzy. Earlier so I don't get you at school."

"Sounds good."

He heard whispers and shook his head. He should've known his hermana was there. The two of them were always together. He had no clue how Izzy had gone out on her birthday without Jacinta. If she had, Lee knew he wouldn't be in this situation. His hermana would never have let it go as far as it did. But somehow he didn't regret it.

He laughed. "When Jacinta's not around."

"Good idea. Good-bye Lee."

"Good-bye."

He heard his hermana telling Isabelle to hang up already. Lee couldn't help smiling as he pressed end call. His stomach had settled down during the conversation.

Their conversations had become easier the rest of the week. Lee knew she wanted his baby as much as he did.

They just had to figure out a way to make it work. Lee pulled his tray toward him and quickly polished off his supper.

Should he call her? Before he could think twice he dialed Isabelle's number.

"Hello."

"Izzy?"

"Yes. Hold on, let me pay for my lunch."

He heard the phone clatter on her lunch tray. Lee grinned. They could share a meal together even if they were thousands of miles apart.

"I'm glad you called."

"Me too."

"So, you're pregnant." Lee couldn't help himself. Each conversation he brought it up.

Isabelle giggled. "Um, yeah. Are you mad?" Her standard line. Now she said it to tease him. Her voice happy through the phone. A grin spread across his face. He was going to be a daddy. Now that they'd established he was excited about it, Isabelle seemed much happier.

"No, Izzy. Not at all." The warmth spreading through his chest let him know it was fantastic news. He'd had a bit of time to get used to the idea. Hearing Isabelle confirm it each time stole his breath. "I can't wait to hold our baby."

"That's good."

"Yeah, it is." Lee grinned. God, talking to Izzy made his day brighter. "Call me when you want to set up your computer tonight."

"I will."

"We will." His sister's voice ran over Izzy's. Lee didn't think Izzy was ever alone. He laughed.

"Brat."

"Hey don't call Isabelle a brat."

"I wasn't. I was talking to you."

Lee could hear a crinkle sound on the line. "There must be static on the line. I think you're breaking up."

He doubted it. Lee could hear both girls laughing in the background. He recognized the cellophane of a cookie bag being crinkled.

"I'll call you later, Lee. Jaci won't give me back my phone!" Izzy shouted above the noise.

"No, it's breaking up."

Jacinta hung up. Lee stared at his phone and laughed.

* * * *

"See? It's going to be okay."

"Sure, if you keep your nose out of it." Isabelle couldn't keep the smile from her face. She thought that maybe, just maybe, Jacinta might be right. She hadn't expected Lee to call during the day. He usually called early in the morning. Not at lunch when Jacinta would butt in.

The day flew by. Lee was going to call that evening to

walk her through setting up Skype. They'd be able to see each other then. She was nervous. Hopefully, when he saw her, he wouldn't change his mind.

She hopped on the bus and sat next to Jacinta.

"I'm going to head home."

"You're coming over later, right?"

Isabelle nodded.

"How is home going?"

"Dad has been talking to the adoption agency."

"Haven't you told him you want to keep the baby?" Jacinta shook her head, the frown on her face showing her disapproval.

"I told him I didn't want to give my baby up for adoption."

"And he ignores you?"

"Yeah, he does."

"He's not going to listen until you put your zapatas down, chica."

"You mean foot."

"Nope. Zapatas. Those big ass black motorcycle boots you own. You know, when you thought you were a bad ass."

Isabelle snickered. Freshman year and bad fashion choices. Her tummy roiled thinking about her dad, though. What could he do? Eighteen gave her the right to say yes or no. If she had to, she'd beg shelter from Mama Rosa. It wouldn't be ideal. Isabelle wasn't sure she'd want to live with so many people. Then again, she wouldn't worry as much. Everyone in Lee's house had experience in handling babies.

"For now, let him be happy so it's peaceful at home."

"Ja ja ja." Jacinta pursed her lips. "I hope that doesn't back fire."

"Me too." Isabelle rubbed her belly, trying to settle her nausea. Her throat burned, acid reflux seemed to follow each bout. Her baby bump barely showing but the rest of the symptoms had hit with a vengeance. She got home every day and puked up a storm. Then made supper. Most of the time she couldn't eat it.

"I'm hungry, let's grab a bite before you go. I bet, Mama Rosa is in the kitchen."

Isabelle laughed. "Your abuela is always in the kitchen."

"True."

Isabelle pushed off the seat, hands gripping the back of the bench to steady herself. The lurching of the bus and fumes through the window enough to bring lunch to the edge of her throat. Thank goodness they were the first stop. Hopefully she only had morning sickness for the first trimester.

Jacinta grabbed her hand and pulled her toward the house. "Come on mamacita!"

"Jeez, not so loud. I don't want anyone to know!" Isabelle tugged at Jacinta's hand.

"Can you imagine how hard it will be to hide in the next few months?" Jacinta eyed her belly. "You'll get huge."

Isabelle pushed open the front door. "Thanks, I really don't want to think about it."

Jacinta rolled her eyes. "Like that will help. You hungry?"

"Not really."

"You have to eat."

"I do. I just don't want to right now. My stomach is protesting again."

"Okay."

Jacinta grabbed a plate, piling food on it.

"You talk to Lee?" Mama Rosa came over and sat down.

"Si, Mama."

"He did good?"

"Yes. He asked me if we were having a baby." Isabelle giggled. "He asks me every time we talk."

She appeared to ruminate then nodded her head. "Good." She pointed a spoon at Isabelle. "You take care of the bebe, si?"

Isabelle nodded. "Yes."

"Good."

Mama Rosa stood and walked back to the stove, obviously dismissing her. Isabelle glanced at Jacinta. She only rolled her eyes and waved. "Sure you don't want some?"

"No. I'll see you later. Bye Mama Rosa." Isabelle waved and headed out the door of the kitchen.

"See ya later."

Isabelle walked home. Her house was just a couple of blocks away and the weather was too nice to bother driving. Isabelle took a deep breath. The air fresh and clean after the surprise rains yesterday. The barest hint of damp earth teased her nose.

She noticed some of Jandro's friends playing soccer. They waved and called to her to come watch. Waving back, she shook her head and continued on her way. Isabelle didn't feel like being up close and personal with the smell of a dozen sweaty men.

She stopped and sniffed the azalea's on Mrs. Juarez' fence. The buzzing of bees adding to her contentment. Talking to Lee helped. She didn't know what would happen, but just knowing Lee didn't blame her, or hate her, helped. That he was interested in her and not just because of the baby thrilled her to her core. Snapping off a small bloom, she twirled it as she continued home.

Isabelle turned the corner. Four houses away and her steps slowed, a car she didn't know in her driveway. Her gut churned. Stopping and stepping behind a palm tree, she called her sister.

"Caroline, who's over?" She couldn't help but whisper.

"Where are you?"

"Who's at the house?"

"Dad invited a couple over that wants to adopt your baby."

"What?"

"Yeah. So, you're giving it up? I thought you wanted to keep it."

"I do. Dad won't listen."

"Where are you?"

"I'm in front of the Gonzales's."

"I don't think you should come home right now. He's got papers and everything. They even brought a lawyer with them."

"Shit."

"If you're gone long enough, they'll leave but dad will be pissed. He figured you'd be here. You have to be sure you don't want this."

"I don't. I want my baby. Lee agrees with me."

"Fuck. Lee Santiago? He's the father? If dad finds out, he'll be pissed."

"Then don't tell him."

"You better not come home right now."

"Can you pack me up some clothes and my backpack? I'll stay at Jacinta's tonight."

"He'll notice if I leave with that. I don't want to get in trouble."

"You never want to know your niece or nephew?"

"Don't be like that. You know that's not true."

"I have a bag packed. I was planning on staying over at Jaci's anyway. Put it at the side of the house along with my computer. I'll sneak around and get it."

"Okay. But don't get caught."

"I won't. Thanks."

Isabelle wiped her eyes, hung up and headed back the way she'd come. Damn her dad. She didn't think anything she said would make him listen. She'd go watch the soccer game after all. Maybe one of the guys would go get her bags. Caroline was right. Better she wasn't anywhere near her house for the night.

She waved at the guys, settling in at a picnic table near the game. Ricardo waved back. Jandro's best friend, her neighbor. If she asked, she'd bet he'd get her stuff. Isabelle texted Jacinta. The response made her laugh.

At the park. Soccer

???

I need to talk to Ricardo

WTF?

My dad.

??

Tell you later.

KK

Isabelle figured Jacinta would be over in five minutes or less. She wasn't disappointed when she saw her running out of the house and jogging over.

"Okay, chica, what gives?"

"You're not going to believe it. My dad had a couple over that wants to adopt my baby. And their lawyer!"

"What? I told you, you have to tell him."

"I have. He won't listen."

"So why you want to talk to Ricardo?"

"I'm going to see if he'll grab my bag. Caroline is hiding it outside the house for me."

"What if your dad finds it?"

"He won't. He never goes outside unless he's mowing. Ricardo sometimes cuts through there to get home. Dad won't even think twice if he sees him."

Jacinta nodded. "Good idea." She watched the game for a bit. "You know, you have to settle this. He'll keep doing it until you do."

Isabelle watched the ball fly across the field, the men running after it. She couldn't look at Jacinta. "Do you think I'm selfish to want to keep my baby?"

"Fuck no." Jacinta grabbed her arm. "It's your baby. Not your dad's. It's your choice. Don't let him strong arm you."

"Lee didn't want to put the baby up for adoption either." She glanced over. Jacinta's mouth hung open. "Better shut it or you'll catch flies." She tapped her chin and laughed. She couldn't believe she'd shut Jacinta up.

"How often do you talk to him?"

"Every day. Lee calls me before school. Sometimes at night." Isabelle gave Jacinta a sly grin. "When he knows I'm not with you."

"Bitch."

Isabelle cracked up and Jacinta joined her.

A cheer rang out and Isabelle looked up. A goal and the final one, evidently, with the men heading off the field, slapping each other on their backs. She waved at Ricardo.

He pointed at his chest and she nodded. He broke off talking with his friend and trotted over.

"Hola, Isabelle. You want me?"

She rolled her eyes at the hooting from his team mates walking by. She called them men? They were definitely boys.

"Yes. I can't go home right now. Would you grab my bags from under my window and bring them to Jacinta's? Don't let my dad see you grab them."

He plopped down, the sweat running down his body. He grabbed his shirt from the table and wiped his face and chest.

"Tell me why."

"He has some people over I don't want to see."

"That's not the whole story." He looked at her and raised his brow.

"I can't talk about it yet."

"I suppose I can do that. I want you to tell me what's going on though." He raised his hand. "Maybe not today. But soon."

Isabelle nodded and leaned over to give him a kiss on the cheek. "Thank you. I will."

Ricardo stood. "I'll bring them over after I shower."

"Thank you."

"De nada, bebe." Ricardo strolled off with a limp fingered wave.

If he wasn't gay, she would have grabbed him. Jacinta had no such reservations.

"Hey, I'm here whenever you change your mind, Ricky!"

"You can't have a piece of dis, Jaci! It's too hot for you!" A wiggle of his finely formed ass and a sizzle sound as he touched his finger to it and shook it, had both girls laughing.

With the sky going black, they headed back to Jacinta's.

Ricardo stopped over at Jacinta's an hour or so later. "Here you go, girl." He perched on the arm of the sofa. "So, why did I have to grab this for you?"

"My dad is trying to force me to do something I don't want."

"Give up the baby?"

Isabelle gasped. "How did you know about it?"

"Girl, you know I cut through your yard. All. The. Time. I heard your dad yelling about it."

Isabelle's stomach tightened. "You haven't told anyone have you?"

Ricardo reared back, frowning at her. "Of course not. I figured if you were telling people I'd have heard. I know better than to spread rumors."

Isabelle threw her arms around him. "Thank you!"

"You're welcome." Ricardo stood, gently pushing Isabelle back. "I have to go to work. I'll see you later."

He grinned. "Call me if you need any more secret missions done."

"Bye, Ricardo. Thank you." Isabelle waved him off.

"Why is he gay?" Jacinta mourned, watching him walk away. "He's so fine."

Isabelle laughed. Ricardo was just Ricardo. "You just want him because you can't have him." She couldn't imagine him any other way. "Let's get my computer set up." Isabelle grabbed her laptop and headed into Jacinta's room.

"Why the rush?"

"Lee's going Skype me today. Once we get it working on my computer."

"That's dead easy girl." Jacinta flopped back on her bed.

Isabelle shrugged. "I couldn't reach Lee when I tried. He's going to make sure we connect. Have you heard from any of the job applications yet?"

"Yup. I just got off the phone with Toys 'R Us when you texted me. I go for a job interview tomorrow after school."

"Exciting! I hope I hear from one of them soon. Before no one will hire me because of the baby."

"That's illegal you know."

"Doesn't mean it doesn't happen." Isabelle set her laptop on the bed where she and Jacinta could see it.

Jacinta shrugged. "True."

Isabelle's phone rang.

"Lee?"

"No. I'm sorry. I was trying to reach Isabelle Rivers."

"I'm Isabelle." She made a face at Jacinta, mouthing 'not Lee' and pointing to her phone.

Jacinta giggled.

"This is Martin Chavez. I'm the manager at Burlington. You had applied for a position. I'm conducting interviews tomorrow and wanted to schedule an appointment."

"I can come in any time after school. I get out at two fifteen."

"How about three o'clock?"

"Sounds great. Thank you."

"No problem. Just ask for me at the front desk."

"Thank you, I'll see you tomorrow." Isabelle hung up and squealed. "I have an interview too!"

Jacinta tossed her arms around her. "Fantastic! Where at?"

"Burlington. I'm so excited."

Isabelle's phone rang again.

"Hello?"

"Hey, Izzy. How are you doing?"

Isabelle bounced on the bed. "I have a job interview tomorrow." She couldn't help the happy laugh. "Isn't that wonderful?"

"What about school?"

Isabelle rolled her eyes.

Jacinta snickered.

"After school, Lee."

"Oh. Well, cool! Where at?"

"Burlington Coat Factory at Las Puentes."

"That's great. If that's what you want."

Isabelle could tell he wasn't sure why she was excited. "They give an employee discount and they have tons of baby stuff."

"Oh. Oh, wonderful Izzy." He sounded happier at that news.

"Thanks. I just hope I get it."

"You will. How can they resist you?"

Isabelle's cheeks warmed. She wished she could feel his arms around her.

"Enough with the mushy stuff. Let's get Skyping." Jacinta had her face against Isabelle's to talk into the phone.

"Fine."

"I'm putting you on speaker phone." Isabelle touched her screen allowing both her and Jacinta to hear Lee.

"You might as well." Lee laughed. "That was fast."

"I have your Tio Mateo's old iPhone."

"Okay. Let's get you set up. Do you remember your account?"

"No. I never could get the setup done."

Lee guided the girls through the set up amid their giggling and teasing. Isabelle and Jacinta both got accounts. Once Isabelle had hers set up, they did the same to Jacinta's computer.

"Oh, by the way, Jaci. You get to keep that computer. I bought a new one."

Jacinta's squeal hurt Isabelle's ear. "Jeez, girl. Way to make me deaf."

"That's awesome Lee. Thank you!" Jacinta ran out to the kitchen, letting everyone in there know how wonderful her brother was.

"That's sweet of you." Jacinta looked at Lee. He made her heart flutter. Lee was in his room. He'd described it to her but it was different seeing it.

"You look great Izzy." Lee looked down and whispered. "Can I see your belly?"

Isabelle's heart fluttered. Lee looked unsure. "Of course." She stood up and put the computer on the dresser. Standing back she lifted her shirt, showing off her little pot belly. "I look like I'm getting fat."

"No you don't Izzy. You look beautiful." Lee put his hand on the screen. "I wish I could touch you."

"Me too."

Isabelle heard the jingle of keys.

Lee groaned. "I've got to go Izzy. My roommate's back. I miss you."

"I miss you too." Isabelle touched the screen where Lee's hand was. "Thank you for setting up Skype with me."

"My pleasure, Izzy. How about you text me and let me know how your interview goes? Maybe we'll be able to Skype again."

"Okay. Good night."

"Good night Izzy. Sweet dreams."

Isabelle logged off, a smile on her face. Lee looked so good. He looked healthy and happy. A far cry from the last time she'd seen him.

CHAPTER EIGHT

Are you here yet?

Lee sent off the text to his hermano. Jandro had finally graduated in late March. He'd just finished Infantry school and was on leave for a couple of days before he went on to his specialty school. It worked out perfectly for him to attend Jacinta's graduation.

Lee straightened up and shouldered his bag. His instructor had allowed him leave for the weekend. He had flown out on the redeye, stopping to change planes in Atlanta and landing in LAX at 2:00 am. Lee had brought his cracker jacks with.

This was his favorite dress uniform. There was no mistaking him as a sailor when he wore them. He'd always thought the snack was named after the uniform, but it turns out it was the other way around. The Navy called them Service Dress Whites. They were comfortable and cool enough in the heat despite being mainly polyester. The rest of his clothes should still be at home so he hadn't packed anything else. But he wanted to present a good impression, so he'd brought his uniform for the girls' graduation.

His phone buzzed.

Just pulling in.

I'll head to arrivals. American Airlines.

K.

Lee wiped his sweaty hand on his jeans. Why the hell was he so nervous? He'd been allowed leave since his hermana was graduating. But so was Isabelle. His Isabelle, at least he hoped. The mother of his baby. God, he hoped this all worked out.

They'd managed to Skype almost every day. Usually in the mornings. Isabelle was hired at the place she wanted to work, limiting her free time. Her father had come around to the fact that she wanted to keep her baby, even though he still brought adoption up. Lee couldn't wait to see her in person.

Lee stepped outside and coughed. It wasn't nearly as humid as Florida, but just as hot. The air wasn't as clean and his lungs were letting him know it. Ignoring the cursing of the taxi drivers, Jandro slid in to the curb with a grin on his face.

"Yo, squid, get your ass in the car."

Rolling his eyes, Lee tossed his bag into the back seat and hopped in. "Let's hit Tommy's on the way to la casa."

"Sounds good."

Jandro turned back into the traffic flow. Sliding into a space Lee swore was too small for the car. Squeals and curses were left behind in his wake. He quickly locked his seatbelt and grabbed the 'oh shit' bar and held on. That or fly out the window.

"The Jarheads haven't improved your driving."

"I don't drive there. No car. Tio picked me up from base for the weekend."

"Just don't go getting us killed."

"No way, I won't leave Isabelle's baby without a daddy. No matter how shitty he may be."

"Fuck you."

"No thanks. Isn't that how you got into this problem?"

"It's not a problem."

"In what universe? Fuck, why Izzy? There's plenty of ho's around, dude. You have to fuck up the one decent girl you know."

"I was drunk, okay? I don't even hardly remember it."

"Don't go telling Izzy that."

Lee hung his head and mumbled. "She already knows."

"Asshole."

"Crap, she doesn't remember much either."

"How much did the two of you drink?" Jandro shook his head. "Never mind, I don't want to know."

"Come on. Let's go." Lee fumed in silence. He didn't want to fight with Jandro. Regardless of what he said. It felt like forever since Lee last saw him. "Izzy's different."

From the corner of his eye he saw Jandro frown and shake his head. Lee loved his hermano, but the dude sure got on his nerves. Always a goody two shoes, not even a whisper of trouble attached to his name. His bro was

Teflon.

He, on the other hand, call him Velcro. Everything stuck. Shit he hadn't even done was blamed on him. His skin crawled. Never could he come home for good. Lee could swear the air changed the closer they got to Pico. Glad he'd joined the Navy to become the man he wanted to be. He'd get through the weekend.

Lee swore at himself. He shouldn't have gotten Isabelle pregnant. Hell, he shouldn't have touched her. But drunk? He did what he wanted. One of the reasons he hadn't had more than a beer or two since, except for the night he'd gotten the news. Tired of being out of control and letting his desires rage. Getting Isabelle pregnant had been an accident. One he had a hard time regretting. He'd wanted her for a long time. Longer than he even wanted to admit.

Lee smiled thinking about Izzy. She'd had a cute little baby belly on her. Lee thought she looked great, but Izzy bitched about how fat she was getting. Lee just wanted to gobble up her curves. He couldn't wait to get to the house. She was planning on staying with Jacinta for the night. If her father would let her.

Lee hoped she was still awake. She slept a lot now. Isabelle fall asleep even Skyping with him the few times they'd managed it at night.

Lee eyed his bag. Inside, there was something for Isabelle. Whether she'd accept it or not, he didn't know. The little black box wrapped securely inside of his uniform. After graduation he'd give it to her. Somehow he'd steal some time with her. Away from his family and away from hers. Let her know how much she and the baby really meant to him.

If he was lucky, Isabelle would say yes. His luck? Usually shit, so he wasn't counting on it. Hoping, but not counting on it. After he found out about the baby, Lee had saved every penny he could. He knew he had to pay for at least two flights home. Not to mention Isabelle would need everything he could save for baby stuff.

The car pulled up to the drive thru. The bump into Tommy's enough to bring his attention back to the here and now. It didn't matter the time, they were always crowded. Especially at night when bar time closed. Jandro eased up to the ordering speaker.

"Bro, what you want?"

"Chili fries and a burger. Oh, and a chocolate shake."

Jandro leaned out the window and placed their order. Quadruple of everything.

"Jacinta up?" Probably more of the familia too. Lee squashed down the excitement of seeing everyone. Almost six months had passed. It had been the longest he'd gone without being around la familia. Of course, since both Izzy and Jacinta Skype'd him, the rest of the family made an effort to say hi also. But it wasn't the same.

"Isabelle's spending the night."

That came out of the blue. His gut clenched at the news. A light sweat broke out on his brow. He was worried her father wouldn't let her.

"I know."

Jandro slipped a look at him while he pulled out the

money to pay, inching forward in line.

Lee's hands shook as he pulled out a ten and handed it to Jandro. He'd pay his own way now, not like before. No more mooching off of his hermano.

"How do you know that?"

"Jandro, I'm not a complete ass. I talk to Izzy almost every day." He wasn't sure he'd be able to eat now. His stomach tied in knots. Isabelle, at home, his home, six months pregnant with his baby. His. He couldn't wait to see her.

A stop at the window to collect their order and pay, then Jandro sped off into the night. Home, coming closer and closer. The greasy smell of fries and chili filling the car. Isabelle and the reality of how their lives had changed just around the corner. Then they were there.

"I'll take the food. Grab your bag."

Lee listened, all of his attention on the closed door to the house. Isabelle, waiting for him. He grabbed his bag, his hand shaking. Firming his lips and drawing himself up, Lee shut the car door and followed Jandro. He ignored the fast pitter patter of his heart, the lump in his throat.

Isabelle. No one else mattered at this point. He'd see her, see his baby. Touch her. It didn't seem real.

* * * *

"What time does his plane land?"

"Two AM. I told you already, amiga."

"I know, I know." Isabelle drew a finger along the pattern of the comforter. "Are you sure I should have come? What if he doesn't want to see me?"

"He does." Jacinta dropped on the bed. She'd been peeking out the window. "Haven't you guys been skyping?"

"Well, yes. Every day. But what if he's changed his mind? What if he thinks I'm fat?" Isabelle clenched her hand in the blanket, the slick polyester slipping through her grip. "What then?"

"I'll smack him upside the head."

Isabelle giggled. "Don't do that. We're going to be so busy with graduation."

"Make time. You're staying here and so is mi hermano."

"You guys haven't seen him either. And I'm not staying the whole weekend. My dad has a graduation party planned for us too."

Jacinta rolled over and raised a brow. "We all know you two need to talk." She pointed at her belly. "You have things to discuss."

Isabelle flopped back on the pillows, staring up at the ceiling. She could see where the light had been changed out. The paint color was off just a bit. Her eyes roamed around the room.

"Hey, pay attention."

"Yeah, yeah." Isabelle didn't know what to say. It felt weird, Lee coming home. What if he just wanted to go out and party? Isabelle hugged herself. She was worrying for nothing. Lee was just as excited as she was about the baby. They'd even decided not to find out the baby's sex, arguing about names for boys and girls. They had it narrowed down. It was the one thing she was keeping secret from Jacinta, no matter how she begged.

Isabelle continued staring at the ring of color around the light. She heard the sound of an engine turning off, doors shutting. She heard the muted sounds of voices. It had to be Lee and Jandro. The front door opened. She knew from the squeal of the hinge from the iron barred door. She heard other voices joining them, happy chatter that got louder, punctuated by the slamming of the door again.

She pressed a hand against her stomach. It didn't stop the churning. Isabelle told herself to stop being silly. She'd known Lee for years. They'd talked almost every day for the last few months. Her racing heart ignored her. Isabelle took a deep breath and then another. One more wouldn't hurt.

"For Pete's sake. It's Lee. Get up off of the bed and go say hi."

Jacinta pushed at her, rolling her to the side of the bed. Jacinta hopped up and slid in front of her. She grabbed at Isabelle's hands, trying to pull her from the bed.

"Give me a minute." Isabelle slapped at her hands, preventing Jacinta from grabbing her.

"You knew he'd be here. Now he is." She grabbed Isabelle's hands and pulled her up. "You need to see him. Talk. I know he wants to see you too."

Isabelle rolled her eyes. "But I'm so fat now."

"And you've been showing him your belly. I've seen the

pics." Jacinta stepped away and pulled her toward the door. "Now move it."

Isabelle hung back, propelled into the living room only by the firm grip Jacinta had on her hand. Her eyes stayed on the tile floor. They stepped into the kitchen. The voices died. So quiet. Much quieter than she'd ever heard this family.

Her cheeks heating, Isabelle finally peeked up. A snicker echoed across the room. A smile broke out across her face. She couldn't hold back a chuckle. She was being silly.

Lee smiled at her, stepping forward.

Jacinta dropped her hand.

Isabelle saw her step back from the corner of her eye.

Lee pulled her to him in a hug.

"Izzy Bell. You look good."

Her arms crept around his waist. He seemed firmer to her. Much firmer than she'd thought. Isabelle looked up and gasped. She hadn't seen Lee so clear eyed and healthy looking in years. The computer didn't do him justice.

He laughed down at her. His arms tightened around her waist. He leaned down and whispered in her ear. "I've been trying to change. No more drunken nights, drunken fights, and drinking until my liver twists in protest. I told you."

"I can see that."

She didn't know what else to say. She hugged him, feeling his warmth against her. Sending her stomach fluttering. Words stuck in her throat. She realized the kitchen was still quiet. Too quiet. The silence unnerving. Isabelle looked around. They were the center of attention. She cleared her throat and tried to step back, disengaging her hands from Lee's waist.

His hands gripped her waist, keeping her against him, before falling away. He didn't stop touching her for long though. He flung an arm around her shoulder, pulling her close into his side. He looked around at his family in the kitchen. "Don't be so nosy."

Jandro chuckled.

She heard Jacinta snicker. Isabelle rolled her eyes, shook her head and smiled. "You know they can't help it." She gestured at Jacinta. "Especially that one." Lee's family was always in someone's business. Usually a family members and this qualified, she supposed. They'd always treated her as such.

"Mi hijo, mi hija, sit. Eat." Her smile lit up the room. She was obviously happy to see Lee again.

Mama Rosa waved them toward the table. The rest of the family sat there or lounged around the breakfast bar. It didn't seem to matter to them that it was after three o'clock in the morning. Dark as sin outside. They chattered away, catching up with Jandro who had also just returned. A chair pushed out and Lee sat, dragging Isabelle into his lap. Food from Tommy's spread across the table.

Isabelle wiggled, trying to get away. Her cheeks red at the attention. The heat of his body sparked an answering heat in hers. His hard thighs beneath her bottom brought her attention to the growing issue in his lap. Her abdomen tightened. Her sex softened, moisture forming in anticipation. Her nipples felt as hard as rock. Glad she had on her robe to hide the effect Lee had on her.

Lee's hands gripped her waist, settling her, cradling his erection between her butt cheeks.

"Stop moving." His arms slid around her, pulling her back to his chest. "Just sit still." Lee's hands slid over her belly, sliding to cradle the baby growing inside her. "I need this."

Isabelle stilled, then couldn't help shifting one more time.

He grew even harder beneath her.

She hid her smirk. At least she knew it wasn't just because he'd been drunk. Then again, if he didn't have on jeans, Isabelle knew he'd be able to feel the wetness of her panties. She felt naked. Perching on him wearing only her jammies and a light robe. His hands were under the robe, touching her, touching their baby. Inches from where she ached for him. All the while carrying on a conversation with his brother.

A plate was shoved in front of her. Another quickly followed for Lee. Lee's hands slid away, his fingers lightly brushing over a nipple with a tweak.

"Lee!"

He laughed against her neck. The puff of air sent a shiver down her spine. "What?"

He knew what. Isabelle had heard that teasing sound in his voice before. Nothing or no one could stop him when he got playful. She just hoped she didn't come out of it red cheeked and unable to face his family.

"Eat. You've two to feed and you're skinny."

She turned to look at his face and exhaled in a puff of air. "Am not. The doctor says I'm doing just fine."

"I think you're just fine too." Isabelle shivered at the skim of his hand down her side. "You've never looked better, round with my bebe."

She faced forward, trying to ignore the hardness beneath her. Ignoring the racing of her heart. Hoping against hope that everything worked out between them.

"Ready to graduate tomorrow?" Jandro tossed a piece of biscuit to get Jacinta's attention.

"Definitely. Then I have to sign up for fall classes."

"Where did you decide to go?" Lee asked.

Isabelle perked up, this she wanted to hear. Jacinta had mentioned doing her basics at the local college, but she never mentioned signing up. Isabelle had caught a glimpse of envelopes from colleges in her locker, but nothing more. Jacinta had been tight lipped about her college plans. She wasn't sure why, unless she planned on leaving the state. Her family wouldn't like that. She wouldn't either, but she understood. Her plans had involved going away too, until her pregnancy.

"It's a need to know basis." Jacinta flicked water at her hermano. "You don't need to know."

Lee stretched beneath her. His hard muscles evident as he brushed against her.

She thrilled against him. Isabelle fought to hide her reaction. Goosebumps she couldn't hide, but she kept her breathing as even as she could.

Lee yawned, pulling her tight against him. His chin settled on her shoulder, his breath wafting across her sensitive ear.

Her goosebumps spread and she couldn't stop the shiver. Her abdomen tightened.

"I'm beat." Lee yawned again.

It was contagious. Isabelle yawned too. She could hear the tiredness in his voice. Now that Lee had arrived, she couldn't seem to keep her eyes open.

"I don't think I'm the only one." Lee nudged her. "Time for bed. You'll want to be bright eyed for graduation tomorrow."

"Oh God. We have rehearsal in the morning at nine." Jacinta turned to her mother. "Do we have to go?"

"Si." She shooed the girls. "Bed. Now. We'll drop you off so you can sleep as long as possible."

"Don't take the lord's name in vain." Mama Rosa scolded, ignoring the reason for it.

Jacinta rolled her eyes. She grumbled but stood up. "C'mon Izzy. You're falling asleep on Lee."

Heat rushed to Isabelle's cheeks. She struggled to stand. Lee wasn't exactly helping, his hands holding her in his lap.

"Lee, let me go."

He changed his grip, helping her to stand. The softness of his lips brushed against the nape of her neck as she rose.

"Good night."

Jacinta grabbed her hand, once again pulling her across

the house.

Isabelle glanced back at Lee, his grin letting her know he saw. Heat rushed to her cheeks. She raced Jacinta to the bedroom. She jumped in the bed, then back out.

"I have to go to the bathroom."

"That figures."

Isabelle laughed then shot across the hall, sliding in before Jandro and slamming the door.

"Dammit."

"Language, mi hijo."

Isabelle giggled. Mama Rosa always seemed to turn up to scold. If you did something you shouldn't, guaranteed she'd be there. Jacinta had begun calling her Ninja Abuela last year. Mama Rosa shook her head and scolded her.

Finished, Isabelle washed her hands and pulled open the door. Expecting to see Jandro, she stepped back, startled to see Lee.

"Oh."

His grin was pure mischief.

"I thought I'd say goodnight properly."

Her eyes raised to his, widening.

Lee pulled her into his arms. The heat of his lips spread to her bones.

Isabelle melted against him, wrapping her arms around him. His six pack hard against her belly. Six pack? Isabelle slid a hand to his stomach. She couldn't stop the moan. Holy cow, a whole new Lee. She slid her hand under his shirt, her fingers tracing the hair leading down. The glory trail. She giggled.

Lee pulled back, a frown in his eyes. "What's so funny?"

"This." She traced the firm muscles lined with the coating of hair.

"How so?"

"Jacinta and I call this the glory trail."

Lee snorted. "The two of you need taking in hand."

"Good luck with that."

Lee smiled and bussed the tip of her nose. "Believe me, I'll manage."

Isabelle shook her head. "You and what army?"

Lee pulled her into a quick hug and released her. "I don't need an army. I've got the Navy. Go to bed." He patted her butt, earning her glare and laughed. "Go on now. You need your sleep."

She huffed and entered the room, closing the door behind her. She heard Lee's chuckle and shook her head. She'd missed him. Isabelle couldn't believe she'd even missed his teasing.

"That took you long enough." The muffled words came from beneath a mound of covers.

Isabelle shut off the light and climbed into bed, dropping her robe on the floor.

"Lee was waiting outside when I got out."

"Hmm."

Isabelle waited for more words of wisdom. Jacinta

rewarded her with a soft snore. Smiling, she snuggled under the blankets. Feeling warm and safe just knowing Lee slept in the same house, she settled into slumber.

* * * *

Isabelle always gave him blue balls. Her warm weight in his arms, settled across his lap at the table sent all thought to his dick. The feel of his child, his, in her rounding belly had him strutting inside with pride. His baby. His girl.

He could hardly keep his hands to himself. If he was a dog, he'd have pissed all over her, marking his territory.

He didn't want to embarrass her in front of his familia though. Despite wanting to stamp 'Mine' all over her. He knew she'd been putting up with crap from her own father. She needed a place to go to get away from her family. For a minister, Lee thought he should find a little Christian charity, especially for his own daughter. It's not like Isabelle had ever done anything wrong before. Calling her a goody two shoes, Lee snorted, not far off the mark.

Lee wondered if he could feel the baby kick. He didn't remember if Isabelle had even mentioned feeling it. Isabelle had to be close to six months if he counted correctly. He had no clue as to when shit like that happened. He'd never thought to ask. It didn't seem real until he'd touched her.

Leaning back against the wall, Lee stared at the door

Isabelle had shut behind her. He wanted to take her to bed with him. Wrap her up in his arms and fall asleep with her warm body against him. But he'd already taken her to bed. The soft curve of her belly proved that.

He rubbed himself, thinking of the weight of Izzy's breasts in his hands. He groaned and adjusted his jeans, trying to ease his hard on.

"Abuelita won't let you sleep with our hermanas so quit jacking off in the hall."

"Fuck you! Izzy's not my sister."

Jandro snickered.

Big brothers were a pain in the ass. Lee tightened his fists. He wanted to wipe that smirk from Jandro's face. If he did, he'd show his familia he hadn't learned a damn thing since he'd been gone. For Izzy's sake he would behave, no matter what kind of shit Jandro dished out.

"I should hope not or that would be gross. But she might as well be mi hermana now."

"Remember that. Izzy's mine."

Jandro laughed and shoved him toward the bedroom. "No need to bear your teeth at me. She's always been a little sister to me. Obviously not to you."

Lee's shoulders relaxed. He let Jandro push him to the bedroom. His eyes drooped and he felt punch drunk. His body shutting down. God, it had been a long day. His hands were clumsy as he wrestled his clothes off. Lee finally managed to strip down to his skivvies. He fell into bed. He heard Jandro drop onto his mattress with a sigh.

The familiar softness of his bed felt damn good.

"Night, Jandro."

"Night, asshole."

Lee grinned. Now he knew he'd come home.

CHAPTER NINE

Graduation day, sunny, warm, and it came too soon after a late night. Isabelle burrowed deeper into her pillow, pulling up the covers to block the sun spilling in the window.

"Time to get up sleepy head." Jacinta chirped.

"Don't want to."

"We've got rehearsal."

Isabelle pulled her pillow over her head. "How hard is it to walk up when they call your name?"

The blankets were stripped off of her. Jacinta tugged at the pillow. "C'mon. You only have a half hour to get ready before we have to leave. I let you sleep as long as I could. I even made sure the shower was empty."

"Nooooo."

"Up." Another tug on the pillow.

"Nooooo."

"I'll take care of this." Strong arms slid beneath her and lifted her off of the bed. Isabelle screeched and dropped the pillow.

"What do you think you're doing?"

"What? No good morning?" Lee looked obnoxiously alert. He went to bed after she did.

She heard him and Jandro talking in the hall. The soothing bass of their voices had lulled her to sleep. Isabelle curled toward him. She could still sleep here. Lee laughed, the rumble in his chest making her glare up at him.

Lee let go of her legs.

Isabelle threw her arms around his neck, her body sliding down his. She dropped her head on his chest.

"I don't want to go."

"You only graduate once. At least from High School."

"Fine."

"Get in the shower or you won't have time." Jacinta tossed a towel over her head. She opened her dresser, tossing out underwear on to the bed. "Lee, get out of here. I need to get dressed."

Lee stepped back, pulling Isabelle's arms from around his neck. "I better get out of here."

Isabelle grunted and sat on the edge of the bed.

"Izzy, go!"

"Okay, already." Isabelle stood up, stretching. Now that she was awake, the urgency on her bladder wouldn't let her laze around. "I have to pee anyway."

Jacinta snorted behind her. "Not a surprise!"

Isabelle ran to the door and flung it open. She wouldn't be able to wait much longer. Her bladder ready to pop. She ducked under Lee's arm and shut the door in his face. Pulling down her panties she plopped on the toilet. She sighed in relief. She'd made it. Isabelle shivered; her bladder eased.

"Are you going to be long?"

Really? Really? His fault she was in this condition, mostly.

"What did you say?" She didn't care how snarky she sounded.

She heard arguing on the other side of the door.

"Never mind."

Isabelle snickered. Someone out there seemed smart enough to set Lee straight. Probably Jacinta. Rising and flushing she stripped and turned on the shower. She might as well go to rehearsal. She was up now. Not like she had a choice, either.

Isabelle hopped in the shower. The temperature warm enough already that a cool shower was a relief. Her skin cooled, the water wiping away the grunginess of the night sweat. The rough scrub of the puff and the tingle from her lime shower gel refreshing.

Graduation and the polyester gowns were going to be awful. Sitting out in the football field with the sun glaring down, for the birds. But Lee was right. She would only graduate High School once. With the baby derailing any college plans, it might be her only graduation. Years down the line she wouldn't want anyone to say that she hadn't graduated because she didn't walk. She'd have the pictures to prove it.

Most of her teachers didn't even know about her pregnancy. She'd seen a couple eying her waistline.

She'd only started to show recently. No one had had the nerve to ask her yet. She wondered if today would end that. Isabelle ran her hands over her belly. It felt like she'd popped overnight.

The door banged.

"Get a move on. We're leaving soon." Jacinta was a pest, her voice easily heard through the door even with the shower running.

"Okay. I just have to dry off."

Isabelle turned off the shower, rivulets of water running from her hair down her back. Grabbing a towel she leaned over and wrapped her hair. Wrapping another around her body, she opened the door and darted across the hall into Jacinta's room.

"I'm almost done."

"You're not even dressed." Jacinta shook her head. "Get a move on."

"Just give me a minute. I have to put on a sundress. It's too hot for anything else."

"Fine. I'll grab breakfast burritos for us and meet you at the car."

"Okay." Jacinta sounded like she had one in her mouth already. She probably did. Isabelle didn't know where she managed to put it all.

Isabelle tossed the towels on the bed and grabbed her bra and panties from her duffle bag. She slipped them on. Pulling her dress from the hanger on the back of the door, Isabelle slipped it over her head.

She quickly brushed her hair, slipping a ponytail holder

in her hair and pulling it up in a high pony. She didn't think she'd be able to stand sweaty hair sticking to her neck today. Dropping the brush on the dresser, Isabelle grabbed her purse and ran out the door and down the hall.

Her stomach was churning. Biting her lip, Isabelle tried to keep from bouncing. Lee, really here. It wasn't a dream. And graduation day, finally. She had no idea what the rest of her life would hold.

Flinging open the front door, Isabelle stepped outside. She couldn't stop the grin from spreading on her face. Jandro, Lee, and Jacinta were sitting in the car, doors open, radio running, and eating Mama Rosa's breakfast burritos.

"Here baby, I saved one for you." Jacinta fluttered her lashes, making kissy noises. She held out a burrito to Isabelle.

Snickering, Isabelle grabbed it and slid into the back seat, pushing Jacinta in.

"Thanks." Isabelle dug in, moaning as the spicy egg and chorizo mix hit her tongue. "So good."

Lee closed her door with a wink and slid into shotgun position next to Jandro. The car started up.

Leaning over the floor board to keep from dripping on herself, Isabelle scarfed hers down.

"Seat belts, ladies."

Jacinta snorted at Jandro's comment but Isabelle heard the click of her belt. Licking the flavor from her fingers, and wiping them dry on a napkin Lee handed her, Isabelle then locked hers in.

"I could eat a hundred more of those." Isabelle sat back, belly full and content. The sun shining, her morning sickness gone, and today, the last day she'd have to go to high school. Life was good today.

Lee leaned over the seat, his eyes twinkling. "I have another. Do you want it?"

Isabelle thought about it, rubbing her belly and trying to decide. "Nah, I'm good. Thanks."

"No problem."

She could feel the taunt skin change under her hands.

"Oh!"

"What's the matter? Are you okay? The baby?" Lee leaned over the seat to ask.

Isabelle looked into Lee's worried face.

"No. I think..." Isabelle could feel the smile spread across her face. "Lee, I think I felt the baby kick."

"Oh my God!" Jacinta's hands slid across her. "I want to feel."

Lee was reaching back and stopped. "Jaci don't you have any boundaries?"

Jandro made a raspberry. "Seriously, Lee? Have you been gone so long? You know she doesn't."

Isabelle giggled. Looking around, joy filled her soul. Her best friend felt her up, at least her belly! The man she'd been in love with most of her life looked like he wanted nothing more than to pull her into his arms, and Jandro, well, once again, laughing. His curly dark hair buzzed to nothing, he looked happier than he had been in a long time.

She realized that Lee wore the same look. Happiness and health showed in their faces. Even though they had left home, they hadn't left the ones they loved. If they did, neither would have bothered to come home for Jacinta's and her graduation. A sense of peace, something she'd not felt for the last few months settled over her.

Surrounded by people who cared, Isabelle knew everything would be all right.

* * * *

Lee wanted nothing more than to feel his baby moving inside Isabelle. To think he'd made it home to experience that. Well, if his hermana would let her go. He couldn't crawl over the seat while the car moved. He was too big to do that easily in his hermano's car. Even if he managed it, he didn't want to hurt Isabelle. Three would not fit in the back seat comfortably.

He stamped down the ache of jealousy that Jacinta felt his baby move before he did. Looking at Isabelle's glowing face and the teasing the two were doing eased the ache in his heart. His time would come.

She'd told him first. She hadn't been speaking to anyone else. His sister just happened to be there. No one could control Jacinta's actions. Plus, the two of them were best friends. Lee knew that. He just hadn't expected to feel left out.

He slid back in his seat as Jandro whipped around a corner. "Dude, watch it. Pregnant lady in the back."

"Pfft. She's sitting properly and buckled in. You're the only one sitting screwy."

"Izzy doesn't need to be jerked around."

"My milkshake brings all the boys to the yard..." Jacinta started singing, off key as usual.

"Shut up Jaci." Isabelle was giggling, watching his hermana wiggling in the seat, her hands waving in the air.

"C'mon bro, turn another corner, make me shake again." Jacinta fluttered her lashes at Jandro.

Jandro rolled his eyes. "Lee, you win, I'll slow down. I don't need Jacinta shaking or breaking in my car. Especially when she tries to sing."

"Hey!"

Lee laughed. He'd forgotten how much he enjoyed his familia. Thinking about it, Lee sobered. He had forgotten, and not just for the months he'd been gone. His last couple of years in high school and after were a haze of alcohol ridden memories. None of them good. Fights and tears at home, drinking and puking and waking up in the backs of cars, alleys, and parks were the hallmark of his last few years. His gut twisted.

Glancing back over the seat, his eyes traced the delicate line of Isabelle's face. How could he even think he would be good enough for her? He swallowed, his gaze travelling down her breasts and landing on the barely showing belly. His baby. The corners of his lips tipped up. His gaze locked on Isabelle's. His brain turned to mush. He knew he wasn't good enough, but he'd do his damnedest to change.

The car stopped with a jerk.

"Move it, unless you're staying in the car." God, Jandro would never stop being bossy. Lee thought the Marines were making it worse.

"I'm moving." Lee unhooked his seat belt. The girls were already scrambling out of the car, chatting away. Standing up and shutting the door, he heard the locks engage. "Don't you want to roll up the windows, bro?"

"Nah, too hot. It'll be fine."

"As long as it's here when we get back."

Lee walked toward the girls, intending to grab Isabelle in a hug before they headed in. She disappeared, swept up and away in a group of chattering graduates.

A hand landed on his shoulder, pulling him to a stop. "Dude, let her be. It's her last day to spend with her classmates. You have all the time in the world to make her future yours."

Lee stopped. His shoulders drooped. "Crap, you're right." He leaned back against Jandro's car.

"So you do want a future with her?"

"I've always wanted a future with her. I just thought she was out of my reach. We watched her growing up. She's Jaci's best friend." Lee shook his head. "Damn. She's Jaci's best friend."

"You said that already."

"I'll never have peace with Jacinta hanging around."

Jandro laughed, leaning back against the car. "Shit, no you won't. You won't ever be able to get rid of her.

Those two are thick as thieves. Just learn to live with it."

Jandro leaned in his window, opening the cooler on the seat. He reached in and pulled out a couple of bottles. "Agua?"

"Si."

Lee caught the bottle Jandro tossed.

"So, what are you going to do?"

"I'm going to ask her to marry me. She'll have to stay here until I'm done with training. Once I get orders, we'll see what happens."

"And you really want to get married?"

"Fuck, of course I want to. Never figured I'd have the chance." Lee pulled himself up to sit on the hood of the car. He absentmindedly played with the bottle in his hand.

"Why is that?"

"Think about it. Izzy's sweet and good. She always does the right thing. I'm a fuck up. I'm trying to change, but I haven't proved it to anyone yet."

Jandro laughed. "Are we thinking of the same girl? She may be sweet, but she's as much of a hell raiser as our hermana."

"Don't talk about her like that."

Jandro shook his head. "You've got it bad. Fine. Maybe that's what you have to do, just keep trying."

"Ya think? Will it be enough?" Lee pressed the cold bottle against his head. The condensation felt good, cooling down his heated blood. He cracked the lid off and drank. The cool liquid refreshing. The cold went down his throat, settling in his abdomen. It beat back the heat, even if only for a moment.

"Only Isabelle can decide that."

Lee thought about that. Months before, he'd crack a smart ass remark about not caring. Sobering up had wiped the fog away. He cared. He needed Isabelle to choose him. Despite his flaws, his temper, and the shit he had done. He thought he had a pretty good chance. They'd become close the more they'd talked.

"Yeah."

"Buck up, bro. Spend the rest of the weekend doing the woo thang. Maybe a little bow chica wow wow."

Lee snorted. "Ass." He tossed his empty water bottle at Jandro's big head.

Jandro knocked the bottle away before it hit him. "I'm wounded! I'm giving you great advice and that's the thanks I get."

Lee grinned. It felt good to be joking around with his hermano again.

Jandro leaned in and grabbed more agua, tossing him another bottle.

"So, you seem like you're doing good."

"Yeah." Lee squinted into the sun, not looking at his hermano. "I've stayed sober since I joined. Had a couple of beers one night, but that's about it."

"Good. How are you liking the Navy?"

"It's good. I like school. It's interesting."

"Do you know where you'll be stationed?"

"Nah, how about you?"

"About that."

Lee looked over. Jandro was fiddling with his bottle, picking at the label. His silence wasn't good. Lee's stomach flipped. He didn't have a good feeling about this.

"Spit it out."

"I've been stationed at Pendleton."

"That's not so bad."

"Yeah." Jandro was silent. "My unit already has orders to the Middle East."

"Fuck." Lee felt the bottle squash between his fingers.

"Yeah. But I figured I'd be going there."

"When do you leave?" Dumbass Marine. "Don't get yourself killed over there."

"Hey, I'm not that stupid."

"Doesn't take stupid. Look at Nico. He's not stupid."

"He's also not dead."

"Pure luck, dude. You know it, I know it, and Nico knows it."

Jandro turned and gave Lee a dirty look. "I know. But it's something I have to do. Fuck, I should have been with him."

"Ever think that maybe you weren't supposed to be? Maybe, just maybe, you weren't there for a reason?"

"Like what?" Jandro scoffed. "I'm finally living the life I

want. I'm away from here. The drugs, the hoes, the shootings."

Lee laughed. "Dude, really? The shootings? What the fuck do you do in the infantry? Knit?"

Jandro snorted then laughed. "Okay, okay. Fine. Gang shootings."

"Still not seeing a difference. 'Specially heading out to the armpit of the world."

"Hey, at least living here, I've had practice staying alive."

Lee shook his head. "Just come back in one piece, okay? My baby will need a tio and you're the only one he'll have."

"Yeah, yeah."

Lee sighed. What a fucked up world. No matter where you went, someone was fighting. Home in the streets, across the world in different streets, someone shooting at someone.

"I'm probably going to end up on a ship." Lee twirled the bottle, watching the water spin.

"Wonder if you get seasick?"

"Not something I worried about. Thanks a lot."

"No problem. Just wanted you aware of all possibilities."

Lee saw his grin. His brother really was an ass.

"What should I do about Isabelle?"

"What the hell? What do you want to do?"

"I want everyone to know she's mine."

"Put a ring on it."

"Duh, like I never thought of that. I just don't know where I'll be going. Maybe she won't want to come with."

"You won't know until you ask her."

"I know. I just don't want her to think it's because of the baby."

"It's not?"

"Fuck no."

Lee watched the last of the stragglers sneak in through the doors. He winced. The squeal of the microphone resonating too close to the speakers could be heard clear out to the car.

Jandro swore. "Damn, you'd think they'd learn how to use those things."

Lee nodded his head in agreement, the shriek making him grit his teeth. He didn't know how he was going to ask Isabelle. They'd been Skyping, and talking every day but that might not be enough. Hopefully this weekend would make her realize that the best thing for her and the baby would be him.

CHAPTER TEN

Her hands were sweating. The trickle down her neck itched. The polyester gown hotter than she'd expected. The walk down the aisle and up the stairs to receive her diploma seemed anti-climactic. All that rehearsal and it was over so fast. She stopped for pictures with the photographer at the bottom of the platform. Every student took a graduation photo. Hoping the parents ordered them.

Isabelle smiled. Lee hadn't worn his uniform after all. He had come outside in it, mopped his brow and swore before going back in and changing into shorts. Isabelle giggled. He'd looked wonderfully yummy in it. She turned and headed toward her chair. She stopped at his wave.

Lee stood on the floor, snapping pictures. The proud gleam in his eye had her pulling her shoulders back and standing straight. Isabelle would do her best to give him a picture to remember. Behind Lee, her dad stepped down the bleachers.

"Isabelle, let me get a picture."

Isabelle didn't know if he didn't recognize Lee or just ignored him. Her dad moved around him and stepped in front, waving at her to get her attention. He had it. She couldn't believe he did that, so rude. Even if her dad didn't recognize him, he shouldn't treat anyone that way.

"Dad, you stepped right in front of him."

"He already had a picture."

Isabelle started to protest. Lee, behind her father, shook his head. She subsided. Right. She didn't want to start a fight today. She wanted only happy memories for her graduation.

"Smile into the camera." Her dad clicked away, her in her gown with her diploma.

Isabelle couldn't help but smile. She had only hope going into the future. She blinked. The flash on her dad's camera too bright. He took a bunch of shots if the blindness in her eyes was any indication.

"Dad, enough. I've got to get out of the way." Isabelle blinked. The line from the stage moved toward her. "I have to get to my seat."

"One more shot."

She skirted past him, ignoring his request. Her dad, the shutter bug. Her whole life could be seen documented in photos. Every church event clearly documented in photos. You just had to say no and walk away.

Isabelle passed Lee. He gave her a pat on the ass with a crooked grin. She turned her head to stick out her tongue and saw her father's glare focused on Lee. Turning away from them, Isabelle made her way back to her seat. Time enough later to deal with both of them.

She sat, squirming uncomfortably in the hard metal folding chair. Walking had created a breeze of sorts. Now sitting, the air was once again stifling. A trickle of sweat inching down her spine.

"Have you decided on where you're going to college yet?" Marina had been sitting next to Isabelle since middle school. Rivera and Rivers, the bonding of alphabetical last names.

"Haven't decided." Isabelle wasn't about to announce the upcoming change in her status. She'd made the last half of the year without questions. A few suspicious looks and a couple of snide comments, but no one bothered to ask. Suited her to a T. Her unexpected pregnancy all her business. Hers and Lee's.

Marina glanced at her stomach and gave her an inquisitive look. Isabelle moved her hand away from her belly. Unconsciously she'd been soothing the baby. Since she'd first felt movement it all seemed so much more real.

"Pay attention!" Jacinta hissed from behind them. She had just returned to her seat. Jacinta sat behind her in every class they shared. Finally in high school they could choose their own seats. They sat next to each other instead. The rest was history.

Isabelle smirked, and faced the stage. She got ready, pulling out one of the bottles that had been surreptitiously passed to each graduating student during rehearsal. The last of the class plodded across the stage. Joe Ziwicki. A roar erupted and thousands of bubbles rose to encompass the graduating class.

A cheer and feet stamping on the bleachers only encouraged them. They had their diplomas. There was nothing the school could do to stop them. Isabelle could hear Jacinta laugh. Marina giggled beside her.

"Attention please. Audience, family, and friends, I present to you the graduating Class of 2016." The principal gestured his arm encompassing the gymnasium. "We ask that family please stay seated until the students have all left. You'll be able to meet them in the cafeteria. Refreshments are there for those that would like them. Graduation photo ordering information will be posted there also."

He took a deep breath.

Isabelle could see it from where she sat. She wished he'd get on with it. She had to pee again.

"Class of 2016 please rise." The students stood up. The sound of chairs scraping on the wood floor had him wincing. "Please exit the room."

Relief! Just the movements of the people around her cooled her a bit. Swaying, Isabelle grabbed the back of a chair. Too hot in the room to even breathe. The unplanned change of venue wasn't any better in her opinion. Due to the heat, graduation was moved indoors. The school didn't want any students or their families to get heat stroke.

A legitimate concern given the polyester nightmares they wore over their clothes were black with gold trim. Hot and stifling in the overflowing room. Steadying herself, Isabelle shuffled forward. The exit from the gym happening fast. Thank goodness. She needed to breathe.

Turning into the aisle, Isabelle tipped, jostled by people who were descending the bleachers, interrupting the exit of the students. Dizzy, Isabelle reached out to steady herself.

"I've got you." One of Lee's strong arms slid around her waist, anchoring her against him. "Let's go." He led her forward, keeping pace with the exodus out of the room.

"Thank you."

"What happened? You looked unsteady."

"The heat and the people."

"It's almost over."

Isabelle nodded. Grateful for Lee's quick actions. She snuggled next to him, ignoring the glare from the teachers. She held on or they'd end up calling an ambulance when she fainted.

"Thirsty?"

Her mouth did taste like sandpaper. She nodded.

Lee handed her a bottle of water. She drank, savoring the cool water with each swallow.

"Move. You're holding up the line." Marina poked her.

"Sorry." Isabelle started moving again. She handed Lee back the nearly empty bottle. "Thank you."

"You're welcome. I know how hot it gets sitting down there."

They finally escaped out the doorway. Isabelle pulled him away to the left. The orderly line had dissolved. Students, no, graduates, bee lined to the cafeteria for cookies and drinks. Isabelle needed the restroom more than a cookie, though she wouldn't turn one down.

"I have to pee." Pulling away from Lee, Isabelle pushed open the door. She ignored the girls primping and dove into an open stall with a sigh. She relaxed in relief, the pressure on her bladder dissipating.

"So, Isabelle, what's going on with you and the hottie?"

Hottie? She giggled. They must not have recognized Lee.

"Yeah, did you see the butt on him? Yum. Spill it girl."

"Don't you recognize him?" Isabelle flushed, drowning out their answers.

She opened the door to see them all staring at her. "What?"

"No. We don't recognize him. Who is it?"

"Seriously. He hasn't changed that much."

One of the girls shook her head. "He seems familiar, but I can't place him."

"I'd like to place him in my bed."

A round of giggles erupted. Washing her hands Isabelle just shook her head. She headed toward the door. She held her amusement inside. She gave them to the count of three.

One.

Two.

Lisa slid in front of her, blocking the door.

"Who is it?"

Isabelle pushed her away from the door. "Lee Santiago."

Gasps and sputters erupted.

"No way!"

They circled back together, chattering, obviously excited.

They glanced at her, shaking their heads.

"I don't believe it."

"What happened to him?"

"He doesn't look wasted anymore."

"He doesn't look fat anymore, either."

Isabelle laughed and decided to give them another tidbit to gossip over. "Lee's sober now. He joined the Navy." She pulled open the door and left. The chatter and squeals her pronouncement made cracked her up. She couldn't help the grin she knew spread across her face.

"What's up?" Lee stepped forward and pulled her into his arms.

"Nothing."

He snorted. "Tell another one."

"The girls just wanted to know who you were." Isabelle shivered.

Lee rolled his eyes, shrugging off the comment. Lee's hands rubbing up and down her back, had her snuggling against him. "Let's head to the cafeteria. What plans did you have today?"

Isabelle pouted when he released her from his embrace.

His chuckle definitely let her know he'd noticed.

"I have to go to the church. We're having a pot luck for all graduating students at noon."

"Can I come?" Lee's hand slid around hers. His rough warm fingers intertwining with hers and sending her pulse racing.

"I don't know if that's a good idea." She knew it wasn't, but he made it hard to resist him. The six months he'd been away had changed him for the better. She may have crushed on him forever, but now she couldn't help but drool too. It wasn't just his body, but his attitude had improved. That he so openly wanted her? That would take getting used to.

"Is Jacinta going?"

"Yes."

"I'll be her driver then."

"You know he doesn't like you."

"He doesn't really know me."

Isabelle sighed. Did he really have to have it spelled out? "He knows of you. Your reputation isn't the best." She tugged on his hand, trying to get him to stop moving.

"Maybe he won't recognize me."

"Right. Like he didn't know you when he cut you off."

Lee was getting that stubborn look on his face. "Let me deal with it. I'm a big boy. I can face the consequences of my actions."

Ignoring the sense of unease those words gave her, Isabelle stepped into the cafeteria. It teamed with noise. Isabelle couldn't see her dad or Jacinta. Shrugging, knowing they would eventually find her, she headed for the refreshments. Pulling Lee along behind her, she ignored the electricity that travelled between them. The growls from her abdomen wouldn't be ignored.

"Slow down, I'm trying to find mi hermana."

"Jaci will find us. Knowing her, she's by the food already."

"Si, true."

He stopped resisting the tug of her hand and came alongside her, easily clearing a path. Watching him, Isabelle could see two people. The boy she'd always wanted and the man he'd become.

* * * *

Soft and warm. Lee tightened his hand around Isabelle's. He never wanted to let go. He pulled her close and headed toward the smell of fresh cookies. He didn't want to let her out of his sight. He had less than two days to convince her that he was the right man for her. Lee had no fucking idea where to start.

He glanced down at Isabelle's delicate form. The graduation gown hid his growing baby. He wanted to shout it to the world, but he couldn't. Isabelle hadn't told anyone she was pregnant. His family and hers knew. No one else.

Lee would be the first to admit he was worried. Why would she hide the pregnancy from everyone? Could she really be thinking of giving up his baby and didn't want to tell anyone? Tell him? Lee shook his head. No. Isabelle couldn't have hid that from him. She was too excited about the baby. No one researches names for a baby they are going to give away. No matter what, Lee wanted Isabelle and his baby. The baby was icing on the cake.

Flashes of soft skin and desperate moans rolled through his mind. The scent of honeysuckle teased his memory. Somehow in his memories it was always her. Even fucked up, shit faced drunk, it was her face he saw. This time it had been true. It was his Isabelle. She had wanted him as much as he'd wanted her.

"There's Jaci." Isabelle pointed.

Lee found his hermana holding court by the food. Face full of cookies, a Dixie cup of something orange in her hand, Jacinta was chattering away. Isabelle's hand tugged and she was free. She grabbed a handful of cookies and a bottle of water.

"Have you seen my dad?"

Jacinta shook her head. "No. I see you found Lee."

"I never lost him."

Her impish reply had him wanting to pull her to him. He had to play it cool. If he wanted to spend the day with her, he couldn't give her father any reason to get rid of him. Lee knew he was around here somewhere.

"I saw you holding her hand. Don't think that just because some son of a bitch knocked her up, she's free game."

Lee stiffened. The whispered words in his ear were venomous. Isabelle's father had recognized him all right. Her dad, the biggest reason he'd never asked Isabelle out. One whiff of misconduct and her father would have had him in jail on statutory rape. Lee knew that he wouldn't have been able to keep his hands off of her. It had been better to stay away.

Too late now, her padre would have to learn to deal with

it. A servant of the Lord, wasn't it his duty to forgive?

His jaw tightened. Lee wouldn't say what he really wanted to. He had to tone it down. Lee was in this for keeps.

"I never thought of Isabelle as fair game."

"She's not for a screw up like you either."

"You don't know me." His fists clenched. He'd like nothing better than to plant a facer on her hypocritical padre.

"I don't like what I do know." Lee could feel his eyes on him. His face hardened. "It was you, wasn't it?"

He had never heard the words that spilled from her padre's lips spoken so fluently or so venomously. Lee wouldn't respond in kind. He knew why Isabelle hadn't told her padre. His reaction was everything she feared it would be. This way, directed at him and not her, her graduation wouldn't be ruined.

"Yes." Lee nodded grudgingly.

"What are your intentions? I wanted her to give the baby away. She's determined to keep it."

Lee nodded. "We both want the baby." He turned to her father. "I have a ring with me. If she'll accept it."

Her father grunted. "Good."

Isabelle turned, spying her father.

"Dad, where were you?"

Lee casually stepped away, removing himself from her dad's immediate vicinity, stopping the flow of vitriol spilling from him.

"I was talking to some of my parishioners."

"Okay. Hey, Lee was going to drive me and Jacinta to the church. You don't mind do you? He's only in town for the weekend."

Lee saw her father frown. "Why is that?"

"He has to get back to base by Monday, right, Lee? I'm pretty sure that's what Jaci told me."

Lee nodded. "She's right. I fly out tomorrow night."

"What base is that?"

"Pensacola, Florida."

"What are you doing there?"

"Dad, why the third degree? Lee joined the Navy. He's going to school there."

"Hmpf." He narrowed his eyes at Lee, looking him up and down.

Lee wondered exactly what he saw. He knew it wasn't the same man that left. He'd worked hard to change.

"That's fine. He's welcome to come as long as he behaves."

Lee tried not to roll his eyes. About as welcoming as he'd ever get from Pastor Rivers. It was infinitely more welcoming than he'd ever been before. Maybe knowing he was stepping up to the plate and not leaving Isabelle to face the consequences alone probably helped.

"What time should I have the girls there?"

"By one o'clock." He nodded his head stiffly and looked down at Isabelle. Lee swore his face softened. "I ordered your graduation picture. I thought you might want that."

Her smile sent a pang to his heart. He wanted her smiles to be all for him.

"Thank you, Dad." She hugged him. "We won't be late."

He nodded and walked away.

Isabelle seemed to love her dad. Lee didn't know how. His demeanor was off putting and he never seemed to have a kind word for anyone. Not that Lee had ever seen at any rate. Of course, that could just be because her father didn't like him.

Glancing down at Isabelle's baby bump, a fierce protectiveness ripped through him. Then again, maybe her dad sensed he'd always been interested in Isabelle. In his place, he'd warn off all men from his daughter. God, he hoped they were having a boy!

Lee watched Isabelle hug and chat with her friends. He wielded the camera, getting photos of her with all of her friends. He could fill a yearbook with all the shots he took.

Lee yawned and checked his watch. Luckily Isabelle and Jacinta had stayed near each other. "Time to go. I promised your dad you wouldn't be late."

"One more picture. Please?"

He snorted. Both Jacinta and Isabelle were fluttering their lashes at him. Loco, both of them. "Fine. Hurry it up." He hid his amusement but they were too full of happiness to care. Their eyes shown and their smiles hadn't dimmed one bit since graduation.

They posed. Another shot of the two of them and about five friends who suddenly photo bombed the shot. Then the whole family with the two girls in the middle. Then one of his mom, Jacinta, him and Jandro. Isabelle took that one.

"Done, now move it flakitas!" Tio Mateo shooed them away, laughing at the girls.

They giggled and turned, heading out to the parking lot with their arms entwined. Lee shook his head. Nope, he'd never have his hermana not interfering in his life. Not as long as Isabelle agreed to be a part of it.

Following behind them, watching them, he knew he wouldn't have it any other way. Lee hit the clicker, unlocking the car.

"Shotgun!"

The girls started racing toward the vehicle, pushing and shoving at each other while their laughter trailed behind them.

Lee shook his head, exasperated. He'd let them fight it out. He knew they wouldn't hurt each other. Every time they were driven around, this same scene played out. They seemed to have a system that worked for them. He'd learned years ago to stay out of it.

Sliding in the driver's seat, Lee started the car. Doors opened and the two slid in.

Isabelle turned to Jacinta. "Loser."

"I let you win, prego."

Good lord, they were both sore winners and losers. He'd forgotten that. If Jacinta had gotten shotgun it would have been the same scenario.

Ignoring their banter, Lee pulled out. The parking lot was starting to empty out. He'd parked close to an exit to prevent having to wait. He looked over. Isabelle was still hanging over the back seat yapping with Jacinta. Jandro had begged off of going to the party at the church, handing Lee his keys. He was going to catch up with Ricardo while the house was quiet.

"Hey, sit straight and put your seatbelt on."

She pulled a face, but did as he said. Amazing.

He checked the rearview mirror. "You have yours on back there too?"

"Yes, Dad." Jacinta stuck her tongue out at him and grinned. She knew he wouldn't do anything to her.

Lee gripped the wheel tighter. A good swat on the behind is what she needed. As an adult she needed to feel the consequences of her actions. He'd take satisfaction that at some point Jacinta would meet a man that wouldn't take her shit. He grinned thinking about it. He'd welcome him to the family whole heartedly.

"What's so funny?" Isabelle poked him in the side.

Lee glanced at his sister in the rear view mirror, oblivious to his thoughts.

"Nothing, nothing at all. Just enjoying the company."

Isabelle smiled at him, thankfully taking his words as truth. It wasn't too far from it. Content sitting next to her, even with his hermana tagging along. It had been that way for years, since they had first met. Now he no longer had to hide it.

Pulling up at the church, Lee walked around and opened Isabelle's door.

"Thank you."

"What about me?" Jacinta stuck her head out the window.

"Roll up the window and I'll let you out too." Lee smirked at her. What a brat. Jacinta's smile told him she knew it, and Isabelle's laughter confirmed it. Brats behaving badly.

Graduating didn't make them grownups overnight.

"C'mon Lee."

Both girls were running toward the church, graduation gowns flying and caps grasped in their hands.

"Yeah, I'm famished." Isabelle laughed, reaching the door first.

"I know, right?" Jacinta followed before the door managed to shut.

Lee followed at a slower pace. No need to run when he knew his welcome came grudgingly. The girls disappeared inside. It became quiet. As quiet as it could get anywhere around here. Lee stopped and listened. The sounds were different here than in Florida. Parts of the base he'd wandered over, the only noise came from the sound of the ocean and a quiet hum of life from the buildings. Nowhere near as noisy as here.

The LA basin gave off a weird vibe of constant energy and sound. He'd never noticed it until he came back. It lit a restlessness in him. He wondered if that was why his life had always seemed out of his control. He hoped his assigned duty station kept him far from here. Keeping him away from the temptation of not being clean and sober.

Opening the doors sent a wave of sound to him.

Following the noise, Lee noticed all of Isabelle's and Jacinta's girlfriends standing in a group, laughing and chattering.

"Thank you for getting them here on time."

Lee started. He hadn't noticed Pastor Rivers coming up behind him. He turned to face him. He got the creeps when he stood behind him. "You're welcome."

His tone, while not friendly, held none of the viciousness that Lee heard in the cafeteria. He wondered if he was bi-polar. It could explain a lot.

"Are you really turning yourself around?"

Lee frowned at him. "Yes. The Navy has helped me. I'm on a clear course and Isabelle and the baby will hopefully be by my side."

"And what? Go on welfare? Live hand to mouth? What kind of a life would that be for her?"

"I make enough money to support us. It's a good life. Would you rather she gives up her baby and is unhappy the rest of her life?"

"Did I say that?" He narrowed his eyes at Lee.

"No, but that's how it sounded." Lee stared at him. "I'm planning on taking care of Izzy and my baby."

"How would it look if I let my daughter have an illegitimate child? I'm a leader of the church." He was ignoring Lee.

It was pissing him off. "Don't you preach forgiveness? I'm here if Izzy will have me."

"You know nothing. Isabelle will do as I say. No one

even knows about her pregnancy. I've played along with her nonsense until school was out. Now that it is, she won't be in the public eye. She'll stay at home so no one even finds out. When it's born, I have a nice family all picked out. Isabelle will realize I know what's right."

"Do you really think that will happen?" Lee snorted. Pastor Rivers really didn't know his daughter. She'd listen up until she got stubborn. Locking her in the house all summer, or trying to, would be a rude awakening for him. Not to mention, Lee would never agree to giving up his baby.

Glaring at Lee, he turned away, smoothly greeting the elderly couple that had just entered.

Lee marveled at the quick change of expressions. Pastor Rivers hid his emotions at the drop of a hat, a consummate actor.

The scent of honeysuckle preceded her. A small arm wrapped around his waist. Her soft body pressed against his back. His body reacted, the stirring in his groin inappropriate in a church, surrounded by the congregation, regardless of why they were here.

"What am I going to do?" Her head pressed against his back.

"What do you mean?"

"I heard him. He still thinks he can take my baby away."

"Our baby."

"Our baby. What am I going to do?" Her head dropped against his back.

Lee could feel her tears in the dampness on his back. He

wanted to rip her father a new one. She didn't need his crap. Lee stood there, taking comfort in her arms wrapped around his waist, from her coming to him for comfort. He wanted nothing more than to pull her in his arms. But that would just make it worse.

"Izzy." Crap, what could he say? He kept his voice low. "Honey, I want to pull you in my arms, but your dad would go crazy. We'll talk tonight, okay? For now, ignore what he said. I won't let him take our baby away. Go grab mi hermana, head into el baño together like you always do and wash your face. Enjoy your graduation. We'll figure this out."

He felt her nod. Her arms slipped from his waist and he mourned the loss of her warmth against him. He turned and watched her head toward his hermana. He wanted to beat the crap out of her father.

Isabelle kept her head down and slipped her arm through Jacinta's pulling her toward the bathroom.

Good. She'd apparently listened. Lee hoped she believed him. His jaw firmed. He would do everything in his power to protect her and his baby.

CHAPTER ELEVEN

Other than hearing her father's belief that she'd willingly be house bound and give up her baby, the day had been fantastic. Isabelle was a bit apprehensive about the talk with Lee. He'd kept his distance at the church. Thank goodness! She didn't know what her father would do if he found out Lee had been the one who got her pregnant. He'd have a meltdown at the church in front of all of his parishioners. He'd never forgive her.

It's not like he wouldn't ever find out. Isabelle had all intentions of letting him know. Just not yet.

Isabelle sighed and rubbed her belly. She had eaten until her bursting point. After they left the church, Jacinta's family had lit the barbeque for a graduation party. They'd even invited her dad, but he turned them down. Thank goodness, she could finally relax without him around. The weight of his disapproval tired her out.

She held the plate with the rest of her carne asada on her lap. So good, she couldn't help but nibble on it. Any more and she swore she'd explode.

"You're going to pop." Lee teased her, flicking her nose. He grabbed her plate and popped the last bite of her sandwich in his mouth.

"Hey, that was mine."

Lee chuckled. "You weren't going to finish that."

Isabelle rolled her eyes. So what if he was right? She wouldn't admit it now. "Yes, I was."

"Tell you what, if you want more I'll make you another bolillo, okay?"

"Sure." There, she didn't admit she wouldn't have finished it, but didn't have to demand one that she knew would destroy her if she ate so much as one more bite.

"Here, let me throw this out." Lee took her plate and threw it away.

Isabelle admired his legs leaving and returning. She couldn't really check out his butt. His shorts were obviously a pair of old ones. They were too big and he kept having to hitch them up. She wouldn't ever tell anyone she hoped he'd miss and they'd fall to the ground. She giggled. Wouldn't that be a show?

She hadn't realized Lee lost so much weight. She knew he looked and felt good but the reality hadn't meshed until she saw him in his old clothes. Clothes she wished were gone.

"Thank you."

"You're welcome." Lee crouched down next to her chair. "Izzy, how about that talk?"

Her teeth pressed sharply down into her lip. Isabelle took a deep breath and let it go. "Okay."

What did he want to say? This wasn't like skyping. Lee stood up. His warm hands reached for hers. He pulled her up, slipping his arms around her.

"You feel so good, Izzy."

Her heart fluttered. Could he really mean it? "Lee?"

His arms eased from around her. Stepping back, he slipped one around her waist, pulling her against his side. "Let's go in the back yard. There's no one else back there. We can talk."

"Okay." Isabelle ignored the butterflies in her stomach and slipped her arm around Lee's waist. She saw the flash of his white grin and he pulled her tighter against him.

They slipped into the shadows of the yard, ducking under the banana tree gone wild, and headed to the back. Lee was right. No one else was taking advantage of the backyard. The lounge chairs she and Jacinta liked to lay in, were still out. They would be all summer long. Most days were spent talking and sunbathing. That would change. She sighed.

Lee sat in one of the chairs, pulling her into the V of his legs and settling her back against his chest. It wasn't really cold out, but Isabelle snuggled into his warmth, contentment spreading through her.

"So…"

Isabelle tilted her head back to look at him. The cockiness that normally surrounded him was gone. She looked down. His arms were wrapped around her, his hands caressing her stomach. Isabelle slid her hands over his, slipping their fingers together.

"So…?"

"What are your plans Izzy? Do you really want to keep our baby?"

A pang shot through her heart? Did he not want the baby? Why would he even ask that?

"Of course I want the baby."

Lee swore. "I didn't ask because I didn't want him. I just want to make sure you and I are on the same page. "I asked because, well..."

Isabelle couldn't ever remember Lee being at a loss for words. They may not have been nice words, but he always had them.

"Well, no one even knows you're pregnant. You haven't told anyone but my familia and yours. No one but my family even knew I'm the father until today." Lee's voice rose at the end. He wasn't shouting but Isabelle could tell he was upset and trying not to show it.

"No! Of course not. I just didn't want everyone at school knowing. You know what high school is like. Everyone all up in your business. Telling you what they think you should or shouldn't do. I had to decide. I didn't want everyone's opinion. I just needed mine." Isabelle swallowed. "And yours."

"Thank you." His voice rough, emotion laden. Lee's arms tightened around her. His chin rested on her hair. "I thought that was it, then I found out your father didn't know I was your baby's dad."

Isabelle let out a breath she hadn't even realized she'd been holding. Her heart lightened. Lee really did want the baby.

"You really do want the baby?"

"Of course I do. It's part of you. I'd want you even if you weren't carrying my baby."

Her eyes widened. She never thought that he cared more for her than the baby. "Do you really mean that?" She whispered it so low, Isabelle wasn't sure Lee would even hear her.

"Yes." He kissed the top of her head.

"You're sure? It's not just because of the baby?"

"No, of course not."

Isabelle chewed her lip. Tendrils of hope wound around her heart. Isabelle repeated his words, happiness warming her insides, then frowned. "What did you mean, no one but your family knew you were the father until today? Who else did you tell?"

"Your father."

"Oh my God! Lee he hates you. I don't know why." Isabelle shook her head. "I can't believe he even let me come over with you. Especially now that he knows. "

"Maybe because I told him that I would take care of my responsibilities, Izzy. I joined the Navy, well, not just because mi familia made me, but because I wanted to become a man you'd be proud of. A man that had a future. So that maybe, some day, you'd want to spend your future with me."

Isabelle swallowed, stunned. Lee had always been her dream man. "Lee, I've always wanted you to be my future."

"I was a shit."

Isabelle giggled. "But I wanted you to be my shit."

Lee's laugh rang out. He slid down, flipping Isabelle over so she lay on top of him.

"I'd be happy to be yours, Izzy, just say the word."

"Word."

"Snot."

Then he kissed her.

* * * *

His Izzy, his. Lee's arms circled her, hands roaming down her back to her fine ass. The soft pillows of her breasts pressed against his chest. Her nipples tight buds against his pecs. Her sun dress thin to ward off the heat. He inched her dress up until he was able to grab underneath.

He thanked God his shorts were so loose. His dick was hard as a rock but he wasn't strangled. He perked right up, seeking the heat of Isabelle's pussy. His hands grasped her ass, arching up to rub against her. His shorts and the front of her dress separated them. Desire filled his belly, his cock aching to sink into her heat.

Lee ran a hand down, following the edge of her thong, sliding in the slickness of her desire.

"Fuck." Lee rubbed his hand over her lips, separating them to tease her, rimming her juicy opening. "You're so wet." He slid his middle finger in, all the way up to his hand.

"Oh." Isabelle wiggled and moaned. "Lee. Lee. That feels so good."

"Fuck yeah, it does."

Her pussy, warm and soft against his rough digit. Wet and sucking him. He wanted his dick in there, strangling him until he emptied himself inside her.

Lee groaned. Isabelle's hand had slid into his shorts. Fingers grasped him, tugging inexpertly on him. Didn't matter, he wanted more. So hard, the soft grip of her hands had him ready to shoot his load like a virgin.

"Izzy." Lee grabbed her hand. He squeezed and groaned. Would it be so bad to cum in his pants? Her soft hand jerking him off almost convinced him it would be worth. "No, wait."

He pulled her hand off of him.

"Lee?"

"Fuck. I want to be in you."

In a flurry of movement, Isabelle's panties were flying. They'd have to find them before his abuelita did. But for now, fuck it.

Lee tugged down his shorts to his thighs. Isabelle's feet pushed them down and Lee pulled his feet out of them. As usual, he'd gone commando. He never had been one for tighty whitey's and all of his boxers were too big now.

"Mmm." Isabelle slid up, her body still clothed.

Despite the desire to strip her bare, they were in his abuelita's back yard with a party going on in front. No one would see her naked but him.

"Izzy." Lee grasped her dress and pulled it up. Her naked stomach pressed against his. Lee's eyes widened. "Oh my God. I felt him move." Lee pulled her up until his lips caressed the swell of her belly. "Thank you, Izzy."

Isabelle wiggled in his hands. Scorching heat pressed against his chest. The scent of honeysuckle had him growing even harder.

Lee tightened his hands on her hips and brought her pussy to his mouth. The trail of her juices down his chest turning him on even more. He pressed her down, his tongue frantically licking her juices away and tunneling inside her.

"Lee."

Her cry and the contractions of her on his tongue had him diving deeper. His teeth scraped her clit. He was rewarded with a jump and a cry and his whole mouth worked to French kiss her pussy.

Isabelle cried out, her body bowing in his hands. Her tunnel convulsed around his tongue. His mouth flooded with her thick honey.

"Mmm. So good."

Isabelle gasped and Lee shifted, suckling her clit. More honey spilled across his chin.

"Lee, oh my God." She was shivering above him, panting and shaking with each suckle. "Stop, stop. I can't take anymore."

Lee licked her once more, lingering on her bundle of nerves, circling it with his tongue.

"Beautiful, Izzy. God, you're beautiful."

He lifted her, pulling her down until she lay sprawled across him. He tugged, pulling her dress up, making sure they were belly to belly. His cock pressed against

Isabelle. Her pussy lips sharing their slickness while the top of his cock flirted with her cheeks.

Isabelle wiggled, rubbing against him.

"Are you planning on doing anything with that?" Her flirty tone and wiggle emphasized exactly what she meant.

"Not too tired?"

"No."

Lee grabbed her hips, shifting her so she rubbed up and down on his stiff member. Lee could feel his pre-cum dripping down his cock.

Isabelle squeaked. She scrambled, moving so she was on her knees, pelvis tilted. She slid back, engulfing him in her hot, tight, silky snatch.

Fuck, she felt so good. He never wanted to be anywhere but deep inside her. She rocked on him, gasping when she bottomed out. He filled her up, snug inside her. She leaned down and kissed him. A soft sweet sensation that drove him out of his mind.

Lee moaned. Nothing tasted as good as Isabelle.

"Cowgirl up, sweetheart." Lee shifted her hips, showing her what to do.

Isabelle giggled and slowly started to move on him.

Her hesitancy turned him on. She was his, only his. Her movements, unsure and inexpert as she tried to ride him had his dick rigid. Lee sat up, his arms cradling her and laid her flat on her back. Her legs slid off the sides of the chair, spreading her.

The sight of her sparse black pubic hair, trimmed in a fucking heart no less, had him swearing.

"Dammit. You're so fucking beautiful." He ran a hand over her pussy lips swallowing his dick. "Soft and pink. Look at this." His finger dusted across her clit. "A tender morsel to be nibbled on."

She moaned and arched. Her juices glistened in the light from the street lamp. Her body followed his finger, her pussy tightening on him with each stroke.

"Lee." Isabelle slowly started moving on his dick, twisting to impale herself.

"Take what you want." Lee leaned over, and suckled on her breast. It called to him. Nibbling on it, he pulled back, grinning at the damp spot highlighting her beaded nipple. "Mine."

His hands tugged, pulling down the top of her dress, popping her breasts out. Lee feasted his eyes on them. Dark red nipples drawn up tight, made his mouth water. Plump breasts that would cradle his dick as he fucked them.

He slid his legs up, shifting Isabelle. He nuzzled her breasts, nibbling on her nipples. Each nip tightened her core around him.

"Please, Lee, fuck me."

Isabelle's breathless begging brought Lee to a frenzy. He sank into her. Holding his body up so he didn't squash her, he flexed deeper.

She shifted, her legs encircling his waist, pulling him to her. Soft as satin ropes, they encircled his body and his heart. Never, would he give this up.

"More."

Fuck, he couldn't resist. Lee rammed home, again and again. Sank into the heat of her, the heart of her. The chair rocked with their frantic movements. God he hoped it didn't collapse.

Her hands in his hair, grasping, tugging, releasing. Lee buried his face in her neck, biting and suckling the cords of her throat. Arching in and out of her slick, tight heat. He was going to blow. He wanted to fill her with his seed, watch it coat her pussy and drip down her ass. See the shimmer marking her as it dried. Show the whole world she was his.

Lee dropped to an elbow freeing one hand. It wandered down, smooth soft skin against his fingertips. He circled a nipple, watching it tighten at his touch. Down to slip through the silky fur protecting her treasure. Lee grinned, the one he was plundering.

He pistoned faster, his finger slipping down to press on her clit. Isabelle tightened on him, strangling his dick. So tight he could barely move out then in again.

"Fuck."

"Lee!" Her hands gripped his hair dragging his head down, smashing his lips against hers.

His balls tingled, pulling tight. He jerked, his dick swelling then exploding, coating the inside of Isabelle with each thrust.

"God, Izzy." Lee pumped his hips, not willing to leave the haven between her legs. He could feel her grasping him, with each spasm of her dying orgasm.

Isabelle's arms dropped to her sides, slipping off to hang

from the chair.

"Boneless, Lee."

He chuckled, nuzzling her neck. "Me too, Izzy." He dropped down, elbows propping him up. Her plump breasts pillowed his chest. Her tummy pressing against his. God, he could stay like this forever. Isabelle in his arms, his baby percolating in her belly, his dick still snug inside her warmth.

"I don't want you to go."

Lee sighed.

"I don't have a choice." He pushed himself up, gazing into her deep blue eyes. "But I don't want to lose you." He held his hope that she'd agree inside. This had to be her choice.

"You're at training for three more months." She looked down, not meeting his eyes. "The baby's due about then. What will we do?" Her nails dug into his back.

"I don't want to lose you, Izzy. You or the baby. I want you both. I want you to be mine. We'll figure it out. Together." His gut twisted. She was saying no. He wanted to beg, plead with her to choose him. The roll against his abdomen, his baby just starting to move tied him in knots. He couldn't lose her.

Her arms tightened around his waist. "I don't want to lose you either."

"Promise?" Lee kissed her nose. He could feel his chest loosen. "What do I need to do?"

Isabelle struggled to sit up, pushing at his chest. Lee pulled back, sighing as he slipped out of her warmth. He grasped her hands and helped her sit up.

"Get dressed Lee."

Fuck, that didn't sound good. He slid back, the vinyl of the seat cushion pulling at his skin. He swung his legs over, careful not to kick Isabelle. Lee stood, and swiped his pants from the ground and slid them on.

Isabelle stood, tucking away her luscious boobs.

Lee watched mournfully while she wiggled and tugged hiding them away from his sight. He sighed. He'd have preferred them left out for him to feast on. Isabelle obviously had other ideas.

She smoothed down her dress, peering around the yard.

"Watcha looking for?"

"My panties."

Lee would bet that she turned and adorable shade of pink. He loved when she blushed. Her whole demeanor screamed 'don't look at me!' Lee felt his lips curl up. God, she was beautiful. Lee walked away from her, glancing around the yard. He leaned up and pulled up a scrap of lace.

"These them?"

"Yes."

Lee put them to his face and breathed deep. "Hmm. Sweet."

"Lee!"

He hid his grin behind the tiny scrap. "Yes?"

"Stop that!"

"Fine." He took one more deep breath. He could smell her on them, her tangy sweetness. He shoved them in his pocket. He shoved them to the bottom. He bet on her natural rambunctiousness reasserting itself. "I think I'll keep them."

"Hey, those are mine." Isabelle pouted at him.

"Maybe I want to bring them out later and remember taking them off of you."

She narrowed her eyes. There, that look. Any minute now.

She snorted and rushed at him. Her hand slid into his pocket. "I want them back."

Her hand slid along his dick. The thin pocket and the heat of her hand had him perking back up.

"Do that again. Grab my dick like you mean it."

Isabelle choked, trying to keep her smile from showing. But he could see it in the dimple in her cheek. Her hand teased him.

Lee grabbed her forearm, pushing it in deeper. He bucked up, giving her a wink. "Here it is."

Isabelle snickered and squeezed.

"Fuck." Lee grabbed her pulling her close. Hard again, all her doing. He rubbed against her. Her hand moving in his pocket and then pulling out. Crap. He forgot his plans. Her talented hands had fogged his mind. "Not so fast." He pushed her hand back in.

"Lee, let me have my panties."

"Fine, but I think rocks got in my pants. If I let you have

your panties, make sure my pocket is empty, okay?"

Isabelle rolled her eyes and nodded.

Lee released her arm.

She reached in and pulled out her panties. "I'm just going to put them on first." She blushed again. The dim light showed just enough for Lee to see the darkness tinting her cheeks. She leaned down and slipped them on. Tugging them up underneath her dress.

Damn, he didn't manage to get another peek.

Isabelle smoothed her dress down.

"Come on, you said you'd clean out my pockets."

"For Pete's sake. You don't need me to do that."

Lee winked at her. God he loved to tease her. "No, but I want you to. What are you afraid of?"

"Fine." Isabelle stomped over and shoved her hand in his pocket. She felt around and grabbed the stuff in his pocket, pulling it out. She splayed her hand out, showing him the contents. "There, see. Nothing but…"

Isabelle trailed off, staring at her hand. She raised her head, a question in her eyes.

Lee had to make this good. He'd had honest intentions to talk to her but one touch of her hands turned into a fuckfest. Not that he regretted it. Oh no. His muscles clenched. For God's sake, his hands were sweaty. He got down in front of Isabelle, on bended knee.

"Izzy. Isabelle." He cleared his throat. Crap, harder than he thought. The words wouldn't come out right. "Fuck. I want to marry you. Keep you. You're mine, dammit.

Shit. That came out wrong."

Isabelle bit her lips, giggles escaping though she tried not to laugh.

"Dammit. Izzy, will you marry me? Now, tomorrow, a year from now? Name the date. I'll be there." He had totally fucked that up. He wouldn't be surprised if she dropped the ring he'd bought in the dirt. He stared at it, sparkling in the palm of her hand.

So dumb. Like Isabelle would accept him after he'd made her play pocket pool with his dick to find the ring.

"Yes, Lee." She leaped forward, wrapping her arms around his neck, spreading soft wet kisses across his face.

"You will?" Lee pulled her harder into him, squeezing her until he remembered the baby. How had he gotten so lucky? "You will. Of course you will."

"Don't get cocky." Isabelle nuzzled his collar. "Now, why don't you put the ring on me?"

Lee smiled into her hair. How could he help but be cocky? Isabelle chose him. He released her, and slid the ring on to her finger. A perfect fit, just like they were.

CHAPTER TWELVE

God, he missed her already. The plane banked over the ocean, ready to turn inland. Across the country all the way to the other side of the States. Lee watched the land change, from ocean to desert, mountains to fields. He slumped back in his seat, his mind going over the moments they'd shared.

An empty hole filled his chest. He'd missing seeing Isabelle grow and change. He'd finally felt his baby move. A delicate flutter underneath the soft skin of Isabelle's abdomen. It stole his breath away. His arms had tightened around Isabelle, holding her gently to him. Knowing there was nothing more precious in that moment.

His phone pinged. Lee glanced down, pulling it from his pocket. Reading the message, he sat up, a smile twisting his lips. Happiness bubbled up, expanding his chest.

Miss you already.

How could he not respond?

I wish I didn't have to go.

Dad saw my ring.

What did he say?

That since we'd already made a baby we better get married sooner rather than later.

So he doesn't hate me?

I didn't say that lol.

Lee sighed. *You didn't have to.*

LOL. He'll get used to you.

He better. I'm not going anywhere.

Good. Gotta go to work. Luv u.

Lee's breath caught. He hoped it was true. *Luv u 2.*

The miles didn't really matter. Well, they did, but Lee was determined to make his future better. He didn't want to end up a pathetic loser, wasted out of his mind, found dead in an alley. Frozen to death in the cold of a winter's night.

Lee snorted. He was getting just a bit melodramatic. Jacinta must have rubbed off on him. He glanced out the window. Clouds obscured that land. Lee sat back and closed his eyes. He might as well grab a nap.

Lee took a taxi back to his barracks. He just wanted to

crash. He'd spent most of the weekend awake and visiting with him familia and Isabelle. He dragged himself to bed, stowing his bag in his closet, stripping and dropping down with a groan.

Lee woke up to an insistent beep. His alarm. Groaning he rolled over and out of bed.

"Shit." Lee pulled himself up, shaking his head. He quickly made his bed and ensuring the head was clear, hopped in the shower. He let the heat permeate his muscles, groaning at the sensation. The water beaded and ran down his back.

The knob rattled. Lee huffed. "I'll be out in a minute."

It had been too much to hope that he'd been the last one to get ready for classes. He turned off the shower and unlocked the connecting door before heading into his room. Wrapping his towel around his waist, Lee brushed his teeth and shaved.

Dressed, Lee headed to class. It would be a long day.

The clocked ticked, the noise capturing his attention. Lee swore the hands weren't moving. Finally, finally it was noon. Time for lunch.

"Dismissed." The chief waved them away. "Tomorrow we'll be conducting field exercises."

Lee quirked an eyebrow, but nothing further was given.

Shrugging he straggled behind his classmates heading to the chow hall. Grabbing a tray, he piled food on it. Sitting down at an empty table, Lee dialed.

"Hello." Isabelle answered.

"Hi babe. Miss you." Lee wished he could grab her through the phone.

"Miss you too." Isabelle laughed. "I don't know what to do with myself. No more school, I don't have to work, not sure how the day will go."

"You'll probably hang out with mi hermana."

"Yeah, probably." Lee heard what sounded like the refrigerator close. "If she doesn't have to work."

"Just relax. You're working just growing my baby."

A soft giggle hit his ears. "Not so hard, not now that my morning sickness is gone."

"I'll remind you of that when you're complaining."

"Oh no, no I told you so's!"

Lee laughed. Just talking to Isabelle made his day better. "Fine. I'll try to keep it in."

"I've got to go. I have another call coming in."

"I see how I rate."

Her laugh wound around his heart. "You rate just fine

Lee. I've got to go. Bye."

"Bye. Talk to you soon."

A click and she was gone. Lee sighed and slipped his phone back into his pocket.

"So, did I hear mention of a baby?" Groves slid in across from Lee. Smyth was right behind him, pushing him over and hogging most of the bench.

"Yeah." Lee couldn't stop the grin. "She's six months along. Hopefully I'll get home on leave in time to see him born."

"A boy? Good job." Smyth grinned.

"We don't know, but it's not like you can keep calling the baby it."

"Congrats, man." Groves grinned. "No wonder you don't want to go out and party with us."

Lee smiled. "Thanks. Pretty much, yeah."

Lunch, then back to class.

Every day was pretty much the same.

* * * *

Isabelle missed Lee. He'd only been gone a short time.

"Hmm." Her dad grabbed her hand, raising it to get a better look. "Better get to it before the baby's born."

"Dad."

"What?"

"Nothing." Isabelle shook her head. No congratulations. Nothing. At least he seemed to calm down, knowing that Lee was claiming the baby.

"I'm going to work."

"Okay, bye."

Isabelle kept busy. Her hours increased at work. She made sure she kept the house picked up. She didn't want to give her dad any reason to complain about her working. She managed to mooch rides from him, Caroline and Jacinta. She'd walk around the mall until her shift started.

"Isabelle."

"What?" She turned toward her dad.

"Come outside, please."

Shrugging, Isabelle put down the towel she was drying dishes with. "Okay."

Her dad was standing in the driveway, next to a small

silver sedan.

"What did you need?"

He walked over to her and handed her keys. His voice was gruff. "For your graduation."

"Really?"

He nodded his head.

Isabella threw her arms around him and squealed. "Thanks Dad. This is awesome."

He nudged her toward the car. "Go check it out."

Isabelle hurried over, admiring the car. She circled it and then opened the driver's door and sat in it. Perfect! "Want to go for a drive?" She couldn't keep the smile off her face.

"Finish looking it over."

Isabelle got out and sat in the passenger side. Plenty roomy. She got out and admired it. And four door, that would be awesome once she had the baby. She opened the rear door and stared. Tears welled up in her eyes.

"Dad." Isabelle turned and threw herself into her father's arms. "Thank you, thank you."

"You're welcome." He awkwardly hugged her. "I figured you were going to need it."

Her dad had bought her a car for graduation. It was overwhelming. The best part about it, was the brand new baby seat sitting in the back seat, already buckled in.

"Thank you." He didn't say anything, but the car seat said it all. Isabelle couldn't stop her tears.

"Let's take her for a spin."

"Do you want to drive?"

He laughed. "No, you need to feel comfortable driving it."

"Let me get my purse." She ran into the house and grabbed it. Running back out and scrambling into the driver's seat, Isabelle drove to the mall. She showed her dad the crib she had on layaway. He nodded, admiring it. He looked a bit uncomfortable, surrounded by all the baby stuff, but he didn't object.

"It's nice and sturdy."

Isabelle agreed. "I like it. Plus, since I work here, I get a discount."

Her dad nodded, looking around. "That's good."

The drive home was quiet. Isabelle parked in the driveway and turned to her dad. "Thank you." She glanced toward the seat. "You don't know what this means to me."

"You're welcome." He sighed. "You're an adult now. You have the right to make your own decisions." He glanced at her hand. "And you won't be on your own. I'm glad Lee is stepping up to the plate. If he stays on the straight and narrow."

Isabelle tried not to roll her eyes. "Thank you. I love the car."

Her dad unbuckled and stepped out. "I have to go to work. I'll see you for supper."

Isabelle smiled. "I'll have it ready."

He left.

Isabelle sat in the car, thrilled to her toes. She had to let Lee know.

Dad bought me a car for graduation.

With a babyseat!

She knew Lee would answer when he could. He was probably in class.

Excited, Isabelle didn't want to go home. She had to show her BFF. She'd be so jealous! She drove over to Jacinta's, pulling up into the empty driveway.

Sticking her head in the door Isabelle called out. "Is Jacinta home?"

Mama Rosa looked up. "Si. In her room."

"Thanks." Isabelle headed down the hall.

"Hey, girlfriend, I have something to show you."

"Don't want to see another stretch mark."

Isabelle laughed. She plopped down on the bed next to Jacinta. "Not this time. It's outside."

"Fine. It's too hot to be out there long though."

Isabelle tried to hide her glee, following Jacinta outside.

"Who the heck parked in our drive? What did you want to show me?"

"I did!" She hit the button on her fob, unlocking the car. "Dad bought it for me for graduation. Here's the best part." She opened the back door. "Look."

Jacinta peeked in and squealed. "Amiga, that's awesome." She grabbed Isabelle hugging her tightly.

"I know, right?"

Her phone buzzed.

Fucking awesome. What kind?

Isabelle looked at the car and texted back.

Toyota Camry

Nice. TTYL. Luv u.

Luv u 2.

"Let's take it for a spin."

The girls hopped in, driving around until dinner time. Isabelle dropped Jacinta off, heading home for the night.

Lee called her every morning, texted at odd intervals and they Skyed on Friday and Saturday nights.

"C'mon, show me. Please." Lee's voice wheedled. "I can't be there, how else can I share the experience?"

"Fine." Isabelle huffed. She stood up raised her blouse. Just enough to show Lee her growing belly. Every time they Skyped he asked. She didn't really mind, but she felt really huge this week. The baby was moving around even more.

"You're gorgeous, every bulge and ripple…"

Isabelle glared at him, dropping her shirt back down.

"Every precious, sexy curve." Lee snickered.

"Too late, bucko."

"Aw, Izzy, you know I was just teasing. I think you're beautiful."

Izzy might have believed him more if he could wipe that grin off of his face. She felt fat and his teasing made her wish he was here. To strangle him. She didn't feel beautiful. She didn't think she looked pregnant, just fat. She plopped back down on the bed.

"I just feel fat."

"You're not. You're pregnant. With my baby. And that makes me the luckiest man in the world."

Isabelle sniffled. "Lee."

"Oh, flakita, don't cry."

Isabelle scrubbed her face. "I'm not. Stupid hormones."

Lee blew her a kiss. "So, they guys came up with a few names."

"Oh no. Groves and Smyth?"

"Yup."

"I don't want to hear."

"Sure you do."

"Their suggestions are horrible. I'm not naming my baby Istanbul or Rocco."

"No, they came up with more."

Isabelle shook her head, a smile lurking on her lips. "That's not good."

Lee laughed. "Just hear me out."

Isabelle rolled her eyes. "Fine. Get it out."

"Landis, Lachlan, Langdon."

"They're up to the L's now, I see."

"No, no. It's not like that."

"Larz. That's not bad."

"It's not good."

"How about Dill? Clover? Breccan?"

"No, no and no." Isabelle giggled. "Where are you guys finding these?"

Lee grinned. "Around."

"I assume inspiration strikes depending on where you are?"

"Exactly!"

Isabelle heard her dad yell for her. "Lee, hold on, my dad's hollering."

"Okay.

"What do you need, Dad?" Isabelle stuck her head out her door.

"Did you make supper?"

"Yeah. Your plate is in the microwave."

"Thanks. What are you doing?"

"Talking to Lee."

Her dad grunted.

Isabelle heard the microwave door open and shut. The beep of numbers signaled her dad heating it up. She shook her head and closed her door.

"He just wanted supper." Her door opened. "What do you need, Dad?"

"Are you still talking to Lee?"

"Yes."

"Good." He came in the room and leaned over the computer, looking at Lee. "When are you planning on getting married?"

"Dad!" Oh my God. Isabelle wanted to sink into the carpet.

Lee laughed. "As soon as we possibly can. I graduate the last week of August. I'll be flying home the same day to start leave."

"That's cutting it close."

"I don't have a choice."

"Let me know when you two decide. I have a fellow minister that is willing to marry you. You just need to get a license."

"Sounds good."

Her dad grunted and left.

"OMG. I'm sorry."

"I'm not. We need to set a date."

"Are you sure?"

"I wouldn't have asked if I wasn't sure. You do know I love you, don't you?"

Isabelle's heart raced. Her smile went clear to her soul. "I love you too."

"Done yet?" Isabelle heard Jameson, Lee's roommate.

"In a minute. Izzy, you heard, I need to go."

"You have a good night."

"You too. Love ya." Lee touched the screen. Isabelle put her hand on his. A virtual caress.

Isabelle's smile blossomed. "Love you too."

Lee's picture went down. Isabelle shut off her computer. She was so glad that they were able to Skype as often as they did.

Isabelle curled up in bed, grabbing a book. Time to relax. She nodded off.

Isabelle didn't work today. Jacinta and she were planning on picking out everything they could think of that she'd need for the baby for her registry. Plus lots and lots of diapers. Most of her friends and family knew she was expecting.

Jacinta and Caroline had a baby shower planned. It would of course be at the church. Easier clean up and plenty of parking. Isabelle was excited but wished Lee could be there too.

Isreal.

No.

Isabelle giggled. Lee would text at odd times of the day. Sending baby names. Weird, ridiculous names she would never, ever use. At this rate the baby's name would be baby. Lee texted again.

Can we get married the day after I graduate? Is a Saturday okay?

That would be wonderful.

Let your dad know. Find out what we need to get to make it happen.

I will.

Does he still hate me?

LOL. Maybe?

Sad face. Let my mom and Mama Rosa know.

LOL. Okay. Luv u.

Luv u 2. TTYL

Isabelle hugged herself. OMG. They'd set a date.

CHAPTER THIRTEEN

She missed Lee so badly. He graduated today and she couldn't even be there. Her doctor wouldn't give her permission to fly. She said it was too close to her due date.

He'd be home soon though. Isabelle glanced at the ring he'd given her. A sparkling solitaire. Simple and elegant. She loved it. Turned out Lee had chosen it himself.

Her stomach muscles tensed. Her groin tightened. Isabelle took a deep breath. Her muscles eased. She exhaled through her mouth. Her abdomen hardened. She tried to relax. The Braxton Hicks contractions had plagued her for the last trimester of her pregnancy. Her body felt foreign. All she could think about was the movie Alien. Something monstrous tearing its way out of her belly.

She looked over at the picture of her ultrasound. It wasn't a monster. Her jaw clenched. Her belly once again hardened. She panted breathing through the pain. Little needles prickling from below her boobs made her have to pee. Her new normal.

"What's the matter? Izzy are you okay?"

"I'm… I'm okay. Just Braxton Hicks." She breathed out,

little pants to ease the pain. She had forgotten she was skyping with Lee.

"Who's he?"

Isabelle giggled despite the pain. "Not who, what. They're fake contractions."

"What do you mean contractions? Is the baby coming?"

"No. It's like my body is practicing for the birth."

"That sucks."

Her abdomen tightened. Isabelle gasped. She hoped they would end soon. Nothing seemed to help when they came.

"Yeah, it does."

"Are you sure they're not real? They look real to me."

Lee sounded worried. His face pressed close to the screen like he could hop over to her.

"Just a preview. The trailers before a movie is what my doctor said."

Izzy saw Lee shake his head, a frown on his face.

"How often do you have them?"

Izzy took a short breath let it out and did it again. "Just a bit every day."

"That's really sucks. I'm sorry Izzy."

She made a noise between a laugh and a groan.

"It's not your fault Lee."

"I'm the one that got you pregnant."

Isabelle shrugged. She couldn't argue with that. The

pressure on her bladder built again. She stood up. "Lee I have to go." She pressed a hand against her abdomen and gasped as water dribbled down her legs. Her stomach muscles tightened even harder.

"Izzy, what's the matter?"

"Lee, I think my water broke." Isabelle stared at the puddle between her legs. The baby decided to come early. She bit her lip. It wasn't too early, but Lee wasn't home yet. He had graduation today.

Her father grumbled, and swore, but he'd finally stopped trying to get her to give her baby away. Isabelle figured the pictures of the ultrasound and the feel of her baby kicking had a lot to do with that. Especially once he found out Lee had asked her to marry him. The huge rock on her finger proving she wasn't lying. The baby seat and the car showed he finally accepted her choice.

Once the date was set, he found a minister to perform the ceremony, a longtime friend. Swearing once he gave her away she was Lee's problem. Tomorrow. Crap.

"Shit! Are you home alone?"

"No, I think my dad is here." Pretty sure she'd heard someone downstairs a little while ago. "Lee, how are we going to get married tomorrow?"

"Don't worry. We'll figure it out. Now, hang up. Go get your dad and get to the hospital. I'll call my family to meet you there."

"I'm scared Lee." She could hear the tremor in her own voice.

"It's going to be okay. I'll be there soon as I can, okay?"

"Okay. But your graduation."

"Let me worry about that. I'm going to call mi hermana now. Go get your dad."

Her stomach tightened again. Sharp pains had her gasping.

"Gotta go Lee." Izzy closed her computer, hunching over, trying to make herself smaller against the pain. It eased as she stepped toward her bedroom door. She turned the knob and opened it.

"Dad? Are you here?" Regardless she needed to get downstairs. If he wasn't home she could call Jacinta. If Lee didn't reach her first. She planned on being there for the birth, regardless of Lee being there or not. Isabelle grabbed her phone off her dresser. She'd call in a bit. When she could breathe again.

"Yes. I'm in the kitchen. What do you want?"

Izzy leaned against the wall. The pressure in her body not what she expected. Her knuckles were tight on the railing. She didn't want to fall if she rushed.

"Isabelle? Answer me."

She finished descending the stairs. Her body eased, relaxing once more. "Dad, the baby's coming. Will you take me to the hospital?"

Her father turned towards her. A surprised look on his face. She wasn't sure why. He knew this day would eventually happen.

"Yes." He looked at her. "Don't you want to change?"

Isabelle looked down. Her eyes widened to she took in her wet skirt. "I didn't realize."

"I'll get you another dress. Why don't you sit in a chair?" He guided her over and helped settle her at the kitchen table. He turned and Isabelle could hear him taking the stairs two at a time. She set her phone down. Stretching her hand out from how tightly she'd held it.

Taking deep breaths, Isabelle tried to relax. The contractions eased a bit. She still felt weird. Her stomach harder than she'd expected. She heard her dad coming back down the stairs.

"Here's another dress. Can you change?"

He held it up, showing her.

Isabelle nodded. "Yes. Just help me stand, okay?"

"Sure." He father grabbed her hand and gently pulled her up. "Do you need help?"

"No!" Isabelle grabbed the dress "I'll be right back." She headed toward the guest bath in the hall. No way was she changing in front of her father. Ick. The pain seemed to be better. Her stomach not radiating the pain from earlier.

"Where is your bag for the hospital, Isabelle?"

"In my closet on the floor."

"I'll go grab it and pull the car out."

Isabelle pulled off her wet dress, dumping it in the tub. Her soaked panties were tossed in next. Turning on the water in the sink, she let it warm up before getting a wash cloth wet. Lifting a leg and placing a foot on the toilet, she cleaned up a bit. She wasn't going to the hospital all damp. Turning off the water and leaving the cloth in the sink, Isabelle grabbed a towel.

Dry, she pulled on the dress. Her dad forgot underwear.

She'd have to send him back upstairs for some. Isabelle grabbed the edge of the sink. Her stomach tightened. She gulped in a breath, her knuckles white. She curled forward, leaning against the sink. It was time to go. The pain and pressure eased. Uncurling her fingers, Isabelle swallowed. Her hands went instinctively to her belly. Her breath coming in small pants.

The pain eased and Isabelle opened the door and headed outside. Her dad had the car running and her door open.

"Come on Isabelle. I called your sister. She's heading to the hospital."

Isabelle nodded and slid carefully onto the seat. Her dad shut the door and went around the car to get in. Isabelle put on her seat belt. Her dad backed up, the bump from the drive to the street pulling a gasp from her.

"Sorry, sorry."

"It's okay." Isabelle slid a look at her dad.

He didn't look as calm as normal. His hands, red and white, gripped the steering wheel. He took a deep breath and shifted, pulling forward and heading toward the hospital.

"Beverly Hospital or Whittier?"

"Beverly." Thank goodness Caroline knew the hospital. She'd taken her to a couple of her appointments.

Isabelle realized she hadn't talked to her father about anything for the baby. Every previous discussion about giving the baby up. Only recently had he accepted she was keeping her baby. They discussed nothing practical about doctors or hospitals. Isabelle heard her phone ring.

"Thanks." She grabbed it from the seat. Isabelle answered it. "Hello."

"Where are you?" No greeting, Jacinta got right to the point.

"On our way to Beverly."

"We'll be right there. I can't wait!"

Jacinta hung up before Isabelle had a chance to answer. She sighed. She'd bet Lee's whole family would be there. Hopefully her dad would behave. She didn't understand why he didn't like them.

They pulled up to the door of the hospital. Her dad grabbed her bag and came around and opened her door.

"Let's get you settled, and I'll park the car." He helped pull her out, holding her arm as the headed to the door.

"Izzy!"

Isabelle looked. Jacinta and her family were there already.

"Pastor, I can park your car if you'd like." Mateo gestured at it.

"Thanks. I'd appreciate it." Her dad nodded at it. "Keys are in the ignition."

"I'll bring them in." Mateo slid in the car. Starting it, he drove off toward the parking lot.

Isabelle entered the lobby, slowing as another contraction hit. She was preregistered so it shouldn't take long. Panting, she closed her eyes, trying to breathe through the pain.

"How can I help you?"

"Isabelle Rivers. She's registered. You are, right?" Jacinta peered at her.

Isabelle nodded. The pain receding.

The volunteer peered at her over the counter. "We'll get you up to birthing right away."

She picked up the phone and spoke into it. She stood and came around the counter.

"Can you follow me or would you prefer a wheelchair?"

"I'd rather walk."

Isabelle followed her, glad for once of the slow pace of the elderly volunteers. She held her stomach, worried another contraction would hit and her baby would drop out onto the floor.

* * * *

Lee grabbed his cover and tore out of his barracks. He had to get home. He ran to his classroom, hoping to find his instructor. Lee wore in his dress whites, graduation happening in less than an hour.

Lee spied him looking out the window, his ever present cup of coffee in his hand.

"Chief, I have to go."

"Go where Santiago?"

"Home. My girl just went into labor." He paced shaking his head. "God awful. Suddenly, bloody water gushing out of her."

"How do you even know that?" His chief turned toward him.

"We were Skyping."

"Graduation is in thirty minutes. When is your plane leaving?"

"At noon. I can't wait that long. I have to catch another flight. An earlier one."

His chief shook his head. "No. You have to attend graduation. Keep your flight."

"You don't understand."

"I do. You already have your flight booked, right?"

Lee nodded.

"And it's probably non-refundable."

"Fuck."

His chief nodded. "Yup. So finish getting ready for graduation, pack your bags. Be the first one waiting in line to leave."

"Yes, Chief." Lee turned and headed back toward his barracks. "Crap." He stomped down the stairs, taking satisfaction in the sound of his shoes connecting with the concrete. "Fuck. Shit."

He already had his orders. He wasn't surprised to get stationed on a ship docked in San Diego. He'd learned in boot camp that nearly one third of the Navy resided there.

Lee headed back to his barracks. He just needed to pack his laptop.

Finished, he dumped everything on his rack. His orders, flight tickets and laptop were in his carryon. Everything else, stuffed in his seabag. He headed down to the auditorium. The class of graduates were milling around.

The Chief stuck his head out. "Inside and in your seats. We're ready to begin."

They all shuffled in, sitting in the seats in order. One by one they were called up and handed a graduation certificate and congratulations. Speeches were given by the base commander.

Lee glanced at his watch in frustration. The hands of his clock were slow. The last text from his sister telling him Isabelle had been admitted but she hadn't had the baby yet.

Finally, the ceremony ended. Lee stood up and quickly exited. He headed to his barracks to grab his bags and orders. A taxi waited at the door.

Lee knocked on the window. "I'll be right down. I just have to get my bags."

"Will do." The driver nodded.

Lee sprinted in the building, taking the stairs. The elevator took too long. Two steps at a time and he arrived. Down the corridor Lee ran, swinging into the open door of his room.

"Hey, you leaving already?" His roommate laid on his bunk. Jameson had graduated a couple of months ago and his new roommate was much easier to get along with.

"Yeah. My girl's in labor. I got to get home."

"Good timing."

"Phft. The baby could have waited one more day. We were supposed to get married tomorrow."

"Best laid plans, man."

Lee nodded. "I gotta go. The taxi's waiting."

"See ya 'round, Santiago."

"Sure. Bye."

Lee grabbed his bags and left the way he'd come. The only thing on his mind was getting home in time to see his baby born. Boy or girl, Lee couldn't wait to take him or her into his arms.

Sliding in, Lee put on his seatbelt. "Airport."

The driver nodded, backed out and headed to the airport. The thirteen mile drive seemed to take forever. He glanced at his tickets. United Airlines leaving at 11:45. It was the flight that got him back in LA the earliest. Thank god he'd been in a rush to see Isabelle.

"What airlines?"

"United."

They were pulling up to the airlines now. Lee tossed some bills over the seat. Enough for the ride and a tip.

"Thanks." Lee opened the door, grabbed his bags and headed in. He had just over a half an hour until his plane boarded. Able to do a quick check in using his ticket in the self-service kiosk he checked his gate number.

His flight left from gate nine. Crap, he needed to get moving. Of course it was all the way at the end of the terminal. Lee stuffed his ticket in his bag, shouldered his seabag and ran. He still had to go through security. He took the stairs two at a time.

Passing the people leisurely strolling, Lee headed straight

for security. Fuck, even the line for military and premier fliers looked packed. Lee got in line. He pulled out his ticket and military ID. He checked his watch, twenty-five minutes to go. He couldn't miss this flight. He checked his phone. His hermana had texted.

No baby yet.

Lee's foot tapped, he checked his watch again. He looked at the line. It moved to slow for him. He couldn't miss his plane.

"Hey, Santiago."

Lee glanced back. He couldn't work up the enthusiasm of a smile. "Hey, Groves."

"Heading home? You're getting married tomorrow, aren't you?"

"Not sure if we can now."

"Sorry to hear that. What happened?"

"Huh?"

"You said you're not sure you're getting married anymore."

"Izzy's in labor. She's having my baby. Like right now." He checked his phone and moved closer to the gate. "I can't miss my plane."

"Shit, man. Why didn't you say so?" Groves started waving and shouting. "Hey, this man can't miss his plane. His girl's in labor. His plane leaves in…" He glanced at Lee.

"Fifteen minutes."

"Fifteen minutes. Can we move him to the front of the

line?"

A path opened up. Lee's throat closed up. "Thanks, man."

Groves slapped him on the back. "Congratulations, man. Let me know how it goes."

Lee smiled, and ran to the security podium. He cleared and went to the security belt. Toeing off his chloroforms, pulling his dog tags off, and pulling his laptop out, Lee placed them in the bins. He went through the metal detectors and grabbed his stuff. He slipped his dog tags on, grabbed his bags, shoes and slipped his laptop in his backpack. He took off, running toward his gate. The plane was already loading and calling for stragglers.

Lee jogged up, showed his ticket to the attendant at the gate.

"I'm here."

The attendant laughed. "You have time to put your shoes on. I won't close the door until you're on. I'll have to check your bag for cargo though."

Lee sat in a hard plastic chair, dropping his bags down. Pushing his seabag toward her. "Here, Thanks." He put his shoes on, tying the laces quickly. "I was afraid I was going to miss the plane." He grabbed his carryon bag and stood up, taking the ticket for his seabag. "My girl is in labor. I'm trying to make it home before she has the baby."

"I hope you make it. Have a safe trip."

"Thanks." Lee headed down the bridge toward the plane. He held his backpack in front and his seabag in back of him. He didn't look forward to walking down the aisle.

The plane looked to be at full capacity.

Walking across the threshold, an attendant checked his ticket. "You're half way down. There should still be room for your bag."

"Thanks." Lee headed down the aisle.

An old gentleman tried to lift his bag into the overhead compartment. Lee slid his arm through the strap on his backpack and gave the man's bag a lift. He looked at Lee, startled. "Thank you, young man."

Lee nodded and hid his impatience. The man finally settled in his seat. Lee header further down, cursing when his bag snagged an edge of a seat. "Shit. Sorry."

Finally, Lee found his seat. He looked into the overhead compartment, full. Maybe he could change that. Lee pushed a couple of bags around and found just enough room for his carryon. He needed to leave room for his feet. Shoving it in, he sat with a sigh. His shoulders drooped. God, he'd made it. Exhaling, he laid his head back.

"Please fasten your seat belts in preparation for takeoff."

Lee sat forward, shoving his backpack under the seat. He pulled off his Dixie cup and put it in the seat pocket. He checked his phone again. Nothing. Dammit. Lee pulled his seatbelt out and clicked it in place, pulling the strap to tighten it.

He dropped his head back into his seat. He glanced at his phone, willing it to tell him something. At least he was on his way. Four hours and he'd be there.

"Turn off all phones and electronics until we are in the air. Make sure all seats and tray tables are in the upright position."

Lee glanced around. The passengers were moving around, settling in. He looked at his phone and shot off a quick text.

On my way

He held down the power button, watching his connection with Isabelle fade away. It was going to be a long four hours.

The engines engaged. The plane began backing up. Lee glanced over at the window. The concrete gave way to scraggly stunted bushes. The vibrations worked up from his seat engulfing his body. Despite his tenseness, Lee began to relax. His hands relaxed. He'd been crushing his phone. Sighing, he released it, tucking it in his uniform pocket. There wasn't a damn thing he could do for the next five hours.

"Are you going home on leave?"

Lee glanced over. He hadn't really noticed the woman in the seat by the window. Hopefully she wouldn't talk all through the flight. "Yes."

He looked forward again. He couldn't wait to get home and take Isabelle in his arms. He'd finally be able to hold his baby. Boy or girl, he couldn't wait. His chest swelled. God, he couldn't believe Izzy was having his baby. Right now. He clenched his fists against the arms of the seat.

He should be there. Dammit. Lee growled. Total bullshit he'd had to stay. There had been an earlier flight, he checked. To be honest, it still landed about the same time because it connected in Houston. A layover would just have gotten him into trouble. At least this flight flew nonstop.

"I am too. This is the first time in fifteen years I'm going home."

Lee started. He'd forgotten about the woman. Evidently she planned on talking to him no matter what.

"That's nice."

"I was doing missionary work."

"Hmm." Maybe grunts would be the way to discourage her.

The plane's engines revved up. It began gaining speed. A sharp lift of the nose and the plane was climbing.

Lee's stomach dropped to his groin. The hollowness in his gut told him man really wasn't supposed to fly. The vibrations didn't relax him this time. His fingers gripped harder. His ears filled then popped. The plane leveled out, the high pitched hum of the engines smoothing out.

"Flying really is safe."

Lee turned his head. The woman looked at him expectantly. "I know." Doomed. She would talk the whole trip. He could tell.

"I've flown all over the world. I've been flying for twenty years and more."

Lee didn't know what to say. He wiggled in his seat, trying to get comfortable. She rattled on. His body relaxed for the first time in days. The sound of her voice caused his eyelids to droop. His head slowly listed to the side and his breath evened out.

The change in the engines brought Lee awake. Blinking,

he rubbed his eyes. Stretching, he arched his back, his jaw popping in a yawn. He rubbed his groin, pointing his toes and tensing his thighs and calves.

"Oh dear."

Fuck, he'd forgotten about his seat mate.

"Sorry." His voice gravelly. His mouth was dry after dozing off. "Forgot where I was."

A nervous sounding laugh escaped her. "No problem."

Lee glanced over. She'd turned to face the window. The touch of pink in her cheeks assured him she was embarrassed. Not a damn thing he could do about it now.

The seat belt sign glowed. He didn't know if it had stayed on the whole trip or not. He glanced out the window. The ocean sparkled below them. They must be approaching LAX.

"Did they say to turn off our phones?"

She glanced at him and looked away again. "Yes."

The engines roared, changing in volume. Power shook the plane.

"Fuck." Lee grabbed the arms of his seat. The plane's nose dipped, the steepness of the descent making him glad he had his seat belt on.

A jarring bump and the plane landed on the ground. The brakes hissed, barely holding back the power of the plane as it coasted in. A couple of turns on the tarmac and Lee saw the terminal approaching.

He slipped off his seat belt. Safe enough now to do so. Lee turned his head, the snap of bones easing the stiffness of his neck. Almost home. Excitement thrummed in his veins. His stomach danced. He'd never admit to anyone his nervousness. Isabelle having his baby. God. And he wasn't even there. His nostrils flared. He had no one to blame but himself.

The plane slowed then stopped. Lee pushed up with his hands.

"Please stay seated. We have a special passenger that needs to debark. If the expectant daddy can grab his bags and come up, we'll then begin debarkation."

Lee sat stunned. Happiness bubble in his chest. A grin spread across his chest. He stood up and stepped into the aisle. He opened the overhead and pulled out his bag. Grabbing it, he jogged down the aisle. A few cat calls and claps and congratulations followed him.

He couldn't stop the shit eating grin. "Thanks!" He stopped at the flight attendant at the door. "I can't tell you how much I appreciate this."

"No problem. They'll be bringing up the bags checked at the gate in a minute. You'll be able to leave as soon as the air bridge is set up and the bags are up."

Lee heard a couple of thunks, something hitting the door, and a scrape. A knock on the outside of the door set the attendant moving. She grabbed the handle and pulled it up. The door slid open.

"Here you go. Congratulations!"

Lee waved and stopped in the tunnel.

"This what you need?" A baggage handler swung his seabag up.

"Yeah, thanks man."

Lee grabbed it and ran down the tunnel. He burst into the terminal. He stopped and got his bearings. Turning right, he headed out of the airport. With Isabelle in labor, he didn't expect to be picked up. He headed to the taxi stands. He'd splurge and take a cab to the hospital.

"Lee!"

He looked up. "Tio." Lee jogged over to him. Tio Mateo enveloped him in a big hug. "I figured you'd be at the hospital."

"I was, but I figured I might as well be useful and pick you up."

"Thanks. I thought I'd end up getting a taxi."

Mateo laughed. "Save your money. With a baby you're going to need it."

A sliver of satisfaction slid through him. "Isabelle had the baby?"

"Not as far as I know. The doctor said first babies can take a while."

"It's been like eight hours!"

"That's nothing according to the staff at the hospital."

"Fuck."

"I know."

"I'm parked right over here. I borrowed Mama's handicapped sign."

Lee laughed. "Thanks."

"I parked in the farthest one. I felt bad enough using it."

Lee snorted. Mateo was always the rules man. Breaking it must have killed him.

"I appreciate it."

They reached the car. Lee tossed his bags in the back seat. He grabbed his phone, strapped in and turned it on.

Mateo maneuvered out of the lot into traffic.

His phone finally powered up. It started dinging with each incoming message.

Tio will pick u up at the gate

Isabelle's dilated to 6

Contractions slowed. Walking the halls.

Isabelle's dilated to 7

She's not happy

Now she's at 8

She's at 9 and boy is she pissed at you!

I'm never having bebes!

Still at 9

I hope you're here soon

Where are you?

Have you landed?

Lee chuckled despite the sourness in his stomach. His guts were roiling, his palms sweaty. Was Isabelle really mad at him? He swallowed. He'd find out soon.

On our way

Lee texted his hermana. He looked up. They were at the hospital. His phone dinged.

She's at 10! She wants to push. Where are you?

Lee jumped out. "Tio, what room?"

"Three-twenty-six."

Lee waited impatiently while the sliding doors slid open, slipping in as soon as he could fit. He ran toward the stairs, ignoring the volunteer at the desk trying to get his attention.

He took them two at a time. Cursing when his dress shoes slipped, almost bringing him down. Grabbing the railing, Lee bound up the stairs. He turned toward the doors and slammed into them.

"What the hell?" Lee pressed what was obviously an intercom.

It crackled and fell silent. "May I help you?"

"Isabelle, she's having a baby."

"Okaaay."

"She's in three-twenty-six."

"Who is she to you?"

"It's my baby."

The door buzzed. Lee pushed it open and ran down the hall. Three-eleven, Three-thirteen, crap. He turned the corner, ignoring the grunts and screams from the rooms he passed. It looked like a full house. Finally! Three-twenty-six. Lee saw Isabelle's dad pacing the hallway, then start toward him. Ignoring him, Lee burst into Isabelle's room.

"Push! A little more."

Lee stopped. The sight of all of the blood turning his

stomach.

"Lee!"

He turned his head and smiled. Isabelle was beautiful. Sweat covered, her smile lit up the room.

"You made it."

He moved forward, grabbing her outstretched hand.

She squeezed, grunting. Nails biting into his hand.

"Fuck."

"Push, bear down." The doctor was talking to Isabelle.

Jacinta held one leg back, and Caroline, the other. Both looked green.

Isabelle screamed, squeezing his hand with strength he didn't know she had. He watched and amid the blood and hands, his baby slid free into the waiting arms of the doctor. He choked, happiness flooding him.

"Congratulations, Isabelle, and I assume this is daddy. You have a son."

The cry of a baby filled the room. His son.

"Do you want to cut his cord?"

Lee looked at Isabelle. She nodded.

"Yes."

Lee followed the directions from the doctor, snipping the bit of blood filled cord after the clips were placed on it.

"Hold him while we clean up momma."

A blanket wrapped around his son and he held in his arms. His heart filled. He swallowed trying to speak. Lee leaned over and kissed Isabelle on the forehead. "Thank you, Izzy."

"Time to finish up momma." The doctor massaged her stomach. "Push one more time, let's get the afterbirth done."

"I love you." Lee whispered to the bundle in his arms. He'd never let anyone hurt him. Lee swore he'd protect him with his life.

The nurses buzzed around the bed. Cleaning up Isabelle and the bed. Suddenly his son was whisked out of his arms and laid on Isabelle's chest.

"A little skin to skin time with mom."

Lee couldn't protest even as his arms felt empty. Isabelle's eyes lit up, her arms wrapping around their bundle of joy. He leaned over and kissed her. "Love you, Izzy. Forever."

She smiled up at him, her love apparent. "Love you too, Lee." She glanced down at their son nestled on her chest. Her face glowed.

His heart was ready to burst from his chest. "Thank you for our son, I can't imagine anything more perfect."

Isabelle beamed, joy shining from her eyes.

She would always be his delight.

Reality intruded, the nurse gently taking the baby. "Time to clean him up and weigh him."

Lee started to follow. Izzy's hand grabbed his while the other tugged her sheet over herself. Lee reached down, and tied up her hospital gown, covering all of the good bits.

"We do it all right here." The nurse gestured at a contraption he hadn't noticed.

"Oh."

Isabelle's soft chuckle tugged at his heart strings. Despite the pain of labor, most of which he thanked God he'd missed, she still smiled.

His hermana stuck her head out the door, gesturing Isabelle's padre in. His familia followed, a thrum of excitement entering with them.

Lee grimaced. Her dad still made him nervous.

Isabelle squeezed his hand, tugging him down to whisper in his ear. "Lee, behave. He's come around."

Lee snorted. He'd believe it when he saw it.

Isabelle's dad headed straight to the baby, cooing softly. Lee's familia followed.

His eyebrows raised. Her father had changed his tune. Then, his camera came out. He took picture after picture. Everything they did was documented. Lee couldn't help but chuckle.

He glanced at Isabelle. "You're right."

"I told you so." Her tired snicker had Lee rolling his eyes.

"So, are you two still getting married tomorrow?" Jacinta bounced over to the bed.

Mama Rosa was blessing the baby, waving her ever present rosary around.

"How can we?" Lee couldn't help the disappointment in his voice.

Isabelle's father cleared his throat. "I can help with that. I called my friend and he's willing to marry you here. If that's what you want."

Lee looked down at Isabelle and quirked a brow. "Izzy?"

"Yes, if you don't mind."

He leaned down, pressing his lips tenderly against her soft mouth. "I don't care when or where. I only want you to be mine."

"Then that's settled. I'll confirm it with him." Her father turned, heading to the door.

Lee heard a soft wail. His son. His heart filled with joy.

"So, what are you guys going to name him?" Jacinta asked.

Lee saw Isabelle's father stop, waiting to hear.

"Asher." Isabelle whispered, nuzzling the baby's head. "It means happy."

"Asher Santiago. I like it." Lee smiled. Asher was a good name.

"Asher Sebastien Santiago. Then his initials will be ASS! He is a Santiago male after all."

Isabelle giggled at Jacinta's mouth vomit.

Lee snorted. Those wouldn't be his initials if he had anything to say about it.

Asher's wail gained strength.

"Time for everyone but Mom and Dad to leave." The nurse held the door open, ushering everyone out.

The room emptied out. Soon it was just him, Izzy, and

Asher.

Lee sat on the side of the bed. He leaned over and kissed her softly on her lips. "Are you happy Izzy?"

"Yes." She gazed down at Asher, crying and fumbling at her breast.

"Think I should show him how it works?"

"Lee!"

Lee laughed. He'd never been so happy. "I'm just saying. I know how to work those babies."

Isabelle couldn't hide her smile. "I think he'll figure it out." Isabelle jumped. "Ow."

Lee chuckled. "I guess he figured it out. Takes after his old man."

Rolling her eyes, Isabelle smiled. Lee lifted his legs onto the bed, carefully toeing off his shoes and pulled Isabelle and Asher into his arms. They were silent, Lee just happy holding the two of them.

"I got a ship in San Diego."

"I'm glad." Isabelle peeked up at him.

"I'll go down one day next week and find out about housing." Lee kissed the top of her head, content. "You will come live with me, won't you?"

"Of course. A wife does belong with her husband. Just ask my dad." Isabelle giggle, tired, but happiness radiated from her.

Lee rolled his eyes and basked in her joy. He had everything he'd ever wanted, right there in his arms.

Isabelle, Asher, and him.

The way it was meant to be.

THE END

Thank you for reading A Sailor's Delight!

If you enjoyed this story, please consider leaving a review.

Author Bio:

Beverly Ovalle dabbled with writing on and off for years when her best friend finally dared her to submit a story to a writing contest. Beverly decided she had nothing to lose and since she'd always wanted to be an author sent it in and agonized for months waiting to hear back. Contract in hand she has never looked back.

Beverly has been obsessed with dragons and romance since she was a young girl, collecting dragon books and reading everything she could find on them even down to the care of real life dragons. She's always been slightly panicked that the world as we know it will end, so has prepped for it, haunting survivalist pages and prepper projects she felt she needed in the event SHTF.

An avid fan of all romance, Beverly's goal is to share her love of the written word and write the hot and erotic romances that she enjoys. She writes what she loves to read and it was only a matter of time before her obsessions crept into her writing for her to share. She hopes you enjoy her tales as much as she loves writing them.

A Navy Veteran, Beverly has traveled around the world and the United States enabling her to bring her settings to life, meeting and marrying her husband of twenty five years along the way for her own romance. Reading romances since the fourth grade she's followed as the genre changed and spread into the vast cornucopia of romance offered today.

Turn the page to see more by Beverly Ovalle:

Love Me Forever
By Beverly Ovalle
Chapter One

The road to Hell couldn't be any worse. Liam wiped the sweat out of his eyes, cursing his helmet, but knowing better than to take it off. He'd seen what happens when a bullet hit a helmet. He didn't think he'd ever forget. He'd much rather have that happen than having a bullet through his brain. He preferred his Stetson but that wasn't allowed in uniform and he'd stand out like a target if he wore it here.

Afghanistan reminded him a bit of the arid desert in Texas. Flat as far as the eye could see. The ground nothing but sand and pebbles, dry as the day was long. When it rained, the whole place quickly grew a cover of green, changing the bleakness to a sparkling jewel of hope. If you travelled far enough, you'd find the mountains. Liam figured joining the military would give him a chance to see the world. He didn't know the world he'd see would look just like home.

Liam wanted to join straight out of high school, but his father convinced him to stay for a couple more years. He took a few classes at the local community college but too many days of butting heads with his father over the ranch management, and Liam decided to follow his dream. The call of the Marines was too deeply ingrained in his soul to turn his back on it. His father should have understood. He had been in the service too, although unlike most of the men in the family, he had been in the Air Force. The men in his family came from a long line of Marines, it was in his blood to serve, no matter how his father argued against it.

Liam rode guard on the back of the supply truck. It was a dirty spot to be in, but they rotated so that everybody had a chance to eat dirt. He couldn't ask his men to do something he wouldn't do. He looked around, keeping an eye out for anything suspicious. Too many damn IED's found their way under the trucks. He had been taught the signs, but the damn terrorists kept upping the ante. Soon as they were able to start recognizing traps they'd change them again.

Nothing looked suspicious, but that just made him more paranoid. It had been too quiet lately. It was one of the reasons he was on lookout. This area had seen too much trouble. They passed the occasional traveler wrapped up in their burkas or dirty denims with keffiyeh's on their heads. You could see a mix of eastern and western influences everywhere. Not a big surprise as troops had been in the middle east for better than a dozen years.

They headed deeper into Helmand province, and the traffic got lighter. They were coming up to some hills, minor but a spot that an ambush could happen. Anytime you couldn't see the other side you'd have to scout. This spot in particular had seen its share of trouble. The tour that was here before them had lost three men in an IED blast. It was one of the spots they had to verify was safe before they crossed it.

Liam jumped down followed by Nelson. The outside duty was dirty, bad all the way around. It was their job to scout when anything suspicious was coming. In this case it was a 'been there, done that, not going back.'

They checked out the area ahead and found nothing suspicious. They turned, heading back to their position on the truck. Liam could feel the hair stand up on the back of his neck but nothing looked out of place. Waving the convoy forward, the Mine Resistant Ambush Protected vehicle in the lead headed out when the explosion hit. Liam and Nelson were thrown from the blast before they could reach the safety of their vehicle.

Liam heard yells and running feet and the crackle of flames as his world turned dark.

He woke up, his body aching, a thousand shards of glass grinding into his body. Trying to turn set up sharp spikes of agony until he once again slipped away.

Liam could hear a steady beep and the air around him was cool. The last thing he remembered was the dirt and heat that surrounded him as he went from FOB, Forward Operating Base, to FOB on the supply truck. He tried to lift his head and the steady ache had him setting it back down. Liam breathed deeply and tried to remember where he was at. Unable to guess, he slowly opened his eyes, squinting against the light.

He looked around as much as he could without moving his head. His eyes widened as he realized he was in the hospital. He recognized a couple of the doctors, so he knew he was still in Afghanistan. Liam closed his eyes against the throbbing pain and tried to remember what happened.

All he could remember was laughing and joking with his team. Then he woke up here. He shifted and bit back a scream of agony. Whatever happened he must've been right in the middle of it. Panting he lay back and tried to relax. If his memory didn't come back, someone would be sure to tell him what happened.

Liam knew they had been going on a run, delivering supplies from one FOB to another. He lay there, head throbbing and pain radiating up from both legs and his shoulders. Wiggling his fingers sent pain up his arms, his left thigh hot and burning. Any movement sent spikes of pain throughout his body. His chest was tight, stomach roiling, and he was afraid to look down. He didn't want to see if he was missing a limb. Liam had heard that even if you lost one you could still feel it. He swore he could wiggle his toes, could feel his leg. The pain and the cramping shooting down his calf. He didn't want to look, anxious at what he would find.

Eyes closed and denying what he knew was a good possibility, Liam listened to the world around him. Groans and constant beeping from machines filtered to his ears. Even through his closed lids he could tell it was daylight, the light shining through the delicate skin. He heard feet come close and reluctantly opened his eyes.

"How are we doing today, McGregor?" Liam could hear the scribbling of the doctor's pen as he made notations.

"Not sure, Doc."

"Explain. What aren't you sure about, Marine?"

Liam had to clear his throat. It was hard to talk through the dryness.

"I don't remember what happened." He turned his head toward the doc despite the ache in his neck. "How bad am I, Doc?"

"Besides the amnesia, which should only be temporary, you had a concussion." Liam realized that would be why he remembered being constantly woken up, feeling overwhelmed with pain only to drift off again. "You were hit with shrapnel from head to toe. You had evidently turned away from the blast point just before it went off. Your back was protected by your body armor. Your legs and arms took the brunt of the damage."

Liam needed to know at that point if his fears were realized. He swallowed heavily, his throat dry. The ache of tears he refused to release renewed the headache into a fierce pounding through his temples. Empty, his stomach was churning with sourness. He had to say it.

"I lost my legs?"

Contemporary romances by Beverly Ovalle:

Love Me Forever
By Beverly Ovalle

Staff Sergeant Liam McGregor doesn't know what hit him. Sent home to recuperate from an IED blast, Liam is stuck in a wheelchair and is sentenced to surgery and physical therapy before he can walk again.

A physical therapist, Abby Worth has loved Liam McGregor since she first noticed boys. It's too bad he's her brother's best friend. She has always been firmly put in the baby sister zone no matter how hard she tried to catch his eye.

Liam sees Abby and when she goes home with him doesn't know how he can keep his hands off of her. She's now old enough to touch and the fire in his blood and the combination of pain killers make him lose control. Abby can't help but take what she's always wanted.

Together they have to overcome their fear of being left behind to grab what they have always wanted-each other.

A Saint's Salvation
By Beverly Ovalle

Corporal Nicholas 'Saint' Santiago needs to go home to reclaim the man he used to be. To be the man he was before Operation Enduring Freedom slowly hardened his heart. He needs to reconnect to the values and the reasons he is doing what he does. Saint also needs to try to forget the courageous woman he fell in love with.

Petty Officer Angelina Jones' life changed the moment Saint saved her life. She survived the blast but now has to deal with the fact that she will never be whole. She can't believe that anyone would want her the way she is now. Digging up her courage, Angelina moves forward hoping against hope that she can live a full life again.

Crossing paths again brings their emotions to a full boil. A coincidence that will have them both reaching for their dreams.

Triple D Dude Ranch
By Beverly Ovalle

Blaire had gotten an exciting assignment, sending her from Chicago back home to Texas. She was taking pictures of a dude ranch for the Tribune, an up and coming vacation spot for the city slicker. Blaire couldn't help the wildfire of desire that ran through her at the uninhibited cowboy she finds in the lens of her camera.

Dan remade his ranch, making it a go to vacation spot being featured in the vacation section in a Chicago newspaper. A freelance photographer was coming to take pictures for the article. Dan couldn't believe the hot and sassy urban cowgirl that arrived, camera in hand.

Texas is hot as hell. But it is nothing compared to the fire that blazes instantly between Blaire and Dan. Just one look, one touch, Blaire was the spark and Dan was the tinder that fed those flames, sparking a conflagration that nothing can stop.

Paranormal Romances by Beverly Ovalle:

Stealing Hope
By Beverly Ovalle
Ardent Books/Assent Publishing

The apocalypse has come and gone.
Those who survived learned to adapt.
Dragons awaken to once again reign over the skies.

Upon eruption of a volcano, Ari awakens to a changed world, and a knowing that his dragon's mate is near. He saves her twice—once as a dragon, and again as a man—and wins her confidence.

Hope cried out, moaning, "just change me with pleasure?"

Hope is restless and unfulfilled until she meets Ari, the man of her fantasies. The sensual tension between them heightens with every touch. When their passion explodes, Hope gets pulled into the dragon's mating ritual...and into a world of erotic sensation she never dreamed existed but now cannot live without. The dragon binds his mate to him with a ritual that shows Hope her true nature in this humorous erotic romance.

Dragons' Mate

By Beverly Ovalle
Boroughs Publishing Group

They had been searching for their mate, but when they find her she is traumatized and scared to be around strange men. They must get her to accept them before they reveal their true natures. Will their love be strong enough to break down her barriers? Could she truly be destined to love two dragons?

Today Annie's dragons will shift and fulfill her every desire, which means a fiery threesome—and true love.

Touched by the Sandman

By Beverly Ovalle
Boroughs Publishing Group

A lonely woman's torrid sexual dreams and fantasy partner await her as a dominant reality in another dimension.

The sandman visits those that need him, assisting them to sleep. Until one night he meets a woman that he cannot help but return to time after time.

She is lonely. He comes to her as she drifts off to sleep, the man of her dreams. Awake or asleep, which is her reality?

He knows she is the one meant for him. He will find a way to make both of their dreams come true.

Lightning Strike
By Beverly Ovalle

For generations Levi's family had guarded a sacred glen in the mountains. Still far from man this isolated area was a favorite spot of his grandfather. Levi grew up listening to his tales and fell in love without ever having stepped foot there.

Now Levi's family, led by his grandmother, wanted to sell the land. With only his grandfather and Levi against it, Levi has to prove to the rest of the family why they needed to continue their guardianship. Believing in his grandfather's tales despite himself, Levi went armed with his camera and his well-known expertise behind the lens and headed out for proof.

Providing that proof and protecting the secrets of the glen from the world, Gaia needs to convince Levi to continue that protection. Daphnaie, the embodiment of his every dream, is sent to show him why, stealing his heart in the process to save her world.

www.ingramcontent.com/pod-product-compliance
Lightning Source LLC
Chambersburg PA
CBHW061320170626
46817CB00001B/241